Uncharted Waters

Theodore Carl Soderberg

Theodore Carl Soderberg (signature)

PublishAmerica
Baltimore

First printing

This is a work of fiction. Names, characters, places, and incidents either are the product of the author's imagination or are used fictitiously. Any resemblance to actual persons, living or dead, events, or locales is entirely coincidental.

ISBN: 1-4241-8251-4
PUBLISHED BY PUBLISHAMERICA, LLLP
www.publishamerica.com
Baltimore

Printed in the United States of America

Prologue

Alcatraz is on our port beam, and Angel Island is on our starboard quarter, and I can see Harding Rock as we shape up for the Golden Gate Bridge. I am the bow lookout on an outbound 900-foot high-speed container ship, and I have the best job in the world. Looking up I can see people waving. I acknowledge with caution, as a natural instinct honed by time. I look upward for that pimple-faced thirteen-year-old kid ready to let go a brick just to see if he can hit a ship. Once we clear the Golden Gate, I will secure the anchors, and head aft and once more have that calming feeling of having left what is known, into the unknown on the horizon.

The year was 1967, "The Summer of Love," and it would be my first time sailing under the Golden Gate Bridge on an outbound ship from San Francisco. As a Navy boot, fresh out of San Diego's naval training center, I was awestruck by the wheelhouse of my new assignment, a U.S. Navy destroyer escort. Most impressive were the low-intensity red lights that were everywhere highlighting sophisticated electronic equipment that, to me, could have been on a spaceship. Orders were shouted to the boatswain mate, and the helmsman clutching a huge polished chrome wheel. Then without warning, a signal man petty officer, in a shiny green bomber jacket, grabbed me by the sleeve, and said, "Look up!" And there, in the night sky, it was magnificent, the underside of the Golden Gate Bridge!

And to the right were the towering Marin headlands, as we could feel a surge in power below decks as the engine room began to answer the bridge's command for more speed. As we began to increase speed I could hear the faint noise of waves washing upon rocks as we made our way in the outbound channel. Providing safety from the jagged rocks we could see the orange Coast Guard lightship off our port bow that was rolling on her moorings. Glancing to our stern, the Golden

Gate was fading into the nighttime mist, as fog signals from many directions were warning mariners.

Fortunately, I have not been jaded with the passage of time, at the marvel and mystery of the Golden Gate. I will always see the bridge as a monument of inspiration.

Whether you are trying to stay out of the prison system, trying to dodge bill collectors and the law, or trying to salt away a fortune, or you are an adventure junkie looking for a quick fix; whatever the motivation, the sea has been the last house on the block for men in transition since the beginning of time. What you are about to read is an account of what happened to a ship and its crew during operation Desert Shield/Desert Storm, and told with the accuracy that only a sailor can tell.

Chapter One

Not unlike many other small boys, I was drawn to water from my earliest memories. As a four-year-old child, I can still recall a carnival in Yonkers, New York, that had a boat ride. I know for certain that I saw a carousel, a roller coaster, and a Ferris wheel, but they were no match for the boats that glided through the mysterious wet stuff. I pleaded with my parents that I might go for a ride, and I can only imagine that my enthusiasm got the best of them. The boats would go 'round and 'round, and I was mesmerized. Once in the boat, I felt compelled to get my hands in the water. The small boats would follow one another in a circular water basin that was five feet deep. As my hands touched the water I could feel the magic flow through my fingers. Hysterical Mom and Dad had the operator shut her down, so their seagoing toddler might come back to the safety of land. And I suspect they thought I might have a thing for the water, or perhaps they might be parenting a juvenile kook. Eight years later, as a grade school mariner in Westchester County, two of my buddies and I discovered an abandoned cement tub that was used for mixing cement. We naturally figured we had salvage rights, and soon discovered that the tub would make a spectacular pleasure craft. As I was surveying the landscape, I can recall saying to my buddies, "I don't see any 'no boating' signs. What do you think?"

Then my sidekick Dickey said, "I bet that sucker floats real good, what do you think, Bobby?"

"Heck yeah," and in chorus we said, "let's do it!"

After we had trundled our newly pirated pleasure craft to the water's edge, the launching and float testing was accomplished like seasoned salts. Carpenters Pond, in New Rochelle, New York, at first glance, was an attractive pond, but upon closer inspection proved to be a shallow mud hole full of duck crap.

Once we got in the middle of the pond, using sticks as makeshift oars, shipmate Bobby wanted to see what would happen if he stood up and did the new dance craze, "The Twist." Before we could tell the knot head to sit down, the water was pouring in over the stern, and we were yelling, "We're going down! We're going down!" And we did, in thirty seconds, like a rock. The three of us remained in the tub all the way to the bottom, that was twelve inches below. I looked at friends Dickey and Bobby, and said, "Well, you guys got any other cool ideas?" On another occasion in New York, at Lake Carmel, Dad and I would go fishing, and this time we were to use a boat, but unfortunately, it was not seaworthy after the effects of a storm. I still recollect looking down at the little boat from the rocks above, and seeing the boat full of the lake. I did not tell Dad, but at the time, I was thinking, "The heck with the fish, let's get the water out of the boat, and go for a ride!"

It was never the fish I was interested in, it was the boat and the water…man against the elements, and the unknown…below and beyond. To me the fish were just an excuse to play in the water. I am still not sure what I saw—power, mystery, raw strength—but for sure, it wasn't fish. I never had thoughts of being a sea captain on a large merchant vessel, or captaining a naval dreadnaught, or an America's Cup sailboat, or any of the other lofty ideas that boys get. For this sailor, it was good enough to be on or near the water, and of course, actually in the water. I have always thought it ironic, that the more position and title one had, the more it would distance them from the water. If I wanted to be in the world of computers and electronics, I would have stayed ashore with the rest of the landlubber geeks. By the age of twelve, I was already accumulating a repertoire of sea stories. As many people go to sea, there are as many stories, and here is one of mine.

Chapter Two

My last assignment was a cable ship in the North Atlantic, in the winter, and I was ready for something in warmer climes. Being an able-bodied seaman in the United States Merchant Marine almost always ensures uncertainty. When a sailor throws in his shipping card for a job all he will know for certain is the name of the ship, and where to board it. He is considered lucky if he knows her destination. The company I worked for supported the United States Navy and its mission. The ships on the West Coast were dispatched out of Oakland, California. It was an unusually damp, gray morning, and I was sitting in the dispatcher's office at 0800 on a Friday. I was having difficulty sitting upright in a chair, as I had a god-awful, skull-crushing hangover, and I would have taken any ship, anywhere.

The dispatcher, Francine, was on the phone. "He beat up the cook, and who else? Look, one guy can't just take over a ship! Oh, I see, and he threatened the captain. I have got someone in mind, and I'll have him meet the ship in Saint Johns on arrival. Okay, bye." Looking straight at me, Francine said, "And what do you want, you look like hell?"

"A ship, and if I wanted to get insulted I would have stayed married, thank you! What's going on, Francine, you going to get me a ship to Japan, or do I have to stay in the pool for another two weeks and watch those stupid training films?"

"Are we having a tough morning, Ted?"

"Look, I'm good to go, if I have to take one more class I'm going to vapor lock. It sounds like you've got a guy out there out of control, and you need someone to coax him off."

"That's right, we've been through this before with him, and it's never pretty. Johnny Morgan, the ship's carpenter on the *Bellflower*, has been drunk for a week, and has already beat the crap out of the cook, and an AB. I've already got someone else to replace him, so don't worry, I'm not going to send you out there to drag Johnny off the *Bellflower*. The *Bellflower* is up in Saint Johns, Newfoundland…you know, you been up there. It's way the hell out by Cape Race, and the temperature is well below zero, but you're going to Japan."

"Great! Let's have the details?"

"You're up-to-date on your qualifications, right?"

"Yeah, yeah, I was born up-to-date on my quals."

"Okay, but I want to look at that training book; I don't need any last-minute headaches from you!" I forked over my training book to Francine; she looked it over, and said, "Alright, you look all up-to-date, okay, this is the way it's gonna go. You're going to be sailing as a watch stander AB. Monday, you and eighteen others are flying out of San Francisco, to Narita in Tokyo, and then you'll be provided ground transportation to the New Nippon Hotel in Yokosuka. You'll be given the rest of the details on arrival, and the ship is the *A. J. Higgins*."

"Eighteen people? That's quite a crowd."

"Sure it is. It's a complete crew-up, and more will be coming."

I thanked Francine, even though she owed me a favor, because of some help thrown my way on my last assignment.

"By the way, what's a vapor lock?"

"It's a car thing, Francine, and it would take to long to explain."

I was a happy camper, I was going to Japan, and the *Higgins* was a new ship, with an anticipated good run, in warm waters. My next step was to get as much info about the ship as I could, and to be done the usual way, by word of mouth, but more importantly, I had to get my shit in one sock. The first order of business was to get to Oakland and put some money on a couple of bar tabs, and then I had to drive to San Francisco and get some work clothes in storage. Second on my to-do list was my first love, that only let me down at gas stations. I had to find a place to store my girl, my 1979, 6.6-liter Pontiac Trans Am. My other girl had already given me the heave-ho, so I was free as a bird, like the phoenix bird on the hood of my car.

I parked my girl underneath a freeway in Oakland, threw a cover over her, and left the rest to the fifteen junkyard dogs, and an eight-foot fence with barbed wire. I could have taken it to another level, setting the car up with trip wires and booby-traps, but I did not have time to play games.

Once at sea, I would be out there for no less than six months, so tying up loose ends was a must, and that included arrangements for my mail and bills. There is nothing like going to sea for six months, and coming home to find out that you forgot to put a hold on your newspaper subscription. There was the time I spent a year at sea, and hadn't patronized my dry cleaner in over a year, only to discover I had four shirts and a sport coat waiting for me. I figured they were either lost or stolen...a nice surprise! I had one more detail to take care of, and then I could enjoy the weekend.

"Hello, Francine."

"Yeah, what!"

"Oh, I'm glad I got you, this being Friday and all!"

"Is that who I think it is?"

"Francine, don't hang up, this is important. What airline is it, and is it Oakland or SFO?"   "How many times do I have to tell you dummies to write this stuff down?" (Sailors are always treated with the utmost amount of respect).

"It's Northwest Orient, flight number 103, and it's out of San Francisco, and be there by 12:30, it's leaving at 2:30."

"Francine, just one more thing, is it too late to get an advance?" I thought the line went dead. "Hello, hello?"

Then after a few seconds I heard, "See you in six months!" And the line did go dead.

I was tapped out, and if I were to make it through the weekend, and still have enough cash to get to the airport, I would have to get creative. This meant I would have to go to plan C; A and B went out the window last week. I would be forced to sell some of my collectables, i.e. books and records. I dialed up an old friend.

"Hi, Cha Cha, how's tricks?"

"Is that who I think it is? What is it this time?"

"Come on, don't be that way. Look, Cha Cha, how would you like to make a little exchange?"

"Like what?"

"Well how's a couple of joints of righteous ganja sound? And all you have to do is give me a ride to the Haight so I can sell some books and records."

"First of all, how would you know if it's good or not? You don't smoke that stuff."

"Trust me. It's from a very reliable source!"

She said, "Do you still live in the same dump?"

"Yeah, I do, and it's not a dump, it's a Victorian!"

She said, "It's a basement room, in a run-down Victorian dump, and I'll be there in fifteen minutes, and it better be good shit."

My exchange went well with Cha Cha, and the sale of my books totaled $37.50. I would now have enough for the weekend festivities, and the airport shuttle.

Chapter Three

Satisfied that my personal business had been taken care of, I was sitting in a very overcrowded and very uncomfortable airport shuttle van on my way to SFO thinking about the years I had spent in Japan. My last day in Yokosuka, Japan, was February 29, leap day, 1970. I had spent exactly two years to the day overseas…well almost. I arrived in Japan February 28, 1968, and when I arrived in San Francisco in 1970, you do the math…my mind was out to lunch. In those two years I had missed everything that had gone on in the States, and spent most of my time traipsing around Okinawa, South Korea, Vietnam, and Japan.

When I got back to the States I read a book that described what I was suffering from; the book was called *Future Shock*, but what I had was called culture shock.

It was now 1990, and I was in an airport shuttle. I was reminiscing of 1968, and daydreaming how great the future would be, and what great things lay ahead, and where my new assignment would bring me. The shuttle was making its last stop before heading to the airport, and Bam! Without a warning, the shuttle bus door opened, and someone jumped in next to me cracking me in the ribs with an umbrella.

I turned around, and great green horney toads, I was looking at Miss Universe. No joke! She had an unbelievably gorgeous set of teeth that produced a smile that would make a sailor grab for his wallet and say, "Here!" By the time I got to her hair and eyes, it was too late, we were already at the altar saying the "I do's." I never really did like airport shuttles, but I was rapidly developing a newfound enthusiasm. When you're in one of these airport shuttles it gives you a chance to socialize and express yourself. I said to Miss Universe, "For Christ sake, what the hell do you think you're doing with that Goddamn umbrella? You're going to kill someone." I glanced at her again. "How about dinner?"

11

Then she said, "I'm sorry, this thing got away from me. Boy, you don't waste anytime do you?" As she was laughing, she said, "I guess maybe a cup of coffee would be okay."

We small talked for while, and then, I could see it coming, that inevitable question.

"And what do you do for a living? And where are you going?"

Here we go! It's off to the races! I don't know where it came from, but the first thing out of my mouth was, "I am a Professor of ceramics at U.C. Berkeley, and I am going to Kamakura, Japan, on an expedition to study a collection of ancient Japanese earthenware. And how about yourself?"

"Japan? Oh my god! What a coincidence! Me too, only I am going to Yokosuka, Japan."

At that point I think I swallowed my gum! I choked and said, "The same Yokosuka that's near Yokohama, Japan?"

"Yes, I have to go to some dirty old shipyard, and check out the digital interface on a ship's keyboard schematic lineup, and the ship's name is the *Higgins*."

I said, "Have you noticed how warm it is in here? I'm having a little trouble breathing."

"Oh, that's okay, let me open this window."

A flood of cold air came into the van, and I had all I could do to keep from not jumping into the oncoming traffic. Miss Universe continued, "I must confess, I am a little spooked. I know you don't know much about ships, but they tell me this one is a bad-luck ship, but who believes in that kind of stuff anyway? It's just a little creepy."

I said, "Actually it sounds adventurous, and interesting, the bounding main and that sort of thing."

Then she said, "This will be all new to me. I am an electronic technician, rather boring stuff, and an adventure would be great. At least my job keeps me traveling." Then she said, "Isn't this great? You like to travel, don't you?"

"Do I like to travel? Oh yes, traveling is my secret passion. If I could just figure out a way to get paid for traveling, and still work for the university, that would be the perfect combination."

"Oh wow, that is just fantastic, it sounds like we have a lot in common."

I was starting to regain what little composure I had, and rekindle my swarthy complexion that had turned milk white, and said, "You know, if I am not mistaken, I think they still serve alcohol in airports. I would be delighted to buy you an aperitif, what do you say?"

"Why, thank you, I would be enchanted. By the way, my name is Blaze."

"Well, how do you do, the pleasure is all mine. My name is Bond, Jack Bond." All the while I was carrying on a conversation in my head. *Bond, Jack Bond? Where the hell did that come from? Who do you think you are, James Bond, and this is some kind of 007 encounter? Am I losing my marbles, or what? But then again this is an airport, and what are the odds of us seeing one another again? Let's just see how goofy it can get.* I was also thinking, *God, these airport shuttle rides are great, I have to do this more often.*

At about this time my acute intuition was giving me the impression that the driver and the other passengers in the van would not regret our departure. My next thoughts were focused on how I was going to extricate my six-foot-five-inch frame from the sardine-can-packed shuttle van. As I grabbed my world-weary sea bag, Blaze said, "You travel light, and why a sea bag? I'll bet you have a sailboat, don't you?"

Do I have a sailboat? I discovered long ago, that when in a tight spot it's always good to mirror a question; it gives you that extra second to come up with something plausible or even more outrageous.

"It's funny you should mention that, and as a matter of fact I do, but when I go on these expeditions it can get pretty rough. This old sail bag here sure beats carrying fancy matching luggage, and my old ketch 42 can get along without this bag for a few weeks." I looked toward my other neighbor, who seemed equally crunched, and I could see that look in his eyes. And if I had to put that look into words, they would look like this, "Will you morons just get out of here, so the rest of us can get on with our lives if you don't mind!"

Blaze said, "A Ketch 42, that's a fair-size boat. You're just playing it down—heck, that's a yacht!"

"Yeah, well as I like to say, the bigger the better when you go to sea." I said, "Driver, this is my stop!"

Blaze said, "That's kind of funny."

"What's kind of funny, what are you talking about?"

"You know, it just seems strange that you have a sailboat and you get motion sickness, ha, ha, ha!"

"Blaze, I don't have motion sickness, I think I might have mercury poison, from last night, thank you, and by the way can you please reach that door handle?" It was so crowded I had to do a jackknife to get out. As I turned around, who was standing there on the curb with a big dopey grin, but my ex watch partner, Farley Cranepool.

"Look, Blaze! My concierge is here, so I have to run. I will meet you in the taproom at 1300."

Blaze, looking confused said, "And what on earth time is that?"

"You know, 1:00, and that's the taproom up at Terminal A, over by that new San Francisco airline, Swish Air, you can't miss it."

"Okay, ciao! See you then!"

Chapter Four

For me, few things in life provide more trepidation than walking across a room to strike up a conversation with an attractive woman, and the attractiveness is directly proportional to my trepidation. It all began in my so-called formative years in grade school, when I discovered that boys shared this planet with girls, and they were both very different.

I can still recall that cute little blond in fourth grade, when I was a little horn pup trying to solve the riddle of the sexes. I still get sweaty palms just thinking about her. The entire time I knew her, I don't believe I spoke more than one sentence to her. Being an almost overachiever, I delivered newspapers on my bicycle after school. Although her house was not on my route, it came within four blocks, and that was good enough for a little kid with an incurable case of puppy love.

When I would get in her neighborhood, I would do no less than three laps around her house just to get a glimpse of little Miss Goldilocks. For my money, she was as good if not better looking than any of the girls in *The Mickey Mouse Club*, and that was the standard of the day. One gorgeous winter that seemed to snow forever, I was on my bicycle in the middle of my second lap around her house, and she came out the side door to dump the family's garbage. Taking a second to look up from her chores, she looked in my direction, and we made eye contact, and it was at that precise moment that everything I had learned about controlling a bicycle went out the window. After nearly going head-on into a parked car, and recovering in a most expert fashion, and quite proud of myself, I gave one glance back, and struck a garbage can loaded with empty bottles, cans, eggshells, and coffee grounds. Garbage was everywhere! At that point, all I wanted to do was pedal my bicycle away and gallantly ride into the sunset, but I knew I could not. I was bound by a higher code, and sense of decency. I knew I had do the right thing, and I had to take the moral high ground, and pick up the garbage.

As I was picking up her neighbor's trash, my true love came over and said, "My goodness, will you just look at all those empty bottles and cans! The Widenfelds sure are keen on their liquor, and will ya look at the size of that bottle!"

I said, "Yessiree, it sure is a big one, and jeepers, look at this big one with the neat name. It says, 'Old Crow Whiskey'?"

She said, "Eww, it's kind of smelly."

While this grand repartee was going on, I was trying to get the mess under control, and the trash back into the garbage can, and wanting to bolt out of there as fast as possible. God forbid that we should actually have a conversation! My mind was racing a thousand miles an hour like an out-of-control engine. What would I say? What could I say? "Gee wiz, this darn bike of mine is always slamming into things!" Or I could have said, "Say, did you see *The Ed Sullivan Show* last night, with that great juggling act? Wouldn't it be great to be able to juggle all those plates up in the air at the same time?" Or "I'll be darned, I didn't know you lived here!" Or "Who do you like, the Yankees or the Giants?" I wanted to speak, but my mouth hadn't caught up to my brain, and my bike was slipping and sliding, and I was trying my best not to fall on my face.

Then she said something incredible! She said, "I see you all the time. Where do you live?"

In complete shock, I said, "Who me?" As I was pointing, "Ahh, back over that way, on Grand Boulevard, by Wilmont Road."

She came back with, "Of course you! Jiminy Cricket, that's not so far away, why don't we go ice skating in that little pond across from the Heathcote Center sometime?"

I could feel the blood rushing to my face, and away from my brain, and I looked down and my pant leg was stuck in my bicycle chain.

I didn't care about my pant leg, and I wasn't so concerned about being able to speak, but I was having trouble breathing, and I said, "Who me, right now?"

"Of course you! No, silly, not now! How about tomorrow after school?"

As my tires were losing traction in the snow, and I was sliding backwards with my pant leg still stuck in the chain, the best I could muster was, "Okey dokey, see you at school!" And I sped off in a hasty retreat, all the while grinning from ear to ear.

As I look back, my social skills with the opposite sex haven't improved much in the past forty years, and more often than not, I feel like that dumbbell kid trying to figure out what to say next, and walking around with my pant leg stuck in a bicycle chain. At least I am no longer suffering from the effects of post traumatic stress syndrome after conversing with a female, so there has been some improvement.

Having this communication impairment makes me wonder how in the heck I ever had any relationships with women, let alone get that first date, the first kiss, or succumbing to the misery of marriage. I like to think I have had a normal amount of relationships, and they didn't all originate as the umbrella-in-the-rib/van type did, or the bicycle/garbage-can variety. I don't pretend to be overly religious, but it could be possible that accidents of the sort just outlined could be God's way of saying, "Wake up, stupid. The girl/boy, man/woman is right in front of you, so don't screw it up!" Life would be abysmally dull and boring without mystery and uncertainty, and allowing the humdrum and monotony of everyday life to creep into our lives spells disaster for couples.

With the passage of time, I can clearly see that there isn't one person alive or dead that knows, or knew one thing about relationships that makes any sense. And all the books, tapes, seminars, and the rest of the how-to nonsense is a pathetic attempt to force an experience that should come natural. What is important for me to know is that when a relationship does work, it has nothing to do with me setting it up; for me, it always comes naturally. I am still working on this theory, and I know I am not alone; I know more than a couple of guys on the planet with this conundrum. And it really begs the question, "How do men and women ever get together? It must be by accident!

And then there is the more obvious question, "Once together, how do they stay together?" Very simple, the answer is they don't! When I hear people say that they have been "Happily married twenty or thirty years," I think, *God, can they really be telling the truth? Or is it so horrible and miserable that they have to lie, and what they really have is a dead shark?* As Woody Allen once said, "A relationship is like a shark; it has to keep moving to stay alive, and once it stops, it dies." It is my belief that most couples are dragging around a dead shark, and not a relationship.

Chapter Five

As the van pulled away, I walked toward Farley, and seeing another half a dozen sailors that I recognized, I said, "What's going on, Farley? Is everyone here heading out to join the *Higgins*?"

"Yeah, and I'm great!"

I said, "Francine said this was to be a crew-up. Have you been on the *Higgins* before, Farley?"

"No, first time, it's a new class ship, and I've heard mixed reviews, so we'll see. We're all going together. There are people from the deck, engine, and steward department, and I understand we're getting a great cook." Then he said, "But hey, listen, you got to tell me, who was the babe?"

"I'm not sure Farley, but we just spent the last thirty-five minutes lying to each other, and I am going to try to get to the bottom of it. Which reminds me, you got to help me out. I'll be catching up with her later, so if I ask you to carry my bags, just play along, I'll make it up to you. Oh, one more thing, Farley, can you spot me forty dollars? You know I'm good for it." (Somehow my $37.50 vaporized over the weekend. Sailors that are waiting for their ship to come in, aren't exactly flush with cash, and I wasn't about to be caught penniless with Miss Universe.)

"You know, Farley, it's very possible I have out-bullshitted myself this time, and I have found someone of the fairer sex that can out-bullshit me."

Farley said, "Anything is possible. Okay, here's thirty-five dollars, but if I got to carry your bag it's going to cost you a hell of a lot more come payback time. And by the way, who is she supposed to think I am? If I'm going to be playing in this soap opera, you have to let me in on it."

"Fair enough. You're supposed to be a concierge—you might not have to, but just in case."

"A concierge? Where do you come up with this stuff? And let me ask you a question. Do all concierges wear Oakland Raider Nation jackets?"

"Good point. You're right, you don't exactly look the part—forget it! Thanks, Farley. You know, you look different, what's going on with you?"

"Well, for one thing, I just got out of detox last Thursday."

"You're kidding!"

"No lie, I'm a new man! I went through a twenty-eight-day spin/dry, and check it out, I'm not even shaking."

"Yeah, and you don't have any broken bones, or black eyes. And that's also why you've got thirty-five bucks to lend. Thanks, this really means a lot. I'll catch up with you by the gate, and I got to go see Miss Universe."

I saw her standing by a magazine rack. I still couldn't believe I met her in an airport shuttle. This is the type of woman you would expect to see in a Mercedes Benz limousine, and not riding around in an airport shuttle van for cheapskates. I walked up behind her and said, "Can you help me? I think my microcircuit has overloaded my flip-flop circuit?"

"You! You know I have been thinking, you don't act very professorial!"

"I am flattered that you were thinking of me. What do you mean, I don't act very professorial? And just how is a professor supposed to act? And are you sure professorial is a word, Miss Electrode?"

"Well, Professor, if it isn't, it should be."

Then I said, "Excuse me, but what flight did you say you were on?"

She said, "I didn't, but it is number 318."

"Well, ma'am, you're boarding in forty-five minutes, and I am on flight 318 as well; we better get a move on. One more thing, my seat is 53A, yours must be 53B, am I right?"

"Wouldn't that be something?" as she rolled her eyes. "I don't know. I will have to take a look."

Hurriedly, we found a table. "So tell me, what does an electronic technician drink in an airport in the early afternoon?

"I can't speak for the rest, but this particular electronic technician will have a kumquat daiquiri."

I said, "What an outstanding selection, that is one of my favorite drinks, but unfortunately my stomach isn't up to par today." The waiter, a lovely little thing that looked as if she might have originated South of the border, approached our table, and I said, "Can you tell me if kumquats are in season?"

And she said, "I believe they are, sir, and if I'm not mistaken I think we got a load in today."

I could tell this gal was a bigger bullshitter and more of a wise ass than me, so I left her remark alone!

"Perfect. The lady would like a double kumquat daiquiri."

Blaze said, "A single will be fine!"

"And I will have a Glenfidrich on the rocks please." I figured a UC Berkeley professor of Asian antiquity didn't drink four fingers of whatever rotgut was in the well, and as I was trying to stay in character, I ordered a high-quality spirit. The airport taproom provided the perfect setting for a romantic interlude for a couple caught up in the high-speed blender of life.

In the limited time we had, we became more acquainted and were feeling at ease, and we teased each other about our professions, and were having fun. Then in a moment of stupidity and overconfidence, while feeling the effects of the first drink jarring my skull, that was already rocked from a weekend of reverie, I took a long shot, and tried to bluff Blaze.

"You want proof that I am a professor? I'll give you proof!"

As I reached for my wallet, she said, "Fuhgededaboudit, that's silly. Of course you teach at U.C. Berkeley, anyone can see that—you have professor written all over your face."

I was thinking, *Wow, I like this girl. She bought it, I still have that salesmanship edge; maybe I shouldn't have given up selling pristine creampuffs to credit criminals after all. But forgetaboutit, what's up with that? Maybe this fine filly has her pedigree roots on the Right Coast?*

Then she said, after fumbling with her airport paperwork, "Forty-five A—well, at least it's a window seat."

Of course I wasn't paying attention to her I was to busy thinking of what was really important. I still had the touch, but how was I to keep this up? I knew I was getting in over my head, and I needed to step back and regroup and figure out a new game plan... I did not want to screw this up.

Another light bulb went off! The perfect place to regroup would be on a fifteen-hour flight to help me for round two when we hooked up in Japan. Blaze and I only had a couple of minutes before we would have to board, and we exchanged contact numbers in Japan.

"Just one more thing, Blaze. What was that seat number of yours?"

"Oh yes, let me look again." She fumbled through her ticket and baggage claims, and said, "Oh, too bad, 45A, and you're 53A. It looks like we won't be next to each other."

In a way I was relieved; this would at least give me time to reevaluate my situation, but I almost fell off my chair when she said she would be staying at the New Nippon Hotel in Yokusuka. Now this was getting spooky. The way things were shaping up, I wouldn't have been surprised if Blaze had been quartered on the same deck with the rest of the rogues of the sea that were to board the *Higgins*.

Chapter Six

Thirteen years have passed and I can still recollect my time served on the *A. J. Higgins* as though it were yesterday. I haven't attempted to tell this tale sooner, only because I couldn't come to appreciate what had happened after the smoke had cleared. Even before I set foot on her decks I had heard some of the stories, and the ship's keel was only two years new. The new crew was to join the *Higgins* at Sumitomo shipyard in Japan. I say new crew, because the ship had been in a shipyard in Japan under going major repairs, and the original crew had been flown home.

As the story went: A man had been electrocuted while working with high voltage in after-steering while in the Philippines, and the unfortunate incident was attributed to an improper electrical tag-out. The disabled *Higgins* was then towed to the Sumitomo dry dock in Yokosuka, Japan, for a complete electrical overhaul and routine maintenance. After flying in from the States, the crew was lodged in The New Nippon Hotel in Yokosuka, Japan, waiting for completion of the repairs. The new crew was being assembled and was getting acquainted with one another and the natives, and doing what sailors did best. Being a new class of ship, and most of us would undergo a learning curve...some a little ahead, and some a little behind. Speaking for most of the crew, I can say we were happy to be assigned to a ship that was built after the Second World War. Our indoctrination would introduce me to the ship and the crew, and it was this time that I met him! Him being Murray Katz, a person I will not soon forget. Even today, when I meet people that exhibit so-called abnormal behavior, I am brought back to my days aboard the *Higgins*. Fortunately, I had prior experience in the mental health field that prepared me for mother nature's misfits and head cases. In my younger days, with a tremendous amount of potential, and short on common sense, and being a big gawky youngster of nineteen, I was the perfect match for a criminally insane ward in New England.

Newtown, Connecticut's, mental hospital had seen my potential, and put me through their extensive training program to become a psychiatric aid (white uniform, keys, and all). Kent 3-C warehoused the most dangerous and deviant of the fellers, and for nine months I would be performing all the necessary cannon-fodder duties commensurate with the title "psychiatric aid" in the Connecticut mental hospital system.

People tend to look at you funny when you tell them you worked in a nut house, looney bin, or funny farm, or any of the other euphemisms associated with the mental health field. So I would simply say that "working with psychopathic killers was just a filler job, until something more challenging and exciting came along." This was just prior to being sent overseas to join a Navy amphibious Seabee battalion that was nine miles from the Demilitarized Zone in Vietnam.

By the time I got to the *Higgins* I honestly thought I had seen the alpha and omega of crazy. Boy, was I wrong! And Mr. Murray B. Katz would prove me wrong. Maybe Murray didn't burn his house down with his family in it, and just maybe he didn't shoot two of his best friends while hunting for an Alaskan Moose. And I could believe he hadn't robbed every drug store from Del Boca Vista, Florida, to Bridgeport, Connecticut, and kill a guy with a lead pipe when thrown in jail. Murray had his very own special brand of crazy!

Eighteen of us flew to Tokyo, and transited to Yokusuka in a military bus in heat that would make the devil hide in a corner. The midday heat was brutal, those that lived to tell the tale remember sitting in that gray bus perspiring gallons of recycled alcohol that was oozing out of our pores. In spite of my uncomfortable state, I was looking forward to Yokusuka, and the changes from the late 1960s to the 1990s.

During the Vietnam War, my unit had a permanent detachment in Yokosuka, and we would make outings to Southeast Asia, and return to Yokosuka, our home away from home. Japan has never been the "bargain basement of the Orient," but the current prices had made it impossible for an average U.S. citizen to enjoy, let alone a poor struggling sailor trying to eke out an existence. In the 1960s, the exchange rate was 360 yen to the dollar, and over the years the Japanese just kept adding zeros. With current prices, we would not be taking any expensive shore excursions into the hinterlands of Japan, and would stay close to home.

Home for us when not aboard ship would be the New Nippon hotel and Honcho Street, and they both provided to our every need. In the hotel vending machines were stocked with beer and coffee, adult flicks hooked up to the TV, plus numerous other services that would require more time to detail. We were firmly dug in, and it would take more than a crow bar to pry us out of this fine establishment.

The hotel was adjacent to Honcho Street. Honcho Street was the residence of hundreds of bars during the Vietnam War...actually there were ninety-three, and they were nasty. Thirty years later it was pared down to twenty-five, and the bar girls of yore were the momosans of today. The current prices might have been high, but our spirits were even higher; short of getting an FHA loan, nothing could keep thirsty, love-struck sailors away from Honcho Street. A group of us were looking for the first bar we could find that had a "traditional sailor atmosphere."

Cleverly, the Japanese named the bulk of the bars on Honcho Street after states in the US. We decided to bivouac at "The Bar Texas." During the apex of the Vietnam War, every state in the Union was represented on Honcho Street, although, now that I think of it, I didn't recall ever seeing the Connecticut, or the Rode Island. Our group was a random collection of traveling companions, and we were beginning to become acquainted. One by one we walked in and surveyed the Texas to make sure we would feel comfortable, and once discovering the bar was well supplied, we dropped anchor, and went with the tide.

My new acquaintance, Murray, said, "This place looks great. I'm buying a round, what do you guys want?"

Farley, the twenty-eight-day spin dry, who bank rolled me thirty-five dollars to buy kumquat daiquiris, nervously said, "That'll be an ice tea for me, thanks."

Joe Bones went straight for the pinball machines and said, "Thanks, but I'm fine. No, on second thought make it a Wild Turkey." Then he took a second look at Murray and said, "Make it a double Wild Turkey!"

Jim, who has already enquired twice about my duty-free liquor purchase on the airplane, had a double bourbon, and insisted that the bartender turn on the karaoke.

I had a beer coming, and in walked a new shipmate, John Hill, just in time to announce he would arm-wrestle anyone in the bar for a hundred dollars. This was quickly put to rest when a nasty snaggletooth-looking bar girl corralled John with a plan of her own; he didn't have a chance. John was a tough little scrapper, but that evening he met his match in the form of a tough old wizened bar girl, that wouldn't hesitate to slap the bejesus out of him if he made one wrong move.

Most of us had been to Yokosuka before, and we thrashed around how pathetic and expensive it had become, and we shared some fond memories. Jim began telling a story, "Right here in this very bar, in this shit hole, in that booth right over there, this chick hit me with one of those thick heavy beer bottles."

Then out of nowhere this funny-looking guy Murray said, "What did you do to piss her off? She would have to be pretty angry to do something like that."

"Let me finish will yah! And...."

"Hey, I was just trying to be friendly an...."

Jim said, "Who the hell are you anyway? And more importantly, what are you doing here?"

"I'm Murray B. Katz, that's who I am, and I'm on the *Higgins!*"

"What's the B stand for?"

"It stands for BenGurion, but you can call me Murray the K. I suppose you have a problem with that?"

I said, "Alright. Well, shut the hell up and let Jim tell his story!"

Jim started again, "Where was I? Oh yeah, well this little trollop damn near gave me a concussion. I came here all the time; they really had some killer-looking babes in here. I was stationed on the *Oklahoma City*, and it was the flagship of the Seventh Fleet, a big cruiser. Anyway, I came in here one night, and I was having a beer with this gal I used to run with, and she said, 'You butterfly! You butterfly!' And she hits me right on the forehead with one these goddamn war-club beer bottles, and I'm telling ya, I saw stars. I said to her, 'You got some nerve. You're calling me a butterfly—who the hell do you think you are, Mary Poppins or something? You're a bar hog scamming for bucks.' And she went to hit me again, and the momason came over and grabbed her."

Joe joined in, "What's a butterfly anyway?"

I said, "You been here before, you should know what a butterfly is. It's someone that goes from person to person spreading the love— butterfly, get it?"

Joe Bones said, "Oh yeah, sure, it's just been awhile. You were lucky you weren't drinking Akadama plum wine—if you got hit with one of those war clubs you wouldn't be here today!" Jim continued, "Can you imagine the nerve of her? She's doing a half a dozen guys every night, and she whacks me over the head for flirting."

I said to Jim, "Jim, old buddy, I think you missed the big picture. Did you ever stop to think that just maybe she thought you were special, and she wanted to get serious?"

"You're nuts. If that were true, then how come every time I dragged her out of the bar all she wanted to do was go to the Alliance Club and play the slot machines?"

"I just thought it might be helpful to look at it from another angle."

Then Joe Bones said, "Hey, any of you guys remember Mattress Marie?"

Jim said, "Who doesn't? And what about that other beauty, Stinky Judy?"

"You know, it's odd—have you ever noticed that everyone remembers them, but I have yet to meet anyone who has been with them?"

"Joe, would you admit it?"

"Would I admit?"

"Hell, I had Mattress Marie and Stinky Judy in the same rack. Once I scrubbed them down with disinfectant, they were beautiful."

"Spoken like a true sailor," said Jim. "There was some really rough trade out there at the time, but you know what? I think it's rougher now," as Jim was pointing out to the street. "Have you guys taken a look out there?"

"I'll tell you one thing," Joe said, "I don't want any of it, at any price. Half these women look as if they should be working with a swab and a bucket."

Jim said, "Oh, how cruel, and unchristian like."

Chapter Seven

Mattress Marie and Stinky Judy got their nicknames and notoriety the old-fashioned way...they worked for it; and they were greatly appreciated by sailors of the Seventh Fleet during the Vietnam War.

Jim said, "You guys know what I'm talking about, you'd spend half the night trying to get a gal out of a bar, just to find out all they wanted to do was go to the Alliance Club and play the slot machines."

"God, I forgot about the Alliance Club. It was fantastic, it had everything. You guys know if it's still there?"

Joe Bones said, "Nah, it's all boarded up and out of business, but inside the main gate you'll find the new sanitized version of the old Alliance Club. This last trip in, I made a stop at the main bar, and I couldn't believe it. I saw these Navy sailors in uniform sitting at the bar watching daytime soap operas. I couldn't take it, and I had to get out of there fast. On the way out I almost threw up, well, actually I did throw up, and sort of made a scene. The sentries at the guard shack were nice enough to give me a ride back to the ship. Of course I was locked up in the back of their van."

"Now that's using the old noggin, you not only got a ride without paying for a cab, but you were safely escorted by marine guards."

"Yeah, I guess your right, but I didn't plan it that way in the beginning."

I said, "It's funny, the goofy things you remember. I can still remember sitting in the cafeteria eating a chili dog, and listening to CCR, and thinking, 'Hell, this isn't so bad!' Of course I had just come from a tour in the Nam, living like an animal, eating out of cans, and using the rearview mirror of a jeep to shave was my reference point."

The Alliance Club had four decks, with a movie theater, barbershop, slot machines, a variety store, and a well-patronized liquor store, and half a dozen restaurants and bars, and stages for shows.

Before I decided to call it a night, and hoist my sails, and stick it in the wind, I took a closer look at my future watch partner, Murray. He was seated to my left, and my inquisitive eye caught the bottom of his pant leg that had white material protruding from underneath his jeans. I said, "Jumping Christ, what the hell is that?"

He said, "What, what are you talking about?"

I said, "I'm talking about the lacey shit on the bottom of your pants."

"Oh that, that's no big deal, it's just a little something I do."

I said, "A little something you do? What the hell is that supposed to mean? What is that down there? And it better be long underwear!"

"Well, see, Mom used to dress me up…"

"Whoa, whoa, hold it right there! Did you just say what I thought you said?"

"Well if you were little more polite, and wouldn't interrupt, I could tell you. As I was saying, Mom would pick out some nice frilly things, and we would make a party of it, but to tell you the truth, with Mom not out here it just isn't the same. So from time to time, just for fun, I'll wear some neat stuff under my street clothes. Check it out— tonight, I have these little doilies on my cuffs. What do you think, pretty cool, huh?"

He had my attention. Then I started thinking, *No way—he's got to be putting me on, and one of these wing nuts in here has put him up to it.*

Then he said, "Do you think this shade of make-up makes me look like a Kabuki girl?"

I said, "I think that just about does it. What did you say your name was?"

"You know, it's Murray!"

"Is that your first name or your last name?"

"It's my first name. It's really Murray B. Katz and you can call me Murray the K."

"I know who Murray the K is, and it's not you, my little friend from outer space. Murray the K was a DJ in New York. Why would you want to call yourself Murray the K?"

He said, "It makes Mom happy; she likes to call me her little 'Murray the K.'"

"That is really sweet and thoughtful that you and your mom are so close, but check it out, you're a U.S. merchant marine, you're about to go on a big long voyage with a lot of strange people, and just look around…Mom's not here. And you're not the DJ Murray the K, and I'm not Cousin Brucey, and this isn't the fairy queen dance."

Then Murray, starting to get wound up, and said, "So you're Mr. Wonderful, with your straight this and straight that, well, all of you are boring, boring, boring!"

Now I was looking right at him, and his eyes were bugged out of his head, as if to say, "Look, I am wired out of my zooky on crank!" And now my attention was somehow drawn to his forehead, and my eyes settled on these spikes pointing straight up. I imagined they were to be a likeness of human hair, but these spikes looked as if they had been plucked from a coarse push broom. I had heard people were having hair transplanted from different parts of their body, and attaching it to their scalp, and I didn't want to dwell on the origin of Murray's donor hairs.

I turned around to talk to Joe Bones. "Joe, have you ever scene anything like this? Will yah get a load of this guy's head!"

Joe said, "Oh, those rows of corn up there? That ain't nothing, wait till he shows you his lingerie wardrobe, and his doll collection!"

Then to Joe, I said, "This is bullshit, those guys aren't going to stick me with this nut job."

Jim came over with a bar girl he found, and said, "What I want to know is, what kind of a name is Murray B. Katz anyway?"

Joe said, "I don't know, it sounds kind of biblical though, doesn't it?"

"Biblical, what kind of Bible have you been reading? I'm no theologian, but I can tell you this, there sure as shit isn't a Murray B. Katz in the Old Testament or the new one."

Jim said, "It sounds Jewish to me, all those guys in the bible are Jewish, aren't they?"

"I never thought of it, but maybe you're right, at least after Judah…whatever!" Now I looked back, and said to Murray, "You realize, Murray, that the 4x8 watch is responsible for all the sanitation on the bridge?"

He said, with extreme enthusiasm, "That's the point! That's the whole point! I have all the cleaning gear, and I've got the best brooms and swabs, and the newest mop pails—everything will be great, you don't have to worry about a thing, I will take care of everything. You don't know how lucky you are to have a partner like me. I know the 4x8 inside and out, and up and down, and you and me will have that bridge looking like a showcase window on 5th Avenue in Manhattan!"

"I didn't come out here to make the bridge look like a showcase on 5th Avenue in Manhattan. It sounds like you have given this a little more thought than I have; we're going to have to talk about it."

Getting louder, he said, "What's to talk about. What is it? You don't like me, you think you're better than me, you don't like the way I dress? Or maybe your just one of those stuck-up California types, huh, that think you're hot shit? I know your type, I seen your type before."

"Wait a minute will yah, what I am saying is that the 8x12 and 12x4 should be involved in the decision process as to who goes on which watch."

Murray moved right along, "They were involved, and you and me are on the 4x8 together."   I could feel my jaws starting to get tight. "The truth is you have got some issues that have got to be talked about."

"Oh sure, try to make a big deal out of a little underwear thing. You're the one with the issues, not me. Haven't you ever heard of the words acceptance and tolerance?"

"Yes, sure I have, but what's that got to do with what we're talking about?"

"Well, because I don't think you have a clue of what those words mean."

"I think I have a pretty good idea. Have you ever heard the words strangulation and suffocation?"

He backed up a little, and went on. "Listen, everyone has something a little out of the ordinary they like doing; everyone has differing hobbies and interests. You need to be more open minded."

"Yeah, well, you're a sicko. You think wearing women's clothes is a normal hobby, and packing around your own cleaning gear is a normal leisure pursuit? There is no possible way we are going to be on the same watch together, and don't say another word!"

He started to raise his voice. "I have rights you know!" and he threw his beer at me.

And with that, I stood up and yanked him out of his chair, my right hand grabbing the back of his belt, my left hand on his collar, and walked about ten paces, and threw him out the front door. And that's the way the conversation ended, and of course Murray B. Katz became my watch partner. Little did I know, that the 12x4 and 8x12 guys already figured out that they weren't going to get Mr. Cross-dressing, Weird Hair, Sanitation Freak as a watch partner. Due to my lack of seniority with the group, I would be stuck with this creature for the next four months on the 4x8 watch, and somebody was going to pay.

Chapter Eight

Like all good things, our hotel stay came to an end, and we bid farewell to the New Nippon, and checked in at the front desk aboard the Hotel *A.J. Higgins*. The upside was that we no longer had to commute to work; the downside was that we had to experience the shipboard crap that happens in a shipyard. The first night aboard was our first memorable experience. At approximately O' dark hundred, I felt the ship do a short snap roll. You might ask, how could this be? We weren't even at sea! Was I having a dream? No, it was for real! Then somewhere in the recesses of my mind, the light bulb came on while in a self-induced alcohol coma dreamscape...an earthquake! It's hard to get hit by a rogue wave when your ship is in a dry-dock. We were sitting on blocks, high and dry, and with zero water under our keel. As the ship shuddered and shook from side to side, someone yelled out, "Earthquake"... They have plenty of them in Japan, and we're in the middle of one! The *Higgins's* general alarm sounded, and we all evacuated the ship, but not in a lifeboat, we walked down the gangway to the safety of dry land that was still fraught with aftershocks. The captain deemed the ship unsafe, and it was back to the hotel, and another round of sightseeing.

As we disembarked across the gangway my buddy Joe Bones said something to me, and I didn't give it much thought at the time. He said, "You're not going to believe the chick I saw just get off the ship. Did you see her? I don't know if she's just visiting, or part of the crew, or someone's old lady or what, but wait till you check her out!"

"No, I haven't, but thanks for the heads up, Joe; anything to beautify the scenery is always a welcome addition." And that was that, and I never gave it a second thought.

While in Yokosuka, I decided to take in some of the local sights, so I jumped on a train and went to Kamakura to visit the "Great Buda." The Great Buda is a fifty-foot statue and likeness of Buddha, and is located in a beautiful sacred Zen park. People seeking spiritually, or some such other nonsense, come from near and far to enjoy the site.

The Buda is large enough that you can walk inside. It has been said, that four hundred years ago a tsunami wave traveled a half mile inland, and flooded the great Buda.

On the way back to the ship I stopped by a local martial art store and purchased a bokkun. A bokkun is a wooden replica of a Japanese samurai sword that is used for drills...and provides an excellent way to practice one's technique without tearing up one's environment. As I opened my wallet to pay the clerk, I saw Blaze's phone number, and immediately I heard that little voice, "Call her, you dumbbell." Then I heard another voice, "You better not. What if she says 'Drop dead?'" Within five minutes I was dialing her number, but there was no answer and no way to leave a message. Whew! I narrowly escaped!

The following day we all piled back aboard the *Higgins*. I can't speak for the rest of the crew, but I was itching to get underway, even if only to anchor. The dry dock was flooded and the ship was waterborne. We then made our way to an anchorage and none too soon, as sailors don't do well with an abundance of time on their hands while pier side. Life is much simpler at sea, and the question of "What to do next?" is seldom a burden. We were waterborne, but not ready for the briny deep, so we dropped the hook just outside the harbor, and a launch service was provided.

One accidental death occurred, as a grim reminder of the consequences of overindulging in John Barleycorn. A crewmember from another ship got liquored up and fell from the back of a crowded water taxi and drowned. We got the sad news a day later when his body washed up on the beach. Then a crewmember in our engine department that same night got all turned around after cocktail hour, and had somehow managed to get himself on the wrong ship and passed out. The unsuspecting engineer woke up hung over and confused (not that waking up hung over and confused was something alien to engineers), but more importantly he discovered he didn't recognize anyone or anything on a ship that was steaming out to sea.

These things happen. Eventually, he had to tell someone that he didn't belong there, and was put off in Kobe, Japan, and mercifully sent back to the *Higgins* without being fired. I don't know what it was, but it appeared that everyone was going nuts.

John Hill, the little feller that almost got mugged by a bar girl in the Bar Texas, would pick a fight with anybody or anything that moved;

he was tough, and he would be fighting mad all the way to his grave.

At anchor, the gangway watch was maintained, and at 11:30 a military launch came alongside, with three marine types, and they were not one bit happy. The guards hailed from below, for us to come down to the end of the gangway to lend a hand. Above the yelling and swearing we recognized John Hill's voice, and knew we were in for a battle. The guards were pushing and shoving to get John aboard while he was hog-tied, and it was no easy chore. At some point however it was comical, because he was threatening to call the Secretary of the Navy and have us all court-martialed for abuse of power and a breach of the Geneva Convention. The chief mate was at the top of the gangway, and it was a bad scene. The mate said, "I want Hill brought to his room. You lock him in there, and I'll be up in a minute!"

We had two more decks to go, and as we were trying to stuff John into his room, the mate gave us some specific instructions. He said to check on Hill every hour, "and just put the back of your hand up to the outside of his wall to make sure his room isn't on fire, because John's a heavy cigarette smoker and he might incinerate himself, and burn up the ship."

The amount of oddball things that had happened was astounding, and it made me think about what Blaze had said earlier about the *Higgins* being "an unlucky ship."

Sailors by nature are a superstitious lot, and after an elevator incident I began to ponder what Blaze had said. The second day aboard, I got stuck in a elevator, and was "written up" by the chief mate for misuse of government equipment. Evidently there was damage on the inside of the elevator, and I was being accused of beating the elevator door with a hammer. I politely asked the chief mate if he was having a momentary leave of his senses, and said as politely as I could, "For Christ sakes, all I did was hit the goddamn button to get to D deck, and who in the hell carries a hammer with them on a ship anyway?"

At that point he assured me there was no reason to shout and swear; evidently there was some prior damage done, and he was trying to nail some unsuspecting dumbbell. Well, it wasn't going to be me, and like the saying goes, "I was born at night, but not last night."

Chapter Nine

At first light the sea and anchor detail finished securing the anchors for sea, and we were bound for sea. Our itinerary looked promising. The Philippines, Pattaya Thailand, Diego Garcia, the Red Sea, Jeddah, plus Djibouti, and a few others no one could remember. Most of us enjoyed the thought of going to a port that no one ever heard of; it was cooler if you couldn't pronounce it, and even cooler if you had no idea where it was! My watch partner and I were trying to get to know one another, and yet stay out of each other's way; we both realized it was going to be a long voyage, and we didn't want it to start out with any death threats.

I had heard the term "obsessive-compulsive" before, but I never fully embraced the meaning until I met Murray. I figured Murray was somewhere between anal retentive and a fixated phobic; we all new he was neurotic—heck, half the crew was neurotic. The ship's nurse said that Murray was a pretentious jerk, but after explaining some symptoms he agreed that Murray was showing signs of being an obsessive-compulsive, and that seemed to make the most sense.

Now that I had a real live obsessive-compulsive for a watch partner, and I was getting a firsthand view of this bizarre behavior, maybe I could have some fun. The 4x8 watch is tasked with the responsibility of stocking and cleaning the coffee mess area, and making sure the bridge is squared away, along with the bridge sanitation. The sanitation is done in the morning, while alternating lookout and helmsman duties with your partner. It sounds easy, and in a normal environment, the thought of chaos in the performance of sanitation would be absurd, and wouldn't be an issue.

However, with an obsessive-compulsive sanitation fiend partner with a proclivity for cross-dressing, with a mother sending him cleaning supplies, everything possible can and will go wrong. At sea, the smallest details can make or break the smooth running of a ship, and one person out of sync can have the same effect. We have an expression at sea, "Mountains are made of molehills, and molehills are made of mountains."

Unfortunately, all I could see as we left Japanese waters were mountains and extremely large molehills. Before we felt that first slow roll of the open sea, Murray had already pissed off half the deck force, and the steward and engine department weren't far behind. As the days turned into weeks, my partner was becoming increasingly interested in the arrangement of the coffee mess. I said to him several times, "What on earth is the difference if the swizzle stirring sticks are on the left side, or the right side of the sugar, or the cream substitute is in the front, or in the back?"

Mongo, another skeptic, said, "What is this, some kind of feng shui, or Asian hocus pocus, or are you just some kind of wing nut that needs a wrench?"

Murray said, "Very funny. It means everything! Look, you might as well understand right now, this is my coffee mess, and this is my plan, and if you can't at least be nice and humor me, then we will go to war, and it wouldn't be the first time I went to war over sanitation and coffee!" Murray had thrown the gauntlet down, and it would be war.

He continued, "The cream substitute has to be in the front row, to the left, next to the spoon in the glass of clean water, the sugar in the right rear corner next to the clean cups, but not too close to the napkins, and all the paper napkins have to be facing the port side."

We of course would never really know, but what was really bothersome, was that you knew that he knew that this sort of thing made people nuts. I asked the second mate, "Don't we have a first-aid kit on the bridge with extra-strength aspirin?"

He said, "Normally we have plenty, but we're out; apparently there has been a run on headache medicine since Murray came aboard."

Murray's unusual behavior got around the ship like wildfire, and it wasn't long before the 8x12 watch caught on, and the next thing you know the 12x4, and then the entire ship was in the know, and everyone wanted to play. The entire episode supported the time-tested saying, "There are no secrets on a ship."

Discovering that sanitation was going to be more than a job for Murray didn't take long. One of the first inklings I had that there might be a problem was when one day Murray announced that for the last two hours he had been fabricating a template in cardboard for the coffee mess. As I looked at the result of his work I was dumbfounded; I couldn't believe that anyone would take the time and effort to craft something so weird.

He had fabricated this thing with an exactitude that would have defied any draftsman. Murray's template for proper arrangement (according to him) of the coffee mess was essential, because, according to Murray, "The problem was that the crew couldn't remember where everything went, and after all, a place for everything, and everything in its place."

It wasn't long before people from all departments couldn't wait to find cause to visit the bridge for coffee, and make minor adjustments to Murray's coffee mess. One day the sugar would be on the left side of the coffee pot, and the next day it would be on the right side. Anything that was out of place and not in its precise location was considered by Murray to be a non-conformity, and would have to be corrected. Finally the chief mate intervened to avoid blood from being spilled, and things settled down. Few things are more important to the smooth sailing of a merchant ship than fresh hot coffee on the bridge. With this crisis behind us we were now prepared to carry out our mission.

Chapter Ten

The *Higgins* was an underway replenishment oilier, and our primary function was to deliver varying types of petroleum products, gas, diesel, and jet fuel to U.S. Navy warships. The transferring of these products was accomplished while steaming at twelve knots, via hoses from rig stations on either side of the main deck. We had a crew of 123 men and women, and our captain was "Touchdown Barney." Why "Touchdown Barney"? The answer was in his body language, because every time the captain got angry and flipped out, his arms would go straight in the air to form perfect goalposts; thus it would be "Touchdown Barney" forever.

Our "floating gas station" was in the process of sea trials, to determine if our ship was sea worthy or not. Once sea trials were completed, we did a 180 and headed back to Japan to refuel. I never found out why, but this would be our last visit before heading into the South China Sea. What was important was that this would be our last time in Yokosuka, and there would be more than the usual amount of inebriated debauchery.

Two of our new hires, expanding their horizons, had no trouble finding Honcho Street. These two knot-heads got so gassed up that they thought it would be cool to rip the rearview mirror off a Japanese national's car. Unknowingly, they did it while the car was occupied, and the driver and two of his ninja friends got out and put a karate ass-whooping on the both of them. After the arrest, and release from the local jail, they were threatened with being persona non grata in Japan. When they finally got to the *Higgins* they were logged in at the gangway, and would then have to deal with the captain.

Then we had the case of two messmen in the steward department that almost missed the ship because they wound up in Kamakura, and couldn't figure out how to get back to Yokouska. Touchdown Barney was not exactly singing sea chanteys, and he connected the dots, thereby arriving at the conclusion that alcohol abuse was our root problem. He explained to us that we had to mend our ways, and if we didn't we would be in deep kimchee, "because I will yank your seaman's documents, and turn your ass over to the United States Coastal Guardians."

Touchdown Barney could be very persuasive, and knew exactly what to say, because for a sailor, losing his documents and being turned over to the Coast Guard was a fate worse than being flogged at the quarter deck at high noon in your jockey shorts. Although convinced, and properly instilled with the wrath of the captain, I didn't relish the thought of dumping my expensive scotch purchased at the duty-free store. But upon closer examination, the captain's threat of taking my sailor documents and turning me over to the Coast Guard was a good enough reason to stay dry. I finally gave the pretentious uppity hooch to my pal Joe Bones; he didn't give a rusty damn about the captain's threats, and I am sure enjoyed and savored every drop of the Highlands brew. Joe's attitude was spirited; he said, "I'm not going to be intimidated; drinking is my god-given inalienable right." It sounded good to me, and I gave him the jug, and wished him the best of luck. We all knew that given enough time things would get back to normal.

As for me, I had bigger problems. Not only did I have to work eight hours a day with my partner, but we shared an adjoining head, and I felt like there was no escape. The head proved to be another battleground that would intensify as time wore on. Before departing for a long voyage it was customary for us to take on provisions for the crew, and varying types of petroleum products for the ship.

We let go our last line for the last time, and were escorted by a tug to the shipping lane. It was strange to be pulling out of Yokusuka; everywhere I looked there was another memory. They say you can't go back, and it wasn't my intention, but it was happening. Reflecting on the past can do strange things; it can make a horrible experience seem like a party, or have a good time appear to have been a goatfuck, of course it's all in perception. Once we cleared the harbor, we were headed past monkey island and slowly made our way out to sea. I was about to rotate to the wheel, I had been on standby, and I was having a leisurely cup of coffee. Joe Bones stopped by to take a look as we were overtaking a small coastal freighter, and I could tell he wanted to bullshit.

We chatted for a couple of minutes, and he said, "So what do you make of that brunette?"

"Brunette, what brunette?"

"God, you mean you haven't seen her yet?"

"No, but you have sparked my interest. I will definitely make a point of checking her out, where does she work?"

"She's in the steward department. I can't believe you haven't seen her."

I said, "I will see her next meal, I'll make a point of it. Look, I've been busy."

"Well, you're going to have to get in line, the entire ship will be scamming on her."   "Whatever. Look, I got to see Murray the K— can you imagine he wants to be called Murray the K."

"Murray the what?"

"You know, you remember that famous DJ in the '50s, and '60s in New York?"

Joe said, "Heck no! You know I'm from Arkansas."

"Oh yeah. Well, like I said, this guy was famous in New York, and all the kids thought he was god, he even had his own hip kind of language." Now Joe was giving me a look like he was lost, so I said, "Furgedaboudit. Look, I have to go to the wheel, catch you later." Murray and I arrived on the bridge at the same time.

"You've got first wheel, Ted!"

"Like hell I do. You have first wheel, don't you remember we discussed this before?" I wanted to grab him by the scruff of the neck, walk ten steps, and throw him out the bridge wing door, but I started chanting mentally and calmed down.

"It's an odd day," (we would rotate odd and even days), "and you have the wheel on odd days."

Murray, getting louder, said, "Why should I have first wheel just because you can't remember?"

"What do you mean, I can't remember?" As the mate, the captain, and helmsman glanced over at us, I said, "Okay, you little shit bird, you win this one, but we're going to write everything down." I knew that Murray knew that that kind of thing made me nuts; he would stand there all day and argue until someone finally hit him in the head with a shovel.

I took the first wheel, and would be at the helm for a full hour; without a ship alongside, we alternated hour for hour. Arrivals and departures weren't as taxing as an underway replenishment, and I could take my eyes away from the course indicator and check the view periodically. Tokyo Bay includes Yokohama, Yokusuka, and Tokyo, and transiting to open ocean is done with a Japanese pilot on the bridge and an escort tug that has a flashing green light that aids inbound and outbound ships.

Once outside into open ocean, the *Higgins* would enter the Sea of Japan, and pass the famous Bongo Straits, home to many a naval battle. The stormy South China Sea would be the next leg of our journey, bringing us parallel to the Philippines, and rounding Singapore, entering the Straits of Malacca, and out to the Indian Ocean, and beyond.

Chapter Eleven

There would be no slack time. We did our first UNREP (underway replenishment) with a U.S. Navy destroyer on our second day out. "It's not just a job, it's an adventure." Those words were plastered over every Navy recruiting billboard from Hackensack to Hayward during the Vietnam era. Training and drills would be accelerated due to a crew unfamiliar with working together, let alone being familiar with the ship and its mission, and when the *Higgins* entered the Indian Ocean she would be ready for the fleet.

Typically, with a full workload for the day, the call-outs would to begin at 0430. On our first run-through, my partner had a total of twenty-five people to call in the deck and steward department...what could go wrong? Murray was armed with the call-out sheets that listed the people, the department, and the precise times, and he was raring to go. And off he went on his mission. To most people, it's not surprising that everyone on the ship doesn't necessarily want to wake up at 0430, but that's exactly what Murray did. He would stand in front of the intended victim's door and begin banging, if you didn't call out in ten seconds, he would start screaming, and after two more seconds he would be screaming and banging on your door. This did not go well with the rest of the crew trying to sleep, and it wasn't long before the chief mate got involved once more. By now the chief mate was beginning to develop an unfavorable opinion of the mighty 4x8. Things have a way of rolling downhill, and things were rolling fast, and it wasn't long before the 4x8 watch was the brunt of everyone's hostility. With the entire ship wide awake, it was time to go to work and refuel our first ship.

We were the "stand-on ship," meaning we would maintain a steady course and speed, and unrep ships would maneuver to us. As usual, the positioning ship would maneuver within one thousand yards of the stand-on ship's stern, and then accelerate within a few hundred feet. Prevailing weather conditions would determine port or starboard approach. Then from a line gun, (a converted M-14), a shot line was fired. The line would be attached to messengers, and phone lines, ready for line handlers to assist, and accomplished in a matter of minutes.

With a ship alongside, only AB's were permitted to steer in hand fifteen-minute rotations, and because ordinary seaman were not qualified to steer they were limited to lookout duties. Fifteen minutes can be an eternity for a helmsman, especially in heavy seas with a ship alongside. I had relieved Murray on the wheel, and was steering 270; a few seconds later I could see a gray mass approaching our starboard side.

I heard the shot from the line gun, and things were happening fast. This would be my first UNREP on the wheel, and I had enough savvy to realize course deviations were unacceptable, and I was ready. During an underway replenishment a helm safety is required; his job is to watch the helmsman, in the event the helmsman has a heart attack, or worse, can't maintain his course. As the approaching warship got closer, the third mate, helm safety, eased over to my right elbow, turned to me and said, "First time, huh?"

"Yup, first time, how can you tell?"

He didn't answer, then he said, "I guess it will be baptism by fire!"

Then I said, "Nice choice of words. Is that supposed to make me feel comfortable?"

He said, "I was just kidding around. Anyway, what's the worst that could happen?"

I was thinking, *Great, another smartass. It must be a prerequisite for this ship!*

He added, "Oh yeah, by the way, this type of warship coming alongside can be tricky, it's an Aegis cruiser, and they have extremely high-powered radars that can knock out your digital readout for steering."

I said, "Oh, you mean that thing up there on the bulkhead that I am steering with?"

"Yeah, that's the one, but don't worry, it doesn't happen every time."

I could feel myself beginning to tense up. My eyes were glued to the course readout, and out of the corner of my eye I could see the captain on the starboard bridge wing. I knew he knew I was a green pea at UNREPs, and I was concentrating so hard that I was beginning to see double.

I quickly glanced at my watch…seven minutes to go, and I heard the comforting noise of my sicko partner rustling coffee filters at the coffee mess. In the background, I could also hear Murray harassing some poor seaman recruit that didn't have sense enough to get his coffee in the galley. Murray was in the middle of one of his diatribes concerning the importance of the empty cream substitute packet, and where it should go, and how coffee filters should be stacked. Then I looked up at the digital course readout, and it went from a steady 270, to 333, to 888, and stopped at 666.

Anyone that knows anything about a compass would know that this was not a good thing! Immediately, the third mate came over, and said, "Oh, wouldn't you know it—looks like you'll have to steer by something else."

"Tell me something I don't know, but what do I use to steer by?"

"Right in front of you, on the stand."

Gripped with anxiety, I would have steered with any set of numbers I could find. My eyes found the compass card, and I began to regain composure, and if for some reason the gyrocompass failed, I would steer by magnetic course. While this was happening, I could feel the advance of the Aegis cruiser, and immediately, our bow was pushed to port, and the captain snapped his head in my direction giving me the evil eye. Luckily, I made the right move, and compensated, as the cruiser positioned alongside. To an old pro it's no sweat; to a novice, it is overwhelming to have ships on both sides, and not know what you're doing… Due to the physics of the side forces, a ship on each side is actually preferred. As the cruiser got into position, the digital readout was beginning to read a solid 270. And that's my "baptism by fire" story, and I was now a pro.

Even though it was my partner's tap on the shoulder signaling I was being relieved, I was glad to see him. We had another half hour to go before being relived by the 8x12 watch, and I would get one more trick at the helm. Typically, four hours was the average alongside time for an underway replenishment, an aircraft carrier could take an entire day.

Chapter Twelve

Changing careers can be a pain in the ass, but nevertheless, necessary. Just before making a change, I had a good idea of what I was in for if I were to start sailing again, and I reckoned I could use all the help I could get. I was merchandising previously owned pristine automobiles in San Francisco, when an attractive Japanese lady walked into my sphere of influence to look at our creampuff of the week. Somehow while demonstrating the features of an exquisite automobile, the discussion took a turn toward religion (a good sign I should get out of the retail sales racket) and spirituality, which I imagine I was in short supply, and she suggested I start chanting. Naturally I said, "Chanting? Why in the world would I want to start chanting? I make a decent living, and I think I am as emotionally fit as the next person. Do I really look like I need to chant, and if so, to what?"

Well, after a lengthy discussion over a flagon of hot sake, one thing led to another, and I found myself two days later seated in a temple getting a copy of an ancient scroll called a Gohonzon, and chanting to the ancient holy immortal ancestors of this mysterious style of Buddhism. Soon I discovered the benefits of chanting, and wanted to express my gratitude to this angel of Buddha, and give her a well-deserved reward. Having not given her a fair chance at the purchase of one of my irreplaceable creampuffs, I gave her another opportunity. Unfortunately she declined my offer of the bargain of the month, and suggested I increase my chanting. I could see my retail sales career was coming to a screeching halt, and decided to quit my job as a purveyor of recycled automobiles, and get a respectable job as a merchant sailor, and as they say, "The rest is hysterical."

My last ship was an old cable ship that had never seen twelve knots in its life of forty-five years.

The ship was an old cable ship of World War Two vintage that was so slow it was hard to tell what direction you were going, and it was horrible to steer. It was my first assignment as a helmsman/watch stander, and did afford me the opportunity to learn how to steer a large vessel. Fortunately, the *Higgins* was completely different; it was new, it had plenty of horsepower, twin propellers with variable pitch, but I still had reservations about my new assignment.

My reservations were born from the knowledge that I would be required to steer with other ships alongside, while steaming at twelve knots, plus transferring highly flammable products. The *Higgins* was a new class of ship that had been designed for speed and maneuverability; somewhat akin to piloting a De Tamaso Mangusta around the Daytona speedway, whereas my last ship was like steering a loaded lumber truck down a goat trail.

To ease my nerves and help with my learning curve, I discovered my newfound religion to be invaluable. And as an adjunct, I also discovered that if I chanted for twenty minutes before I took the helm, I would become more focused, and centered, thereby lessening my margin for a screw-up. As for the attractive Japanese girl that converted me to chanting? Well, that's another book!

Chapter Thirteen

I was famished, and in less than three hours, I would be off watch, and was looking forward to a large breakfast. Normally I would go straight to my rack, but this time I was standing in the chow line, armed with my little tin tray and utensils, leisurely looking at the menu, trying to decide between the powdered eggs Creole or the Spam surprise. The cook had his back to me, and I said, "I'll have the Spam surprise with everything, but hold the kimchee, 'anything for a laugh, ha, ha, ha.'"

The cook turned around, and, Hooky Smokes, Bullwinkle, it was her! "Electronic Technician Blaze, the short-order cook?"

And she said, "My goodness! A professor all the way from UC Berkeley—aren't we honored? Weren't you supposed to be heading to Kamakura? What are you doing here?"

I said, "What am I doing here? What are you doing here? I'm trying to get some breakfast. This is a rare treat; I've never had a Spam surprise prepared by an electronic technician. Are you going to put my Spam surprise on an oscilloscope?"

She hadn't fully recovered, and neither had I. To say we were both blown away would have been the understatement of the century. A frustrated voice to my right said, "You guys know each other from the beach?"

Another voice said, "Wow! That's pretty cool, but the rest of us back here are starving, so could you move it along!"

She said, "Okay, one Spam surprise coming up, with extra kimchee."

"Blaze, that's sans the kimchee."

She completely caught me off guard, and my head was spinning. She was obviously the hot brunette that Joe Bones had been talking about for the last ten days. I didn't know what to do, so I took a seat and waited for whatever I had just ordered, and in a few minutes I heard, "One Spam surprise!" When I picked up my order, she said to me, "How could you tell me such a pack of lies?"

I said, "Well, isn't that the pot calling the kettle through the trees?"

She said, "What is that supposed to mean? You have your metaphors mixed up. It's the pot calling the kettle black!"

"That's right, that's what I am talking about!"

"Well, you started it, with your professor nonsense! I was just trying to keep up!"

And now someone else piped up, "You know there are people back here that really want to have breakfast before it's time for lunch!"

"Yeah, yeah, this ship's loaded with comedians." I said in parting, "I will talk to you later!" Blaze said, with an all-business face, "We'll see!"

I never order Spam, I can't stand Spam, I hate Spam, but I confused the menu for the meal, and the surprise part hooked me, and I was sorry I ordered it. I finished my breakfast as best I could; the only surprise I found that morning was Blaze.

I was still trying to recover from the shock of seeing Blaze, and thought I would go down to the main deck...maybe a walk would clear my head. Then my mind started running again. *"We'll see"* — *what the hell did she mean by that?* I knew darn well she was mad, because I never got in touch with her in Yokusuka. I found out she never registered at the hotel, so what was I to do? I didn't want to blow it, but I wasn't going to look for excuses. I was going on the offensive, and come up with a plan, even if it meant telling my version of the truth. I also had a million questions.

First of all, where did she stay in Japan, if not the New Nippon, and what was she doing on my ship? And what was she doing in the merchant marine for Christ sake? And furthermore, how on earth did she get (in) the merchant marines? And finally, what next? We had to talk, that was certain, and as sure as the sun sets in the West, I would be forced to see her at least three times a day for the next six months unless I wanted to starve. I went back down to the galley, the steward directed me toward the back where Blaze was doing preparation for the next meal.

She was chopping carrots like a wild banshee...Blaze looked up and said, "Ted, I can't talk now, but we can talk after chow, at 1330?"

I said, "You mean 1:30!"
"Yes, smart-ass, then I'll tell you what is really going on."
I said, "Fine, 13:30 it is," and left.

Chapter Fourteen

On the main deck, starboard side, the Aegis cruiser had disconnected, and we could hear her breakaway song (every ship had a breakaway song, and some were hilarious). All lines and hoses were clear, the warship accelerated, and sheared off to starboard with her exterior speakers blasting, "Loaded Up an' Truck'n," by Jerry Reed, of *Smokey and the Bandit* fame. Remembering that the average age of a sailor on a U.S. Navy ship is nineteen is helpful. I thought it was cool. This was a part of the Navy I never saw. When I was in the Navy my duty assignments were somewhat different from a fleet sailor. I was with a naval beach group with an amphibious Seabee outfit, and did a short stint on a destroyer, and was assigned to small combat patrol craft as a brown-water sailor...never a blue-water sailor.

I sat in front of my lunch for not more than five seconds with Joe Bones, then Mongo sat down with a tray overloaded with grub. As the three of us sat while munching on our homemade cheese sandwiches, I still wasn't sure if I should tell them what was going on with Blaze. I had to let someone know, because this thing with Blaze was just too unbelievable to comprehend, and it was making me crazier than a shit-house rat. But before I could confide in anyone, and let them in on my secret, I knew I needed to gather more information.

As I finished my last morsel of heaven, I discovered I was in the middle of one of those tough-guy conversations that can accelerate into a free-for-all. On my last ship a guy had gotten hit in the head with a sugar jar over a tough-guy macho bet. Like most beefs, it started in the galley, where many skirmishes originate. The tough guy said he could take anyone's punch in the gut for $100. The guy that wielded the sugar jar got so rattled by the walking punching bag's challenge, that he couldn't help himself, and as he said, he didn't want to take any chances, so he let fly a perfectly good sugar jar, and split the guy's skull. Both guys were put off the ship and are probably flipping burgers somewhere where they can have day-long food fights.

Mongo asked, "Who's the meanest-looking guy you've ever seen? Joe here thinks he's seen the meanest-looking guy on the planet."

I said, "Come on, Joe, let's hear it, who is this macho mountain man?"

Joe took the cue. "Well, alrighty then! It was winter, and I was on a tanker coming back from Valdez, Alaska. It was horrible up there, freezing rain, and 550 inches of snow that year; it was the worst year ever. Trying to tie a ship up with frozen lines, was an absolute nightm..."

"Come on, we don't have all day. Are you forgetting we've been up there—we know it's shitty. Tell the story."

"Okay, okay okay... Myself and a couple of guys were in a hotel bar in Long Beach, California, and at the time, one of the Navy's big bad-ass battleships was being decommissioned and there were sailors, and fleet jar-heads everywhere. These guys were the guys that sailed on this battlewagon past and present, some of these guys went all the way back to WW Two. Well, there were five marines seated to my right, and my partner was to my left. Then in walked this guy, and he sits next to my partner and he's bigger than me—he was a monster, he had to have been six feet eight inches if he was an inch. I noticed a long scar down the side of his face, as he ordered a drink. This guy was missing half his teeth, and his eyes were messed up; he had a pterygium in each eye, and one of them was really big."

Mongo interrupted, "Wait a minute—what did you say about his eyes, what did he have in them?" Joe explained, "A pterygium—it's a growth on the eye that goes over the cornea, and people in the outdoors get them a lot. So anyway, these marines are about forty-five to sixty years old, and looked like they had scene plenty of action in their day, and they were getting loud. The bartender told them to keep it down as they were telling their war stories, but they weren't getting any quieter. The bar was full, and this Freddy Kruger dude that was sitting to my left, just sat there drinking his drink minding his own business.

"Then this one marine looked left, and did a double-take at the guy, and I heard the jar-head say to his buddies, 'Hey, check that guy out with the scar, at the other end.' I could hear the marine plain as day, so Mr. Mountain Man/ Freddy Kruger must have heard the crack as well. Then he stands up real slow and looks over at them and didn't blink an eye…he just growled at them. And before you could say shit all five of them picked their money off the bar, and damn near ran out the door without finishing their drinks. The big guy sat back down and started laughing, and now he's looking straight at me, and he said, 'Pretty cool huh? You should ought to see what happens when I does my crazy act.'

"With that, I said, 'That's sounds terrific…by the way, can I buy you a beer?' It turned out that he was the nicest guy you ever wanted to meet, and wouldn't hurt a fly, and the three of us had a great old time. He told me he always had a tough time everywhere he went, sometimes people would ask him to leave, just because he was so scary looking, and he was hurting business; it was kind of sad."

"Well, you got me beat, Joe. I don't know anyone that scary. How about you, Mongo?"

"That's easy. You know, I knew this guy one time, that was so big and ugly he couldn't even find a decent hooker with a credit card, so he started sending letters to women in prison."

Joe said, "Well shit, that doesn't make him mean, it just make s him horny and stupid."

"If it's strictly mean looking we're talking about, then that would be my ex-girlfriend in Richmond, California, but she wasn't that tall."

Joe Bones grabbed his tin lunch tray and said, "I have had enough of this intellectual stimulation, I'll see you geniuses later."

"Adios," Mongo replied. When Joe was out of hearing range, Mongo said, "Joe thinks he's some hot shot just because he's writing a book."

I said, "Yeah, big deal, everyone is writing a book these days."
Mongo said, "How well do you know Joe?"
I replied, "A little. I was on another ship with him—why?"

Chapter Fifteen

With Mongo, it was hard to tell if he just had too much coffee, or he was genuinely enthused about something. Whatever it was, he burst into a conversation and said, "Joe's got the craziest background I've ever heard — you want to hear it?"

"Yeah, why not? We have some time, go ahead."

"Okay, I just finished reading part of his manuscript, so this is the real shit."

I said, "Yeah right!"

"You know just because he's from Arkansas don't cut him short, he's got more on the ball than ya think!"

Joe just couldn't resist, "Yeah, like what — the intellectual rights to a Broadway musical?"

"No, smart ass! But his family had gobs of money, and he got into the family business and lost the whole thing."

Joe said, "It's news to me, but if the family had 'gobs of money,' and he lost it, how does that make him a genius?"

"Right, I don't get it. It sounds to me like he has a bad case of the 'dumb ass.'"

"You guys have to hear the whole story."

"Alright, I give up! Let us have the rest of the story."

"Okay, check this out, his father was doing hard time in the South..."

"Oh Christ, not one of those stories?"

Then Mongo said, "Just listen! While he was in the clink, he worked in the prison's laundry, and somehow he got wind that the prison system needed a bra for the females that would go through the heavy industrial steam laundry. So now after spending eight years working with this stuff, Cletus, Joe's father, gets out of the slammer, and started a legit business making these ladies' undergarments. He really had it all thought out. He was using Asian immigrants as laborers — they might have been Vietnamese, or Chinese, it's all the same thing, and I can't remember—but anyway the next thing you know he was rolling in money. He was driving around in limos, and he bought a new house, 'the works,' he even started getting contracts from the federal penitentiary system, things couldn't have been better...then in steps prodigal son Joe."

Getting somewhat anxious, I said, "Come on, what the hell happened?"

"Same old thing—whiskey, and women, and drugs, and not necessarily in that order. Joe became manager of one of the plants, and he got a couple of the gals pregnant."

I said, "A couple of the gals?"

"Yeah, I didn't get all the details—I guess it'll be in his book—and that's just the beginning. Listen to this, he had them selling his bathtub speed at a chain of weight-loss clinics, and then the shit really hit the venticulator."

"Wow, Mongo, no wonder he's out here...bras for women prisoners—that's brilliant, why didn't I think of that?"

"Sounds to me like Cletus had the brains, and his stupid kid blew the whole thing."

"Well yes, up to a point, but it starts to get real interesting when you find out that Joe had socked away a fistful of money in Bermuda, and started a charter service with large sailing ships for the filthy rich...they call them Windjammers."

"Get out of here! I know what they are, and they're huge!"

"I'm not kidding! He started with one Windjammer, and then two, and the next thing you know, he had five."

I said, "Are we talking about the same guy, Joe Bones, alcoholic, shiftless albatross sailor that doesn't have a pot to piss or a window to throw it out of?"

"I'm telling you, that's the guy! He had it all, and lost every red cent, and he's lucky he isn't doing hard time today. He had everyone after him; DEA, IRS, FBI, the whole alphabet soup of bad stuff, but fortunately for him he had the brains to have the right ambulance chaser."

"Well, I'll tell you this, when he finishes the book I'll be the first in line to buy it! How do you know so much about him anyway?"

Mongo said, "One day we were in the ship's library, and Joe and I were talking about books and one thing led to another, and the next thing I knew I was back in my room reading a rough draft of his book."

I said, "That's cool!"

"Yeah, he's been working on it for two years, and he's doing it with pen and paper—you've any idea how long it's taken him? He'll be working on that thing forever. I told him to lose the pen and paper, and get with the program and get a computer."

"Hell yeah, if I had that kind of story to tell I'd get it out pronto, and then go on the talk show circuit."

Chapter Sixteen

So it wouldn't look suspicious, Blaze and I agreed to meet in the crew mess area after chow. I was pacing, and trying to collect my thoughts, trying to figure out what to say. My thoughts were also going in the direction of a romantic outcome, and I was visualizing how this great love affair was going to unfold, and that it was some kind of cosmic destiny that had thrown us together and that our relationship was pre-ordained in the grand planetary alignment of the universe, and a bunch of other romantic crap. I was smitten, and little cupids were dancing 'round in my head.

And holy shit, there she was, right on time! And she looked positively regal in a spectacular pair of coveralls. I almost lost my breath, as she plunked herself down next to the galley's trash compactor. I said, "Mind if I join you for a cup of coffee?"

She flashed that gorgeous smile, and said, "Of course, please sit!" And Blaze began, "Ted, it really is great to see you, but I have to tell you the whole truth."

God, I hated it when a women said that. Why does it always have to be the truth, especially the whole truth? I said, "Sure, no problem. I can handle the truth; after all, isn't that what we're all looking for. I admire someone that can tell the truth…"

"Would you mind if you'd let me get on with it, and tell you what is going on?"

And I said, "Sure, go ahead"

Then she dropped the first bomb. "The truth is, my old man is a mob boss, and he's out to kill me."

I simply couldn't believe what I was hearing, and my first reaction was to stand up and start pacing, and I said, "What!! Well, that caught my attention. A mob boss? You've got to be freaking kidding me. I hope you're not telling another lie to cover up the first lie."

"No, I swear to God. Come on, be reasonable—this isn't something you lie about. Besides, everyone has a few peccadilloes in their background. What the heck do you think I'm doing out here anyway? You really think I'd be on this gray piece of shit with all you morons if I didn't have to be?"

She had a point! She also had a mouth on her.

"Well, who is he?"

Blaze saved the best for last. "His name is Frank Scarpino!"

I said, "Frank Scarpino?" This was like being told you have exactly one day to live, then you'll be set on fire, then hacked into a thousand pieces, and what's left will be shot out of a cannon.

I said somewhat nervously, "You mean 'Frankie the Muscle Scarpino,' the Frankie Scarpino that's always being charged with this or that, and currently under indictment for racketeering, and money laundering, and is going to get busted under the RICO law?"

"Yup, that's the one, along with seven counts of murder. Can you still handle the truth?"

I said, "Who, me? Are you kidding? Of course I can handle it, but I think I am a touch behind the curve on this one, but I can live with it. Are you sure you're not just having a problem with a jealous boyfriend that has a few of whatever you said, pica somethings...?"

She interrupted, "Peccadilloes!"

Then I said, "Well, don't stop now!"

So she began to open up. "Okay, here goes. I was working at the One Night Stand Flower Shop over in Jersey, and making real good money, and after about six months I met the owner, Bernie Simpowitz, and he said he wanted to introduce me to someone special."

"Let me guess..."

She said, "Yeah... that's right, it was Frankie the Muscle Scarpino. One thing led to another, and well, here I am."

Blaze continued, "I didn't realize until about two months after we started going out that he was the leader of the most powerful mob on the East Coast, and by then it was way too late. I mean, for God's sake, what could I do?"

At this point, I didn't know what to think. So I said, "The One Night Stand Flower Shop, what's up with that?"

She said, "Oh come on, I know what you're thinking. It wasn't like that. This place was professional, and it was clean, and respectable, and we really did have beautiful flowers. Plus a fun quirky name like that can sell tons of flowers."

"Look, at this point it doesn't matter. I don't want to make you nervous or anything, but what does matter is that if Frankie Scarpino is after you, and I don't even know why yet, and I don't think I want to know."

She said, "Settle down, you're overreacting."

"I'm overreacting? Are you nuts? Don't you watch the news? His face is everywhere, TV, newspapers, magazines... This is not your average crook; he's got an entire army of highly trained, paid gorillas at his disposal. As a matter of fact, I can't believe you are telling me any of this, and I wish you would have made up another lie."

Then as I was getting lost in her eyes, I said, "Oh great, don't give me that look! Oh okay, how bad does he want to get you? You've told me this much already, level with me."

She nervously lit the first cigarette I had seen her light, and said, "In a bad way, real bad. I'll give you a for instance!"

Blaze moved right along. "Let me tell you, just listen to this, one day George and I were over in Elizabeth, New Jersey — George was my ex-boyfriend — and we were in a bar restaurant kind of place. George was such a great guy, he really was a gentleman; I miss him so. Anyway, we were celebrating my birthday, and in walks Frankie, and he's got two of his goons with him, but they stayed at the door, like good little doggies. I still don't know how he knew I was there, but anyway, Frankie was very gentlemanly and nice to George, and asked if he could sit down. And then he goes and buys us a swell bottle of champagne. It was the Dom Perigon kind, and 1970 to boot — you know, pretty fancy stuff, that was a good year you know, Frankie and I were to go to France, and see where they make that champagne, an..."

"Forget the champagne already!"

"Oh yeah, sorry, and then Frankie leaves, and George and me had a beautiful time reminiscing about when we were together. I was proud of George. You know, that he stood his ground, and didn't get all nervous and weird, you know, most guys would have shown a lot of strain, you know what I mean? With Frankie being there, with his goons, and everything. And that was the last time I saw George alive. George was the first to go."

I caught myself saying, "The first to go?"

"Yeah, that's right. Frankie has methodically hunted down and brutally tortured and killed my last three boyfriends, and Frankie knows that I am sick and tired of it, and I am going to report him to the G men." Blaze was now talking so fast I could barely keep up. "And getting on this ship was my only escape. If it wasn't for my friend that is pretty high up in this shipping outfit over in Bayonne, I don't know what I would have done. And when I told him about my situation, he said, 'No problem, I'll put you on ice for a while; we'll put you on a ship out in California.' Then he told me, the next thing I knew I would be off to Japan, and no one would be able to find me. And so far the plan has worked."

Then she said, "Why are you looking at me that way?"

"I don't know, it's probably because I was picturing you in Little Italy sitting at a table under an umbrella on Mulberry Street at an outdoor café street eating a cannoli with a bunch of Gumbahs."

"Don't be ridiculous... I've never even been to Little Italy. You're talking crazy."

Then I said, "You were sick and tired of it? You know, Blaze, I have heard a few stories in my day, and I have told a few, but that story tops them all. And 'G men'? Who says 'G men' anymore? You got to cut down on the late night TV!"

"I swear to God, I am telling the truth, and Frankie does want me real bad, and I am scared to death. Believe me, I have seen him and his boys in action, and that is part of the reason he wants me dead, but now I have you."

"Excuse me! What did you just say? You know this ship has so much vibration sometimes you think you hear things, and it turns out to be nothing. Oh god, don't tell my you're crying. Will you stop that? Come on, you can't be doing that here."

"Well, I thought you were going to help me, and you said..."

"Okay, okay. Look, I'll see what I can do. Come on, you know crying is not fair!"

She said, "Does that mean you will help me? You are going to help me aren't you?"

I could feel myself sinking.

I said, "I will do what I can."

"Oh, thank you, thank you!" Then out of nowhere Blaze said, "You know I haven't been on the ship that long, but some of these guys give me the creeps. The only guy that is nice to me, and not in a sexy way, is that funny-looking guy, Murray."

"Murray? Of all the people on the ship, why him?"

Blaze was trying to convince me. "Well, first of all, he doesn't ask a lot of personal questions, you know, plus he's more interested in my clothes than my entire social life. I think I can trust him."

"Well that's just great, that just completes the mess I am in. What have you told him?"

"Nothing!"

I said, "Look, Blaze, if you want my advice, don't tell him a single thing, I mean nothing. Don't tell anybody anything."

"You're not just jealous of Murray are you? I bet that's what's going on. Oh, how sweet."

"No, I am not jealous! And if I were, it wouldn't be because of him. Look, stay with me on this, every time someone comes aboard, treat them as if they were an assassin out to kill you, that's the only way you can play this and remain alive, and I'm not kidding, Blaze."

She said, "See, that's what I mean, you know just what to do and how to act."

"Give me a break! It's just simple common sense; any fifth-grade school kid with a team of hired assassins after him could figure this out. The biggest concern of yours will be when we get new crewmembers on board. Just because Frankie hasn't made an attempt on your life yet, means nothing; it only means he doesn't know where you are. When he does find out, and he will, his army of Guidos will try anything to get aboard. As a mater of fact, if I were you, I would think about my next move; you can't stay here and just sit."

She said, "Well, what can I do? I can't just walk away from here."

I said, "There's a number of things you can do. First of all, you could come down with something serious, like a seizure or an attack, and get off the ship, or you could stage your death, and reemerge as someone else, with a new identity. Or how about this, we would say you appeared to be under a lot of stress, and jumped over the side — believe me, it's done all the time. I've seen guys jump a couple of times till they get it right."

Blaze said, "That's comforting. You make it sound like one of the perks of going to sea, so when you're ready to pull the plug, you can just hop right over the side. I'll have to tell all my friends."

"Look, I am trying to be serious. Either way you do it, getting off the ship is critical, and the sooner the better, because even though you are out of sight, your options are limited."

"Yes, I have thought of all that stuff, but I'm going to need help from other people."

I said, "No, you don't! That's where people make mistakes, because when you let other people in on your secret, they can be extorted, tortured, and forced to tell where you are, and right now I am one of those people. Which brings me to the guy that set you up with this ship— what's the deal with him?"

She said, "He's a powerful man, and I shouldn't have to worry."

"That's even worse, because he is more vulnerable than the average schmo… he has more to lose." I said, "Look, I'm going to have to get a couple of aspirins."

She continued, "What makes you think anyone would come out here looking for me? And besides, you need clearances and paperwork to get out here. Not only that, but I am sure people are screened real good what with the military thing, and all?"

I said, "You got here didn't you?"

"Good point." She ended by saying, "I have to meet with the steward. I'll see you at dinner." "Okay, see you later."

Chapter Seventeen

We would spend the next ten days maneuvering, testing equipment, and doing normal shipboard drills before a stop in Subic Bay, Philippines. The Philippines was a virtual home away from home for many sailors and fleet marines for generations, and has always been a welcome sight on the horizon for many a ship. Coming down from the bridge I went to assume my standby duties, making sure critical spaces on the ship were secure, and then I would go to the bow to relieve my partner.

On a pitch-black night, no moon, and very little shipboard light, I was heading to the bow, and just before I got to Murray, I said, "Is there anybody up here on lookout?"

Right away I could tell I startled him, as he stood at attention in the dark, he said, "Of course there is, it's me!"

With that statement we started yelling at each other like a couple that had been married for an eternity, and then blasted each other with white light from our flashlights, and like idiots lost our night vision. These encounters were a pain in the ass at best, but we had a job to do, and we exchanged information, snarled at each other, and as Murray headed aft he never took his eyes off me.

The little childish skirmishes were getting old, but just like in any confined space or institution, it was necessary to keep one's own space from the enemy. Given the choice, between bridge wing or bow, for me, lookout on the bow is the way to go. On the bow, you're away from all the business end of the ship, and it is just you and the elements, and of course your "electronic tether," the radio. The crew on the *Higgins* included civilian mariners, and a small military detachment, which included operation specialists, radio, and weather guessers. Then there was Murray; he really thought he was separate from the crew. Like the time the captain asked for a small voluntary donation to a charity, and if one hundred percent were accomplished by the crew the captain would grant everyone a day off. Murray as a mater of principle wouldn't kick in one nickel, and naturally no day off for the crew, and with two months at sea, a day off would have been huge.

One day, one of the many voices in Murray's head gave him an idea that our adjoining toilet needed a makeover. The following day while in the head, taking care of business, I found it difficult to move, I also discovered an inordinate amount of clutter. There was a broom, a swab, a bucket, and a multitude of cleaning gear that I wasn't even familiar with.

I was sure the naval architect's original designs for the *Higgins* never included the head to be used as a cleaning gear locker, and Murray and I needed to talk. I knocked on his door with two sharp raps, and as he opened the door, based on past encounters, I was prepared for anything that would appear. And once again, he caught me off guard! I never thought I would live to see the day that my watch partner would be sporting bits of tin foil in his or her wet hair, and wearing short shorts, with what I was hoping weren't pantyhose.

This was my first look at the real Murray, and his digs, and as I bent over to pick up my jaw that dropped to the floor, I was stunned. I saw boxes and crates stacked to the overhead. He had floor-to-ceiling mirrors on two of the walls, and how he got them in there and installed I will never know. After getting over the shock of him and his room's appearance, I said, "What the hell is all that crap behind you, and how in the hell can you move around in there? And what's that shit doing in your hair?"

"Don't you make fun of me, these are essential accoutrements for my lifestyle, and it's none of your goddamn business. What do you want anyway, can't you see I am in the middle of tinting my hair?"

Then he slammed the door just before I could reach inside and get a grip at his throat. This would be continued; I needed to let off some steam, and did it my usual way, via a rigorous workout in the gym.

While working out on the heavy bag, I got to thinking, *Don't they ever have room inspections? And how in the hell does Murray get away with all this bizarre behavior, or can I be the only one that knows?* I went to chow, stood the 4x8 watch, and Murray and I glared at each other for four hours on the bridge. That evening as I showered, I couldn't help notice that I was still surrounded by cleaning gear.

Murray didn't just bring the gear into the head in one day; he did it one piece at a time, reminding me of the story about a auto factory worker that stole a car piece by piece. Anyway, as I toweled myself off, I jammed my toe on the metal swab bucket next to the crapper and let out a howl. If I had heard so much as one giggle from his room I would have broken the door down and throttled him. I hopped into my room on one foot and hit the rack, ready for a quiet peaceful sleep far away from the *Higgins* and the ridiculous minutiae of shipboard life.

Not five minutes later, the door opened on Murray's access side of the head, and I could hear metal banging, and Murray cursing. Then in a voice I could hear, "If I don't do it, no one's going to do it." I heard some more rattling and banging and then the door slammed.

I went outside to his main door and I was in front of his door again that was locked, and with a towel around me in the corridor and knocking on his door. I said, "I know you're in there! Open up! What is going on, what is your problem?"

He said, as he was yelling through his door, "It's simple. If you're not going to swab up the water drops when you are finished showering, who will? You expect me to do everything, don't you? Well, I got news for you, buddy, I'm no one's stooge."

I, in a calm controlled voice, said, "Open that door now!"

By this time, a rig captain and the ship's bosun were walking by, and the bosun with a big grin said, "Got your hands full, huh? Ain't he something? Maybe we can help you smoke the little varmint out."

"Yeah, yeah. No, I can handle it."

I figured, as pissed off as I was, the best course of action was to go back to my room and chant at that Gohonzon thing, before I blew a freeze-out plug. The next day I had a chance to talk with some of the unfortunates that had been with my partner before, and it became painfully obvious something had to be done, and so I went to work on a strategy to rid myself of the pest. Don Morse had something interesting to contribute. "So you didn't know Murray was a fanatical survivalist?"

"Fanatical survivalist! What fanatical survivalist? Don, I'm talking about the cross-dressing, obsessive-compulsive thing, and now it looks like he's living in a cleaning locker." I said, "Is there anything else I should know?"

Don said, "You know looks are deceiving. He looks like he doesn't have two nickels to rub together, but that little pervert has a survivalist compound somewhere in the Midwest that I keep hearing about."

"Don, I think that's about enough, I can't take any more."

And Don kept going. "Oh yeah, you got to hear this, he is what you call multi-dimensional, and he is very close to his mom—she sends him cleaning gear—plus there's the pack-rat thing. And just wait to see what happens when we are pier side and you guys have gangway watch." Don said, "I had Murray as a partner for three months, and it was nothing but a battle."

I said, "This guy has more issues than the Library of Congress. When is he due to get relieved?"

"You got me. He's been on here for at least a year, and he's only had the shipyard break, and I don't think he's requested to get off. He's what you call a homesteader...when he gets aboard, he's there for keeps. But I don't remember him being quite this bad. We sailed together a few years ago, but he wasn't this weird."

"That's great!"

"And, oh yeah, let me give you some advice—If you're thinking of putting a head on him, forget it...he and the chief mate have got a history. The mate puts up with the clown, and the rest of us have to suffer."

"Well, we'll see. I'm going to come up with something. If I'm going to be here for the next six months, something's got to give."

"Yeah, well, if you do come up with a plan you'll make a lot of people happy. Hey, listen, we're pulling into the P.I. soon, so forget that idiot and have some fun."

"Thanks, Don, but I have to get this situation sorted out before I can relax. Thanks anyway."

Don and I were having this conversation as we passed the slop chest, and who was window shopping as the ship's store was opening, but Blaze. And, wow! She looked great, even in her galley outfit!

"Hi, Blaze!"

"How's it going, Ted ?"

"Not bad, except Murray is turning out to be a watch stander's nightmare."

She said, "Why, he can't be that bad. What does he do? He seems like such a sweet little guy."

"Sweet! Mother of god!" I went into detail with her, and as she rolled her eyes I could tell she was grateful she hadn't told him anything that could put her in jeopardy.

She said, mercifully changing the subject, "Where and when should I get off, and what's the best way to do it? You're experienced with this stuff."

"To tell you the truth, with my partner being such a head case, I'm starting to think maybe I should go with you. But seriously, I don't know what they told you when you came aboard, Blaze, but six months is the minimum they are going to want to get from you, and to get off early is going to require some tricky work, and will require major planning. Blaze, it just occurred to me, did you change your name when you got aboard?"

"No. I wanted to, but I couldn't get the papers through in time."

"Okay, Blaze, as you know, our next port is going to be the Philippines, and that's where you should make your jump. If you do it legit, they will send you back to the States, and you can regroup there. At least being on the ship will buy you some time to get away from Scarpino. I'm going to give it some more thought, but whatever you do it has to be good, and once back in the States you're going to have to act fast."

She said, "This was the best I could do on such short notice. You have no idea how bad Frankie can make things."

"I've an active imagination, and considering what you were up against you appear to have made the right choices so far. But listen, Blaze, one more thing, Blaze, if you got the job in Bayonne at the other office, how come you were in a shuttle from San Francisco?"

"Oh, that's because I had a twenty-four-hour layover in the city, and I thought I would check out the sights before flying to Tokyo," she said. "Why do you ask?"

"I don't know, I was just curious. Blaze, I have to get up to the wheelhouse and go to work; I'll catch up with you later. In the meantime, do some brainstorming about how you want get off of here."

She said, "Do you have any ideas at the moment?"

I said, "Yes, I do, but I'll have to tell you later. Let's meet in the ship's library at three."

"It's a deal—1500 in the library."

Chapter Eighteen

Four hours later we met in the library. I had gotten there first and unfortunately several people were already there, and we couldn't really talk. At times it can be difficult to be in the same space with someone of the opposite sex. When we were finally alone, I said, "I got it, I got it—here's what you do, Blaze. To be convincing, you plop down on the deck and go into uncontrollable convulsions."

Predictably she yelled, "Whaaaat?"

"Blaze, just listen to me, and stop yelling—it's your derrière were trying to save, not mine. This is a surefire way to get off the ship—it scares the hell out of people, and best of all, it works."

"You can't be serious, you mean sprawled out on the floor and shaking and drooling, and acting like I might swallow my tongue?"

"Yeah you got it, you know what I'm talking about."

"Oh, that doesn't sound very ladylike or nice."

"It's not ladylike, and it's not nice, it's actually horrible. And what's being ladylike got to do with it? The grosser it is the better. You should have more important things on your mind than trying to be ladylike. Look, Blaze, like I said, the bottom line is that it works. I am serious, you have to approach this like your life depends on it, because it does, and you can't screw around. You could just collapse, and try to fake something else, but it won't be convincing."

Then the door opened and someone walked in, followed by another, and we had to end our talk. I quietly asked her phone number, and she wrote down 23, and she also wrote, "And this time call it." I gave her the signal for "in ten minutes," and we left.

Ten minutes later, we were on the phone in the privacy of our separate chambers. She said, "What if I got an awful case of seasickness?"

I said, "No!"

"What if I faked breaking a bone?"

"No!"

"What if I said I was pregnant?"

"No way! All of that is way too lightweight, and it just comes with the territory out here, except for the pregnant thing. Look, Blaze, there are no easy ways to do this, you haven't even been here a month, so this has got to be real. Believe me when I tell you that out here we have seen it all."

"I suppose you're right, but I just want to explore all my options."

"Look, I am already late for the bridge, I have to go now, bye."

I was just getting ready for watch. I had a fully charged battery for my radio, and I had first standby, and I ran into Joe Bones, and he started in.

"So listen, what's up with you and that brunette beauty? You've got something going there don't you, you old dog you?"

I told him I didn't want to talk about it, and he started pressing me hard. So I said, "Okay, Joe, you really want to know what's going on, then listen to this. I was on this airport shuttle, and then, blah, blah blah...."

I told him the works. I told him everything, right up to Frankie the Muscle Scarpino, and at the end of the story he said, "You're going to have to kill me aren't you?"

"No, not for that, but for making me late, and you better not spread this around — this is not just a couple of sailors gossiping, this is serious!"

"Holy shit, you're not kidding. What do you think will happen next? You think they know where we are? You know they have a crew list, did you ever think of that?"

"You think Scarpino knows where we are?"

"Now you've got to keep your mouth shut, at least until we get Blaze out of here."

"What do you mean *we*?"

"Look, as of this minute you're involved as much as I am, and I suggest you help me with this mess before she gets us all killed. Hell, I wouldn't be surprised if Frankie the Muscle Scarpino already knows what ship Blaze is on, and has a submarine come out here and torpedo our ass."

Joe said, "Man, you're freaking me out. Why don't you go for a walk, and make your rounds. I think you're overreacting,"

"Yeah, maybe you're right. I got to find some aspirins; catch you later."

Chapter Nineteen

Just outside of Subic Bay was a sailor's paradise, Magsaysay Street in Ologopo City. This was virtual adult Disneyland, where sailors would have done just about anything to get to this place of enchantment and sublime decadence.

There wasn't anything you couldn't get; booze, hookers of every size, and shape, and description, and of course, weapons and drugs. There was even a place you could go to rent a wife for a daily or weekly rate. This was also common practice in other parts of the world, such as Curacao in the Caribbean. Of course drugs, and just about any other controlled substance known to man, were available for a price.

About the only thing I didn't see in Olongapo City was the Bolshoi Ballet, or a monster truck car crushing, or the New York or Berlin Philharmonic, but I'm sure if you looked hard enough, and flashed enough money, you could find them. Having said this, still many sailors had wives and families, or girlfriends, so we were all looking forward to this upcoming port stay. Guys understood that regardless of the amount of ships and sailors in Olongopo, there would always be an ample supply of ladies. We were really convinced that bar owners would call up to the mountains, or jungles, and say, "Send whatever girls you have, as long as they have a pulse, just have them put on their party clothes, because there's a shitload of sailors throwing money in the air."

Years ago I was in Olongopo, and the town was jam packed. My partner and I sat down and ordered a beer, and two females with their eyes bugged out of their heads and hair going in all different directions came up to us to talk. One of them had a "Princess Dashiki/do-wrap rag" around her head, a jungle dress, and nothing on their feet. We couldn't even figure out what language they were speaking, and neither could the locals. It wasn't Tagalong, it was some kind of hill country dialect, and these gals were wild. I mean wild; I mean the kind of wild like they just jumped out of a tree kind of wild. My partner and I had nothing against women being frisky, but a net should have been thrown over those two.

Frustrated that we weren't making any headway, we chugged our beer, bolted out the door, and rallied at the next bar where at least we could get things going with a fairly normal conversation, and not fear of being the victim of some ritualistic tribal ceremony.

The day before we pulled into Subic Bay, I finally convinced Blaze that a death in the family, faking a pregnancy or, a half a dozen other dingbat schemes wouldn't be as effective as an epileptic seizure. To have a large enough audience and ample witnesses we decided she would have her performance in the galley during breakfast. I also made it abundantly clear to Blaze that if she had any acting talent at all, this was the time to go for the Oscar, and showcase her talent. Everything was set, and I made sure I was at a table near by with Joe Bones, and he was to run defense, if needed.

Blaze hit the deck on schedule, and started flopping around like a mackerel as if she had done it a thousand times. Blaze had taken my advice and made sure she was wearing slacks, so as to not put on a different kind of show. My part in the theatrical production was for me to jam my wallet in her mouth, so as to appear to be preventing her from swallowing her tongue. Little did I know she would bite into a credit card, and my driver's license…truly a great performance! I will cherish those beautiful bicuspids, incisors, and molars for many years. In fact her performance was good enough to clear the mess deck in thirty seconds, beating a ship's record the last time two females got into a cat fight over a peanut butter jar, that ended with one girl getting stabbed in the hand with a plastic fork and had to be brought to the ship's hospital. Blaze had even put carbonated soda in her mouth, to appear as if she was foaming at the mouth, and hers eyes were blinking uncontrollably. She had me convinced! I had no doubt she was star material!

Blaze was then rushed to the ship's hospital, and within a half hour she was down the gangway, and sent to the local naval hospital for observation. The next day her gear headed down the gangway at noon, and another routine day came to a close on the *Higgins*. Blaze might have left, but her memory would be sailing with us, and would not be forgotten.

Chapter Twenty

The *Higgins* arrived in Subic Bay on the 4x8 watch, and was all fast by 1930, and the temperature was still in the mid-nineties. When in port, the bridge watch would shift to the gangway, and the three watches got together to work out the coverage. Murray and I had the night off, and as we both made our way down the gangway, I couldn't help hearing Murray in one of his private conversations with himself. "That's it! Why didn't I think of it before! The Philippines is a great place to find natural sponges for cleaning. That's what I'll do, I'll show these ungrateful dumbbells a thing or two!"

Then out of nowhere, I felt compelled to give Murray some of my invaluable inside information concerning the local tourist excursions. "Murray, hey, wait up. I think I can help you. Do you realize we are in a world-renowned dive spot, where you can go down to a hundred feet and select your own sponges?"

"That's right, but where do you go to get the equipment?"

"Here! No problem, I will write it down for you!"

And that was the last I saw of Murray, until our next watch. Effortlessly, we went our separate ways. I just wanted to leave the ship and go to town.

Olongopo, not exactly a romantic city on the Rhine, was a short bus ride to the main gate, and a short walk on a bridge that traversed a small stagnant river that was an open drainage ditch full of raw sewage, but on the other side, was the mother lode... adult Disneyland! There was one minor drawback; this time of year the Philippines was like a blast furnace, and sitting in front of an ice-cold San Miguel was as ambitious as one could get. I hit the beach with my new acquaintance Don Morse, and once in Olongopo, we walked two blocks, and like the Sirens of Circe calling, "Come in! Come in!"

Don and I found ourselves in the Power Station bar in front of two ice-cold San Miguels, and as my lips touched the crystallized ice on the beer mug, the lights went out. In unison we said, "You've got to be kidding."

And then a voice from heaven. "So sorry, sailor, we have brown out, we fixie soon!" After a full chorus of imprecations by the bar patrons, the lights came back on, and everyone cheered, and proceeded to get down to the business of merriment.

Then Don blindsided me with a question. "Level with me, what was going on with that chick in the steward department?"

Here we go again. Even with Blaze gone, I didn't want to get into the Frank Scarpino thing, because I somehow knew it wasn't really over. Anything was possible; Frank Scarpino could have discovered Blaze was on the ship, and send an entire team to get Blaze...we had no way of knowing.

I knew Don was on a fishing expedition, and would persist, so I gave him a typical outrageous, you-got-to-be-shitting-me variety story, and that seemed to work. Joe Bones and I were the only ones that knew the truth about Blaze, and staying silent in the months ahead proved to be a wise decision. Don and I went our separate ways, and on the way back to the ship I picked up a butterfly knife. When ashore, I always try to pick up something of interest from the local artistry of the indigenous population, like pottery, carvings, fine art, or guns and knives.

A busload of inbound Navy sailors in tropical whites had just arrived in the parking lot with great enthusiasm, so much so, that they were pouring out the windows of the gray Navy bus. There is no higher high for a sailor than the placing of that first foot on terra firma after an extended time at sea. The bars, the girls, the phone calls back home, and the souvenirs are just icing on the cake. I can recall a Christmas at the Yokouska Navy base in 1969; there were three aircraft carriers with their support ships that had arrived for the holiday festivities, and the place was a sea of white uniforms. Sailors in their whites were seen liberally walking around with foot prints on their backs, it was a glorious celebration of the holidays.

The Triple Crown of holidays—Thanksgiving, Christmas, and New Year's—was complete and utter mayhem, and it was a blast. The local Japanese were making money, the sailors were letting off steam, the shore patrol were gainfully employed, and the crazy thing about it was that it all seemed normal. A temporary escape from all the questions and controversy about the Vietnam War (even for those that never set foot on Southeast Asian soil), Yokusuka was much appreciated.

Back on the *Higgins*... in the Philippines, with no more than three hours' sleep, I was ready to stand watch from midnight to 0800. My game plan was to sleep till noon, then go out, and do it all over again. Olongopo in the day time was completely different; you had more time to assess your vices coming at you. Mongo, whom I have known for some time, invited me to lunch with his Philippine family. He had a nice setup; a store, a house, and family with two kids, and two little dogs named Pete and Re-Pete. I called them lunch and dinner (an inside joke); dinner was a pound bigger than lunch. I was certain Mongo had told me he had a wife and kids in Arkansas, but I let it go; sometimes a guy forgets things.

I then went to see an old girlfriend, and found out she had married a marine gunny sergeant, so I went to plan B, which is highly classified. We would be sailing at 0400 in the morning, so I needed to get some shut-eye. In the interim, I discovered my partner Murray had just left the ship's hospital, and the story went something like this.

Murray, equipped with all the dive gear he could muster, went to the beach, and couldn't find the dive shop for his sponge diving excursion, but did find a jug of high-octane alcohol and got blind drunk.

Getting blind drunk is one thing, but he ditched his beachwear, passed out in his birthday suit, and wound up with third-degree burns over most of his body, and that was just for starters. Murray's outing also introduced him to new and exciting people and places. Murray single-handedly managed to get arrested by the local constable for indecent exposure, and would have some explaining to do.

Farley was doing his best to stay away from the evils of demon rum, and he gave us the scoop on Murray and his adventures in the great outdoors. Farley said, "I took a jitney out to the beach, and there was Murray on the beach with his jug. I didn't give it a second thought. I decided to rent a boat with a local girl, and we went out to Grande Island for some fun, and when we returned Murray was passed out under a chaise lounge in the buff. We just got finished with the boat, and were about to go to the snack bar and get some drinks, and that's when I saw him again." Farley said, "I couldn't believe it, the cops went right on the beach and drove right up to him...."

Farley, trying to do the right thing, said, "I went over to help him, but someone had swiped his clothes, and the local police just threw a beach towel over him, and put him in their truck, drove him back, and dumped him off at the shore patrol at the main gate." Farley said, "You know, if someone were to ask me to come up with the stupidest, most embarrassing, and utterly ridiculous thing I had ever seen, that, without a doubt, would have been it. No doubt the old man's going to love this one."

I said to Farley, "So now you have some idea of what I am dealing with every day."

"Oh yeah, I think I do. You'll be in my prayers."

After two days in the Philippines, most of the crew was ready to leave, and the allure of the next port on the horizon was ever present. Singapore would be next, but unfortunately, on arrival we were going to drop the hook, and no launch service would be provided. Few things can piss off a crew more than being in sight of a great port, and not having access. Singapore is on the tip of Malaysia leading into the Straits of Malacca, a waterway second to none in sea traffic. Joe Bones was so mad we were not stopping at Singapore that he could barely talk straight. I heard Joe Bones saying to Farley, "You might not miss it, with your new lifestyle nonsense, but I haven't been to the 'Four Floors of Whores' in Singapore for two years!"

The Straits of Malacca is 550 miles long, and sea captains for centuries have feared it, not only because of its congestion, but the straits are home to cutthroat pirates that would stop at nothing to lay claim to anything they desired. Piracy in these waters is out of control, and next to nothing is being done to stop it; none of the countries that border the straits have taken effective action against the pirates, so mariners have been left to fend for themselves.

Many creative defensive measures have been implemented for dealing with the problem, for example; some ships are lit up like Christmas trees, others have fire hoses charged and ready, some ships even spray water over the side. There are ships that are armed to the teeth, and there are those that have varying combinations. The lone ship, not paying attention, that becomes complacent, soon is an easy target. And just like wolves stalking their prey, once overwhelmed, the determined pirates will stop at nothing; over the years pirates have become more brazen and sophisticated in their attacks.

Not stopping in Singapore was a disappointment to all, and we would get over it; evidently we had orders to proceed through the straits posthaste and join a battle group in the Indian Ocean. My little shipboard drama with my watch partner continued; he was taking sanitation where few had gone before, and I was a very reluctant follower. To say our differences were becoming personal would have been a gross understatement. I had taken the swabs, brooms, buckets, and the rest of the sanitation trappings out of the head.

I knew this would escalate things with my neighbor, but what the heck? Why not have a little fun in an already impossible situation? One day Murray was on the bridge doing his sanitation ceremony; not many things made him happier than a new swab, and armed with his new swab he had just finished swabbing the deck.

I had never seen Murray happier; he was now consumed with a special method for cleaning the inside of coffee pots with ice cubes and vinegar. Murray felt he had been a pioneer of sorts, and had volunteered to give a clinic on his innovation, but was crestfallen due to a lack of interest.

I was on the bridge with Mongo, and he said, "How do you stand that idiot? He's making me crazy, and I don't even work with him." Mongo continued, "You know one of these days someone is going to let him have it right in the snoot."

I said, "It's already been done. Next time you see him, take a closer look at that nose—he didn't break it from picking it."

Mongo did a double-take at Murray, and said, "For Christ sake, now what's he doing over there?"

"Mongo, he's cleaning the coffee pots."

Looking at Murray Mongo says, "You can stay here if you want to, but I can't stay here and watch this. I'm outta here."

Murray would hover around and monitor you while were getting a cup of coffee, and god forbid if the sugar went where the creamer was supposed to go, or even worse, that you should spill something, and if there were water drops in the sink, then you had better be ready for a barrage of bullshit, because it was coming your way.

It didn't take Murray long to discover that his sanitation toys in our head were missing. I'll give him credit for being determined, he was at my door yelling, "Where's my swab and my cleaning gear? I need that cleaning gear, how do you expect me to do my job?"

I told him, "It's gone, and you're not getting it back!"

"Oh yeah? When we get to Singapore I am getting my own swab and I'll put a chain on it!"

"You put another swab in that head, and I'll break it in half and shove it where the sun don't shine, and I'll chain you in your room. And we're not stopping in Singapore, you moron!"

He stomped off to his room. To be continued....

Chapter Twenty-One

Along with two able-bodied seaman, there is another component of the 4x8 watch, and that was the ordinary seaman. The ordinary seaman is the entry-level seaman with little or no experience…some guys will make an entire career of sailing ordinary…and it's their choice. Had it not been for Miguel's Pizza parlor firing Joe Gonzales for eating and drinking up their profits, we might not have had Joe on our crack team. True enough, Joe enjoyed his victuals and a mug of ale, but Joe's real battle was trying to stay awake.

It made no difference where he was or what he was doing, Joe could fall asleep anywhere anytime, on cue. On one occasion, in the crew's lounge, I observed Joe waking with a mouth full of coffee. Joe was so startled, that he shot a mouthful of cold black coffee clear across the room. As unbelievable as it may sound, Joe would fall asleep standing up while in hand steering, and occasionally someone would either yell out at him, or grab the wheel. But Joe's most serious wickedness was falling asleep in the TV lounge, while snoring in the middle of a movie. As Joe's snoring would become louder and louder, guys would start throwing stuff at him to wake him; it would begin with small things you could fit in your hand, pieces of fruit, popcorn, shoes, just about anything that was handy. It hadn't escalated to metal objects, but Joe Gonzales was headed on a collision course with something heavy. Joe was a nice enough guy, but he had all these problems that were hard to overlook. We all have defects, and the most tolerant of sailors could overlook Joe's foibles, but his sight or lack thereof, was asking too much. I never really paid attention, until one day I had to relieve Joe on the bow. Not only was Joe facing in the wrong direction, but he was asleep.

I said, "For Christ sake, Joe, will you get your ass up before the chief mate fires you and sets you adrift in a lifeboat!"

Then Joe said, "Who said that? Where are you?"

"It's me, Ted, your relief, and I'm standing right in front of you, if I was any closer I'd be behind you. Now give me those binoculars and the radio." Joe had a pair of eyeglasses with lenses thicker than the bottom of Coke bottles, and it didn't matter what direction he was facing, he could barely see his own hand.

A three-man watch consists of a helmsman, a lookout, and a standby. The standby's job is to make security checks throughout the ship. The man on standby relieves the lookout, and the lookout would come to the bridge for his turn at the wheel, and so on. Nothing with Murray was a pleasant experience, and relieving him on the bow was the worst. Well, there was this particular time when I had to relieve him on the bow, and I knew it would be an ordeal. I had a handheld radio (we were also using the fixed sound powered phone on the bow).

Murray needed something I had, and all that was between us was a six-foot by four-foot vent on the deck. When I got to the bow, I heard him say something under his breath, and I knew he was "bull baiting" me. I said, "What did you say?"

He said, "You heard me, I know you heard me!"

After chasing him around the vent for ten minutes, I said, "Okay, stop will ya? You have to have this radio for standby, and I need to be on lookout." I put out my hand, and I said, "Shake." It was then that I introduced Murray to my special handshake trick. It's a simple technique that has persuasive results, and can optimize your opponent's attention. Just as you touch the other person's hand, you pull back slightly, then you press your thumb down on the second joint of their thumb, and this should bring the biggest of them to their knees. While he was on his knees, I looked him straight in the eye, and I could see he was in some discomfort, and said, "You're good at sanitation, you little shit bird, but how good can you swim?" I released his thumb, he grabbed the radio, and didn't say a word, and off he went.

At sea, these tit-for-tat conflicts can get out of hand, but sometimes you're up against a wall, and a little violence usually does wonders. In no time, Murray and I got along like old long-lost brothers, and I didn't have a problem for a month. The Germans have a word for something in the back of their mind just waiting to come forward, and it's a hintergedung. My hintergedung was knowing that Murray was setting something up to get even, and it would just be a matter of time.

Word had been passed that three rescue swimmers were needed, and I immediately volunteered. I had always been a strong swimmer, and my logic went as follows: I could earn overtime by sitting in after steering for four hours in 110-degree heat, and usually without a break, or I could be out in the sunshine, and fresh air, and possibly go for a swim. No contest! It was an easy decision, I would rather risk sharks and drowning than be stuck in any engineering space, even under the best conditions. I also knew I had to stay busy, being at sea twenty-four hours a day, and only working eight hours leaves only sixteen hours for rest. I can recall a Catholic nun in sixth grade as she slammed her ruler on her desk with her eyes blazing in my direction as I was staring out the window enjoying the landscape; "Master Theodore, idleness is the devil's workshop. Eyes forward and pay attention!" I can recall another catchy phrase she unloaded on me when I was having a lively debate with a fellow classmate. And once again, eyes a glare in my direction, she said, "Master Theodore, empty barrels make the most noise!" She was really a lovable person with a tremendous gift for having the exact expression for every occasion.

So as I said, it wasn't a difficult choice, a no-brainier, be on the stern in the fresh air, or sweltering in an inferno. I never have been able to understand why normal people would want to work in a engine room. I reasoned that it must be some kind of inside joke, or perhaps an initiation into some obscure club, like the Bohemians, Freemasons, or Rosicrucians. Why would engineers spend half their life in a manmade simulated hell?

For me, tinkering with machines of any size is definitely not a good enough reason. Perhaps if gold bullion bars were passed around every time you descend into the mechanized inferno below I might be persuaded. Apart from that, the only way to get me below is mandatory fire and boat drills, or being threatened with a loaded weapon. Heat has differing effects on people, but extreme heat makes all people crazy over a period of time, and when vibration and noise are added, the combination can have catastrophic consequences.

For example: The Middle East has conditions similar to a ship's engine room, and it isn't an exaggeration to say that these people are volatile and exhibit bizarre behavior to other more temperate climates in the West. Some of the most bizarre, and off-center people I have met have come from engine rooms. I am not trying to make a formal statement, but just a casual argument for connecting the dots that lead from people being exposed to extreme heat to freaking crazy behavior. Shipboard engine rooms have unbearable heat, constant vibration, deafening noise, and oily fumes. I'm not trying to minimize the Mideast's wretchedness, I'm only trying to explain their behavior. The Mideast has sand storms, lack of water, no food, and then just when it cools down and you think its going to be okay, in come the flies, there's plenty of them, and they are aggressive. I think we should all be grateful that there is no engine room noise and vibration and oily fumes in the Middle East, because the world would certainly have detonated long ago, and succumbed to a nuclear winter.

Chapter Twenty-Two

The South China Sea and Singapore were on our stern, and it was time for the fun to begin! We were about to enter the most treacherous 550 miles of waterway on the planet. The waters between Malaysia and Sumatra are called the Straits of Malacca. This hazardous stretch of waterway from Singapore heading north to the Andaman Sea has had more piracy reports than any other navigable waters, and we were about to take precautions.

In the middle of a routine watch, just to my right rear, in a loud voice, I heard something a helmsman doesn't like to hear. "Don't point that thing at me, for Christ sake! Can't you see it's loaded?"

Evidently, the mate, the ships bosun, and select AB's were breaking out the riot guns from the armory, and working out a strategy for security. While behind the wheel, I was visualizing an accidental round being discharged in the wheelhouse, and everyone heading for cover. I didn't have much protection from where I was standing, so I figured dropping to the deck would be the best course of action.

We all had small-arms training, but to me, a couple of hours at a firing range was an introduction to an accident, and it merely informed the trainee how to load a weapon and which end the slug exited. From watching the television shows of the '50s and '60s I always loved the Wild West, and this was the next best thing. Most of us thought it was cool, and couldn't wait for a pirate to ascend the side of the ship, and poke his greasy little head up on deck, and then; BAM! BAM! Whew hoo, what fun! And we were getting paid! "Now, this is why I go to sea!"

Clint Kevlarson, our weapons expert, just arrived on the bridge, and was going over the ship's security plan with the mate, and immediately we knew there was someone on the scene who knew what the hell was going on, because things had spiraled down into a confused macho mess. Clint wore the Budweiser on his cap (indicating he was a Navy SEAL at one time), and we knew what it represented, and respect naturally came his way. Clint had cut is teeth in Vietnam as a Navy UDT/SEAL, and if there was ever a question about weapons or security, he was our "go to" man.

According to Clint, "Most guys worth their salt have 'SEAL envy,' and if they don't, they're either, wimps, liars, or worse, commie pinko tree huggers from San Francisco with a proclivity for same sex marriages." Some of the crew thought our weapons expert had some major psychological problems, and should have been worked over with a rubber hose, but no one would take him on. To the rest of us hard-core nut jobs he had become our hero. I'm proud to say I got rejected by EOD/SEALs. I made it through the recompression chamber, the combat swim, and the rest of the physical requirements, and when I was informed I didn't pass the timed run, my response was, "I thought you guys were fighters, not runners?"

The leader of the pack said, "Look, smart ass, these requirements are the minimum for what will be expected from you."

At that time I had a moment of clarity. It was possible that at thirty-nine I was too old for this outfit, and just maybe I was doomed to be a dreaded wanabee. What the heck, at least it's better than a never-had-the-guts-to-try.

Murray was getting excited, "Mate, if we're going to be up here on the bridge that means we're going to get weapons, right? I'm good with any of those guns, and I know the necessary cleaning procedures, and I would really like a riot gun. If you let me have my own riot gun I would take really good care of it. I have all the cleaning gear, and I can get Mom to send some cleaning patches; we got lots of them back in the bunker."

"Oh, I don't think so, Murray, we have things well in hand. There are people assigned to security, and they will be in charge of the armory and weapons."

"Okay, Mate, but if you change your mind."

"Murray, I am not going to tell you again, you are not to go near the armory or the weapons unless ordered to do so. Do I make myself clear?"

"Yes, Mate, I won't go near the armory or touch any riot guns unless you say so."

Murray with a loaded weapon of any size or description at that point would have put a crimp on my rest periods, and I was secretly applauding the mate.

Chapter Twenty-Three

As we entered straits, the waters were thick with vessel traffic, fishing boats, bum boats, work boats, and plenty of ship traffic...basically every kind of waterborne conveyance imaginable. Additionally, the skies were turning dark as we entered these dangerous waters, and what began as a squall transformed into a Sumatra, a local storm that can bring lightning, wind and violent torrential rain. Working in this kind of weather was not only miserable, but hazardous when driving sheets of rain would last for hours at a time.

At one point, even with the scupper plugs pulled, the rainwater flowed over the fishplates. With rain that hard, there is no amount or type of shipboard raingear that will keep you dry and comfortable. We all had to endure it, and in such conditions it is always important to find a silver lining, such as "You could be soaked to the bone, but at least you weren't cold." Flash lightning was another wonder of Mother Nature, and a common occurrence, and it would turn night into day. But alas, there was indeed an another silver lining in our storm clouds, for tonight was pizza night!

Joe Bones entering the galley said, "Did someone say pizza?" Joe was the kind of guy that was always cracking jokes, but you could never tell if he was kidding or not so at times he was hard to take. Joe continued, "At least we have pizza, and speaking of which, where is the pizza man Joe Gonzales?"

I told Joe, "He's on the bow, ass deep in water, pondering the possibilities of pepperoni, versus sausage, and mushrooms."

Farley Cranepool, looking bored as ever said, "You ever think about that gal Blaze, and what she's up to, Ted?"

I said, "What do you know about her, Farley?"

He said, "Everything—what's the big deal? The whole ships in on it."

I turned to Joe Bones. "I thought I told you I didn't want this getting out, Joe?"

"Well don't look at me, I didn't say a word. She must've blabbed it to someone else; she could have been having a thing with one of the guys, who knows? Or she could have told the captain, but not me, no way."

"Alright, alright!"

"Damn, it sure is true what they say."

"What's that?" says Farley.

"You know, there are no secrets on a ship."

"And to answer your question, sure, I think about her sometimes. She was hot—kind of crazy, and kind of scary—but she was hot stuff."

"Yeah, me too, and I didn't even know her. She was a looker."

Joe Gonzales, almost out of breath, entered the galley.

"Hey, Joe Gonzales, how you doin'? Is it still raining up on the bow?"

"Are you kidding? It was coming down so hard I could barely see my own had in front of me."

Joe Bones said, "So I guess things are normal up there?"

That brought a good laugh at Gonzales' expense. Joe Gonzales took most of the ribbing with a smile, but it wasn't difficult to see that Joe Bones was getting under his skin. Gonzales was an easy target, what with being overweight and a stupid obsession for watching kid movies, and an unhealthy devotion to Laurel and Hardy—he was still an okay guy.

Joe Gonzales asked, "How's the pizza, is it up to snuff?"

"Yeah, great sauce, and that crust ain't too bad for U.S.N. All I need now is a brewski." With a plate full of pizza, Gonzales left for an undisclosed location, and in walked Shanghai Cid. Joe and Cid tipped the scales at 300 pounds apiece, but Cid's weight was wrought from lifting heavy plates of steel, and not plates of pizza. "Hey, what's up, guys? One thing for sure, if there's a pizza in the oven we don't have to worry about keeping Joe Gonzales awake—there went a 300-pound pizza nut. If I am not mistaken, I think he relieved me on the bow with at least one slice of pizza in his pocket last week."

When sailing on military ships, the crew could count on special events; there was pizza night, taco night, and barbeques on the fantail. The Navy takes care of its own, and at least makes attempts to maintain morale. I like what Shanghai Cid had to say about morale, "Liberty is cancelled until morale improves." For sailors of the merchant service, there is a different attitude, because the average age of a sailor on a merchant ship far exceeds the regular navy. Due to the average age of a sailor in the United States Navy being much younger, any similarity to the merchant marines is coincidental. Being homesick, and missing the girl next door, and all the other gooey stuff is rare for the older crowd in the merchant marines.

In the U.S. Navy, Uncle Sam has a vested interest in the sailors' morale, and in the merchant marines things are completely different. It's a business with a different mission and focus. As with regular shore-side jobs, the merchant marines attracts all types. There are the mid-life crises nine-to-five types that say, "That's it, I can't take it any more, and I am ready for a change, and enough is enough." They do a complete 180, and go to the local sailors union hall, and say to the dispatcher, "I want to go to sea, and I don't care what it takes, just tell me what I have to do to get in." And there are plenty of hard-working, so-called normal people that are just looking to earn a honest living. Then there is an entire different group, this group is a rougher crowd, that includes scam artists, lazy slugs, violent bullies, gays, ex-cons, and everything from child molesters to mad bombers. And then there is the more eccentric group, such as Hollywood actor/extras, Rolls Royce salesman, and so-called outlaw bikers, cowboys, and starving rock stars. I once had an author of naturalist books as a watch partner. This guy was something else; he claimed he was in between stories for a popular naturalist magazine. He was no dummy, he had graduated from Harvard, and he told me that he and his wife moved to the desert of New Mexico so he could study snakes and reptiles. Charles, that was his name; I used to call him Chuck, and that pissed him off in a most undesirable way. Chuck told me it took two years for him to convince his wife to move, and when he finally did he was on top of the world.

They sold their beautiful home in Marin County, California, and moved to the high desert in New Mexico. It sounded great...he said they had neighbors, but they couldn't see one another the way the home sites were situated, because each plot was at a different elevation. He did mention that his wife was somewhat reluctant of the move, but was willing to be a good sport and give it a go. Once moved in, it didn't last long, and after the third month of living in their desert paradise being able to see his neighbors was the least of Chuck's problems. In Chuck's words, Millicent said to him, "Charles, if you don't get me out of this godforsaken hell hole immediately, I will divorce you, and bleed you dry for the rest of your naturalist freaking life." I guess that caught his attention.

Charles said, "You know, we had been married for thirteen years and I thought I knew her, but I can still see her face and hear the venom in her voice, and I have to tell you, she scared the shit out of me, and right then and there I knew it was over." When I asked him what she was complaining about, he said, "Oh, she was constantly complaining about the extreme heat of day and the frigid weather at night, and all the little varmints that would surround the house, and that it was impossible to shop for anything without a major hassle."

He thought she was spoiled rotten, and she never really gave it a chance. I asked him what he did, and he said, "Do you want to buy a beautiful desert paradise in New Mexico?" I said no way, but now can say one of two things: I am glad I did, or I wish I had, and today I whish I had!

I might add, there is also a fair amount of bullshit out here as well. Some people are of the opinion that all merchant sailors are a collection of knuckle-dragging, inebriated dope fiends and jailbirds. No doubt, some of that behavior exists, but it is no more prevalent than in the world of landlubbers; the difference is the adventurous mystique. Enough said!

Chapter Twenty-Four

Blaring over the radio at a deafening volume, "I see a guy two points to port!" Then the lookout said, "No, wait! Make that a point and a half; actually he might be a..."

The second mate on the bridge answered directly and to the point, "We got him, bow lookout." Murray continued, "You know, I'm looking at him right now, and I tell y..."

The bridge again answered, "We got him! We got him, Murray, we got him!"

Being correct with location and direction, and rate of speed when calling in vessel traffic when you are the lookout is important, but like anything else, it can be overdone, and Murray was the master at getting things overdone. "Bridge, this is the bow lookout, your guy broad to starboard appears to be turning to his port, actually he is making a full three hundred and sixty... Oh, hold it—he stopped."

"I repeat, we got him."

Again Murray continued, "Wait! Actually he just turned to starboard."

"Bow lookout, for the last time, we got, him we got!"

A bow lookout that calls in traffic like that can make the bridge crazy, especially in seas cluttered with small craft. With heavy vessel traffic, a prudent watch officer will instruct the lookout to report only the critical and most threatening traffic.

The second mate took me aside. "Would you tell your partner what is expected from him, and what is not?"

"Yes, sir, at the first opportunity I will use my powers of persuasion and judgment and have a little chat with my shipmate Murray Katz about the duties and responsibilities of a proper lookout." Now all I had to do was wait for the right time and place to deliver the message.

We would be heading into open ocean, and released from the threat of the straits. With the constant onslaught of small fishing boats on our stern we could breathe a little easier. At night it was not uncommon to see fishing fleets that looked like a string of pearls, with boats stretching from one end of the horizon to the other. We were applying the term "threading the needle," to stay clear of the oncoming fishing boats. Acting as a fishing aid and collision avoidance, smart fishing boats are well lit at night, but on occasion you can be steaming along, and a light will appear without warning. Small boats trying to conserve every bit of energy to the last minute will turn on their navigation lights.

Conserving energy and trying to economize should not be a criteria when sailing at night, especially in shipping lanes. The expression "Might has right" is not necessarily right or correct, although might has advantage of size, and no argument or excuse can make up the difference. Smaller vessels being struck by large ships are paying the ultimate price for inattention or cost-cutting. Many small craft have been sunk because they thought they had the right of way, and could be seen by all. If a large ship can't pick up a target on radar, and lookout can't spot it, the contact doesn't exist. No doubt, a large number of missing boats fall into this category.

At the next available opportunity, I wanted to convey to my partner the concerns of the second mate concerning Murray's lookout duties. I knew, and I was sure the second mate knew, that Murray wouldn't listen to me, but what the heck, I'm a believer in finding fun where I can! I said, "Good morning, shipmate Murray. Would you like to join me for a cup of coffee?"

"No, asshole. What do you want?"

"Now that is no way to talk to a fellow shipmate aboard the good ship *Higgins*, is it?"

"Cut the crap. What do you want?"

"Alright, you little shitbird, the second mate told me to tell you you're fired unless your lookout skills improve."

Murray said, "Who does he think he is? I'm the best bow lookout they ever had!"

I then told him, "Look, I don't have time for your nonsense, and if you have any questions ask the second mate. Let me give you a tip, Murray—you know he can't push you around, you've got rights! Just because they have difficulty hearing you, that doesn't make you wrong."

"That's for sure, you bet I have rights!"

The next day, Murray and I were two hours into the watch, and Murray went up to the second mate while he was standing in front of the radar.

Murray said, "I had a talk with my partner, and I'm going to work on my lookout stuff. I was thinking maybe I am not talking loud enough into the radio. I have heard that there are power boosters that can amplify your voice...."

"Look, not now, we have traffic—later!"

Murray continued, "I'm only think...."

"Will you shut up, I am trying to concentrate!"

Murray wouldn't let up. "Look, I have rights you know!"

"You have the right to get the hell off this bridge right now, or I'll send you home on the next flight!"

I was so startled, I bit my tongue while jawing away on a piece of gum, but I didn't laugh, and I could hear the military types behind us giggling. Then the second mate said, "Look, all of you shut up!" And he picked up the handheld radio. "Bow lookout, what do you see up there?

Gonzales came back, "Bridge, bow lookout, I don't see anything!"

The second mate said, "Two points to port, I have had something for the past half hour, he's now at five miles. You got to see him—use those binoculars!"

"Yes, Mate, there he is. I can see him real good, I don't even need the binoculars!"

"Great, there's more where he came from, so keep a sharp lookout."

"Aye, aye, sir!"

Being in the open water made it possible to stow our weapons with the risk of piracy minimized, and we could all breathe a little easier. The *Higgins* was to join the aircraft carrier *Independence* battle group, which consisted of thirteen ships. Our assignment was to relieve another underway replenishment ship that had been assisting the group for an indeterminate time. We became accustomed to traveling alone, and steaming with a battle group would bring new challenges and tasks, and in a larger sense, a feeling of being in the big picture.

Chapter Twenty-Five

Aboard the *Higgins* there were two types of able-bodied seaman: watch standers, and AB maintenance. I was sailing as an AB watch stander, and ninety-five percent of my duties were on the bridge. Maintenance AB's were responsible for the normal day-to-day maintenance of the ship, as well as line handling on arrivals and departures. Being an unlicensed AB, I was a long way from "officer's country," as they say, but at least I was on the bridge. Watch standers by design are supposed to be observant, and I was not an exception to this rule, and was observant in all my affairs. I was particularly observant to a trend that wasn't going to go away in the near future, and we would all have to endure. My observation became more of a preoccupation with "women on the high seas." Generally woman in uniform, women on ships, and more specifically women on this particular ship are a colossal pain in the ass.

None of us have anything against women; we all love women; some of us even had mothers, and aunts, and nieces and even wives and daughters. But what were the people in Washington, D.C., thinking when they decided to put women on ships with men? Being at sea for months at a time, shut off from normal society, on ships overcrowded with men isn't natural, and it borders on lunacy. I still have vivid memories of my days in boot camp, and I can't fathom how a sexually integrated Navy could work. Having the company of women in uniform most certainly would have enhanced the experience of standing security watch. Our security watch training had a strong emphasis on making sure our clothesline wasn't sabotaged by enemy saboteurs in the dark of night. If that wasn't stupid and humiliating enough, adding a female wouldn't have improved the situation one bit. The fairer sex's contribution would have put us all in the brig. Whew! I had to get that off my chest.

Now I feel better. Back to the *Higgins*...I could see my partner was having a difficult time adjusting to the ladies on the bridge. Normally this would not be worthy of mention, but Murray was having trouble focusing on his steering, and eventually the old man was going to jump on the 4x8 with both feet. We had been assigned crew replacements, and two of the replacements were women, and they were tasked to assist on the bridge during underway replenishment operations. One of the women was a specialist second class, and the other a Navy chief. I knew Murray knew what women looked like; after all, it was his mother that was sending him toiletries. A curious thing was happening; whenever one of them was on the bridge Murray would lose it. He would drop something, or he would start stuttering, and on one occasion he saluted one of them because he got flustered, and didn't know what else to do. Somewhere between the Nicobar Islands and Sri Lanka, making our way into the Indian Ocean things got dicey. My partner and I were communicating minimally at best, and he began to refer to someone on the bridge as Tee Tee. Finally, after hearing Tee Tee being referenced for the third time, I said, "What are you talking about, who the hell is Tee Tee?"

And he looked at me with this big goofy grin, and said, "You know, Tee Tee, 'Thunder Thighs,' on the bridge."

It took about five seconds to register. *Holy shit, this nut job has the hots for the Navy chief!*

This situation had possibilities! And I told him, "You know, Murray, having a Navy chief for a girlfriend would be a great career move, and it would open many doors and endless possibilities." I couldn't stop myself now; I wouldn't get this opportunity again, and I would hate myself for doing it, but oh, what the heck, why not go for it? I continued, "You know, Murray, I really think it is great that you have such great taste, and a healthy outlook, and the chief being a normal woman, and maybe feeling somewhat lonely, and away from home, might appreciate your advances."

He said, "Gosh, you really think so? You know, I bet you're right, and I'm not in the military, so I don't think she can get in trouble for fraternizing with a civilian like me."

"Murray, you're on the right track. I can see the way she looks at you as she checks you out." "Wow, really?"

"Yeah. You know, Murray, I was thinking of putting the moves on her myself, but I know when I'm outclassed. Can't you see, opportunity is knocking at your door? I am sure she would be flattered by your special treatment, and I have it on good authority that she is single."

I laid it on real thick, and I didn't know if he would go for it or not, so I would just wait. With the ladies' lingerie incident still fresh in my memory, I wasn't entirely sure what Murray's orientation was, and didn't really care. I must admit I was out to have a little fun, and if playing cupid worked, well so much the better. I merely thought a little romance would be a nice diversion from his anal-retentive, self-righteous, pretentious sanitation nonsense, and all the weird obsessive-compulsive behavior, plus it would keep the little bugger out of my hair.

Then something happened! It only took a couple of days, but someone had been slipping little love notes under the Navy chief's door signed with Murray's name, and the last note was a beauty. The note cordially invited the chief up to his room for after dinner cocktails, and launched into a description of her finer attributes, and note ended with, "For every Jack there is Jill, why don't you and I go play on the hill?" I am sure she was impressed with his literary talents, and I am sure she was flattered to have this newfound love interest, but had she found out whom the author was, our new Navy chief probably would have given up her career with United States Navy, and disembarked from the *Higgins* in Diego Garcia.

It didn't take long for the flattery to metamorphose into hysteria, as Murray's advances were becoming more detailed as time went on. Just like clockwork he Navy chief finally snapped, and went to her superior, and he of course, went to the captain, and it was a "Touchdown" by the home team. Murray, of course, denied everything, but his intentions became painfully obvious when he tried to put the moves on her during taco night, and the chief, in her dress whites, launched a half-eaten fish taco at him.

All in all, things were going rather well. The captain put out an official announcement about fraternization and harassment, and it wouldn't be tolerated, and the perpetrator would be found out, and punishment would be severe, blah, blah, blah.

Dejected, Murray insisted he was innocent, and he had nothing to do with the notes, and when Murray came to me for advice I could only tell him it was probably for the best. After all, any woman that was lucky enough to corral Murray wouldn't be caught dead on a ship with sex-crazed misfit sailors anyway. I also explained to Murray that it's a shame some people have to resort to such sophomoric and immature tactics.

I don't think he bought one word of it, but in the end we could at least say our minds were occupied, and any diversion from the tedium of duty and boredom is always appreciated aboard ship.

Chapter Twenty-Six

Then there was the case of the gorgeous blond seaman recruit, and the E-5 weather-guessing studmeister. The gal was a knockout, and half the deck department was getting brain damage just looking at her. When these two were discovered by one of their own, to be playing house, it created another daytime drama, but this time it was up to the military to police their own "Horn Dogs."

God knows we had enough of our own. What happened in this case wasn't out of the norm; evidently the couple got busted by one of their own because he wasn't getting what he thought was his fair share of action, and took it upon himself to be the sex police, and subsequently blew the whistle.

As an ardent fan of the opposite sex, it is my belief that women should have equal pay for equal work, and naturally all the rights that they have gained over the years. But what chaps my hide is why people fail to see the stupidity of putting both sexes on a ship, and then to ask them to disregard their sexuality...it's ridiculous. The socialization of the sexes at sea, at the height of their sexually active years, and expect nothing to happen, and when it dose to discipline them, is, at best, inhumane. Trying to be progressive and politically sensitive to everyone's needs is one thing, but the military leadership needs to re-visit its current policies.

In addition to the unlicensed civilian mariners aboard, we also had civilian officers, who proved to be just as colorful as the unlicensed. For the most part, they had graduated from a maritime academy, although coming up through the haws pipe wasn't that unusual. I can recall such case. His name was William, and early on he made it clear that he didn't want to be called Dick. William also made it clear that he might be a dick, but he didn't want any AB's calling him Dick. William had been an AB for some time, and he had decided one day that he no longer wanted to get his hands dirty, and wanted to become part of the white-glove elite. William did his best to break ranks with the Philistines on deck, but when I think of William, the expression: "You can't make a valise out of a sow's ear" comes to mind.

The company required its officer's to wear khaki uniforms, and as a newly appointed officer, having worked his way off the deck and up to Mt. Olympus, William was experiencing a learning curve difficulty that the captain was finding unacceptable. "Goddamn it, William, either put the uniform on, or take the son of a bitch off." With his shirt tail half in and half out, and a three-day growth on his face, with pant legs too long, in the captain's words: "William looked lunchy."

In his street attire, William was equally confounded; he would mix cowboy clothes with biker clothes, and actually wear them. We imagined that before getting ready for the day, William couldn't quite figure out who he wanted to be, or he was getting dressed in the dark. We reckoned it was a good thing he didn't want to be a punk rocker and an Ivy Leaguer.

We also figured William had bigger problems to deal with than his clothes, given the rapid and copious amount of message traffic he was receiving from the States. William had been open about his wife's lucrative antique business back home in Louisiana, and he was excited that he and the Mrs. would be purchasing a new car and a ski boat. But lately things had taken a turn for the worse, when William got an urgent message from the West Monroe County Jail stating that his wife was locked up for selling controlled substances to minors, and she would be needing bail money. Drug dealing was bad enough, but then William got another message from his brother, Ferlin, stating that Amy Sue, William's wife, was having an affair with the local sheriff. Poor William didn't know what to do. Most of us had empathy for William's plight, but as a rule dicks don't get much sympathy. Domestic upheaval is not unfamiliar territory to most of us; romance and finance are a sailor's never-ending headaches, and we figured William would be at sea for some time, with many leagues of water in his future.

Then there was Kevin, our watch officer on the 4x8. Kevin's troubles began with the U.S. Navy, and being Japanese didn't help. He terminated his career with the regular Navy early, but no one aboard the *Higgins* ever got the full story of what happened.

We could only surmise that being full-blooded Japanese might have had something to do with his early termination or resignation. The United States Navy still has vivid memories of December 7, 1941, and I suspect he was feeling the heat and decided to relocate to a different kitchen where things were a bit cooler. It wasn't hard to see that Kevin was still suffering from shell shock, (now referred to as PTSD, post traumatic stress syndrome) from his time in the Navy. While standing in front of his radar plotting targets he would literally pull his hair out. As a helmsman positioned directly behind him, it was strange for me to see a man in his thirties becoming prematurely bald at his own hand.

Chapter Twenty-Seven

The *Higgins* was passing the southern part of India, leaving the Maldives to the south, and steaming toward the Arabian Sea. The thermometer was continually climbing, and so was our workload. Early the following morning we were to perform drills with two warships, in preparation for future operations. The increase in work had been anticipated, and the crew was doing its best to wrench out the last bit of enjoyment it could. The crew, when not working, was provided recreational activities; a decent library, with books and movies, a gym, and a basketball net on the stern.

"Sports fans, Take Caution of Heavy Seas" warning signs were posted liberally, evidence of previous sprains, brakes, and bruises. The *Higgins* had a ship's store that provided the essentials in between ports. Barbecues on the fantail were always first preceded by an announcement to clear the fishing gear on the stern.

Beer-drinking sailors and fishhooks are never a good mix, and rationing beer was the rational thing to do. Life was still good! Murray and I were coming to the close of our watch, the seas were calm, and there wasn't a cloud in the sky. Our drills would start at 0700, and the 8x12 and the 12x4 would bear the brunt of the workload for today. The main body of the fleet was just over the horizon. At 0730 we would be shifting from autopilot to hand steering, the first ship would approach our starboard side and break away; this was called leapfrogging, and would be repeated until it was an old story. We had all been through a lot since departing San Francisco, and now we were preparing to do what we did best...replenish ships.

At 0740 the bridge got a call from the bow that he had a large contact two points to port. The second mate had already had the contact plotted on the radar, and it was the USS *Independence*, a large nuclear-powered aircraft carrier. Within five minutes the rest of her support group was on radar, and the bow called them in as they became visible. By any standard, an aircraft carrier is huge, but more than physical size, it is a show of the flag, and military muscle. My shipmate Don Morse could have cared less about any of the military hoopla, and he was continually getting into heated debates with the military department. In the near future Don would have an experience that would alter his idea of the military in a positive way.

The evening was pitch black, with only the celestial objects for illumination, and for first-time observers, the Southern Cross was instantly recognizable. With the absence of a moon, we were able to see a green light on the *Independence's* flight deck, and it wasn't her starboard-side light. The *Independence* was having flight operations, and her green light signaled that everything was a go. Five of us were on the stern having a smoke to see if we could catch a free air show. In a split second we heard a roar, and then we saw it. I knew right away what it was. "Over there! Check that guy out! Did you see that, Farley?"

"Yeah, that was cool. What was that, a F-18 or something?"

"No! That guy doing that high-speed loop was an A6 Intruder, an A6 all-purpose fighter bomber!"

Farley said, "How do you know all this flyboy stuff anyway?"

"Well, Farley, do you have time for a short story?"

"Yeah, okay, but let me have the abridged version."

"Sure, here goes. My Uncle Bill was the closest thing I had to a father, and he was quite a character. Uncle Bill was a World War Two night fighter pilot attached to the aircraft carrier *Bonhome Richard*. My Uncle Bill would tell me all kinds of stories about torpedo bombing runs, dogfight tactics, and different sorties he had been in. For me, the spookiest thing was to imagine myself landing a plane at night on an unlit aircraft carrier, while the ship was moving beneath you."

"What type of plane was he flying?" Farley asked?"

"An F4 Grumman Hell Cat; it was a cool-looking plane, real dark blue, single prop, it looked like the planes in that TV series *Ba Ba Black Sheep.*"

"The major difference was that on the TV show they were using marine-air Corsairs, and my uncle flew Navy Hell Cats. I asked my uncle about the TV show, and he said, 'Aside from all the Hollywood fluff, the show was true to form. Like the character Robert Conrad portrayed, Pappy Boynton, the men were short and tough. There was a height limit, because of limited space, but what the men lacked in physical stature, they made up in arrogance and toughness.'

"Just before I was to go to Vietnam, my Uncle Bill passed down a bit of sage advice, 'Always watch your back, and always watch out for the little guys!' I said to him, 'Vietnam is an entire nation of little guys.'

"'It's not their little guys I'm talking about; I'm talking about our little guys.' I look back on that piece of advice as priceless, especially coming from a height-challenged person. He wasn't perfect, and neither am I, but he left me with a code and a set of standards to live by, and when I get too much leeway, I make a course correction and get back on track. Uncle Bill was constantly trying to get me to fly, and I still value his efforts even though he couldn't light the spark. Over the years he owned numerous airplanes, and he was in newspapers on several occasions.

"He would commute with his plane to different cities and states, and in the nineteen fifties and sixties that was unique. Occasionally I would go for a plane ride with him, even though it scared the hell out of me. For him, flying was akin to getting in your car and going to the grocery store, and once in the sky he enjoyed the trick stuff. Now look over there—see that plane taking off?"

"Yeah, that's something you don't see every day, that's one of those new Stealth jets."

"Yeah, F-18!"

"Anyway, he would do barrel rolls, and slow rolls, and the worst was the freefalling dives. Luckily we never came upon any barns; I don't know what he would have done, but if the barn doors were opened I am sure he would have flown through."

"Oh yeah, Farley, another cool thing he told me was that when WW Two had ended, he was back here on the West Coast, and he and two of his buddies flew underneath the Golden Gate Bridge in formation. If you got caught doing that today they would probably yank your licenses. He tried everything to get me to fly, and he would say things like, 'You know you're smart, you have great reflexes, and great eyesight, you would make a great commercial pilot.' And my comeback was usually something like, 'Thanks but no thanks, Uncle Bill. You see those ships down there in that mothball fleet? That's where I want to be.' He kept his plane at the Napa airport in

California, and at the time we were flying over Mare Island. At an early age I remember him identifying planes. If there was any air traffic around he would constantly be identifying; 'That's a Beechcraft, see that one it's a Piper Cub, or there goes a DC-3.' Many times he didn't need to see a plane; the sound alone was good enough. His eyesight was the best I had ever seen. He would also explain things to me, like what the difference was between a wing stall and an engine stall. I was mildly interested when it came to piloting a plane, but I wouldn't bite, I am sure it was frustrating for him.

"What I was really interested in were those battle groups and task forces that I saw on the TV show *Victory at Sea*. Big battlewagons with huge sixteen-inch guns lobbing 2,000-pound shells—man, that's what I thought was cool, not flying around in a piece of tin like a sitting duck just waiting to get your ass shot off. Once we went to the Blue Angles air show when they came to town, and it was cool, but not cool enough for me to even consider it as a career or a pastime."

Farley said, "It's great that you had all those opportunities. Do you ever regret not flying for a living?"

"No, never, not one bit; I only want to look at airplanes from the ground upward, or from a cushy seat back aft.

"In 1962 he bought a new Corvette roadster, and I thought that was the coolest car on the planet. Uncle Bill would keep a log on the car just like a log that would be kept on an airplane— you know, maintenance records, miles, hours, the whole bit."

"Yeah, I bet that was cool. Driving a 1962 Corvette is probably as close to flying as you can get."

"That's for sure, Farley. Occasionally he would let me take it for a spin, and I'm damn lucky I didn't kill myself. Naturally, I had to see if the one hundred and eighty miles per hour indicated on the speedometer was bogus or not. Over one hundred and twenty I started to get spooked, and eased her back, there was no way I was going to the top end. To me, that was flying,

"Let me buy you a cup of coffee, Farley."

"Yeah, sure, let's go. You know that guy Bill Braumbauh in engineering?"

"Yeah, I think so. He's fifty-five or so, about six feet."

"That's him. Well, he was telling me he was Special Forces recon or something like that. Why is it no one ever says they were just a plain old grunt, or a dog soldier? Someone had to have been there doing all the thankless shit jobs in the Nam."

"Yeah, I know. You hear it all the time from these guys, either they were in the teams, or back when they were in the bush, or in the LRRP's. I doubt if anyone's gonna tell a war story beginning with, 'This ain't no shit—I burned the shitters for a full tour of duty.' Yes, I was dodging bullets, RPGs and rockets the whole time, and I made sure the cans got fresh diesel every week and burned real good!"

Chapter Twenty-Eight

"I don't want to be an alarmist but…" Joe Bones on his way down from the bridge, passing the sailors' deck. "Hey do you guys know that Farley's been stuck in the elevator for fifteen minutes? And now the engineers got the thing shut down, so you have to walk up to the bridge."

Someone said, "What's happening, Joe? Is he still in there?"

"Well, apart from Farley in the elevator, we just spotted the *Independence* up ahead so things should be happening soon."

"I hope so, I'm bored out of my skull. I could use the overtime money for the stewardess at the Gulf hotel. I'm going to get some ice. You guys want to join me for a toddy for the body?"

I said, "Don't even talk to me about booze; I'm just starting to get my head clear after your last party."

Farley said, "Don't look at me; you know I don't drink anymore. At least for today, count me out!"

"Man, what's with you guys anyway? You're doing some kind of chanting thing, and what are you doing, Joe? Didn't you get hooked up with some Maharishi cult thing, and you're dancing around playing a tambourine. You're all going to the dogs. What you both need is a double shot of Wild Turkey to put your head right. I don't want to see you guys turn into some new age pansies that listen to new age alternative music, and drink hazel vanilla, raspberry coffee, and fag water out of a bottle. If you change your minds, you know where I live. See yaah."

Then Farley said, "You're crazy. Why did you ever tell Joe Bones you were chanting—it will be all over the ship."

I said, "I don't care about a bunch of stupid gossip, if someone's got a problem with my chanting or anything else, it's their problem. Bones said to me one day, 'I don't know how you watch-standers guys do it, spending all your time up here on the bridge having to put up with these idiot officers, and being in hand steering most of the time when it's not required.'

"I only told him I started chanting, and that it has been helping. And I might stop tomorrow or I might, not, but for now it works. He made a big deal out of it; you should have heard him, 'You started chanting?' Naturally he started laughing. 'Oh man, that's it, of course, all you guys are in some kind of weird-ass cult, I knew it, knew it. Come on, you can tell me, what are you chanting?'

"So I told him, 'No Mo Ho Ren Ye Ko, and I do it over, and over again.' He said, 'Well, what does it mean?' I told him I don't know. 'Well what do you mean you don't know what it means? It's got to mean something.'

"'I'm sure it means something, but I didn't get to that part yet. I don't think it matters, that's not the point, it's the effect that matters.'

"There's no shortage of religions, cults, books tapes and philosophies to follow; when Joe is ready he'll find one or maybe he won't, until then he's still on that elevator heading down."

"God, where did you get all that psycho babble from, that twenty-eight-day detox?"

"As a matter of fact I did, and it's not psycho babble it's information that works."

"Whatever, but what can you accomplish in twenty-eight days?"

"Are you kidding? For one thing, you can get your dumb ass out of the revolving door of drinking, passing out, getting well, getting drunk passing out ad nausea."

"Wow, you sound like you were in bad shape."

"I was, and I might be better know, but it's still a one-day program. Back then, I was at what they call the 'jumping-off point.' I was at death's door, my friend. I had a wad of money after getting paid off my last ship, and I met up with this wild Polish girl in Frisco."

(I just had to tell him). "It's San Francisco, Farley."

"Whatever! Look, it's my story. Anyway, we both had plenty of money, and she was a computer genius, and had a high-powered job in a bank, and was pulling down one hundred twenty thousand a year. I still remember I asking her, 'How in the hell can you make so much money in a bank?' And she says to me, 'I'm in recovery.' And I said, 'Recovery, you mean rehab, like the Betty Ford clinic?' She said, 'Hell no, not even close. I recover computer systems when they go down.' She had to carry a pager and a cell phone. She would get calls if there was a satellite glitch, or if the sunspots were acting up, or if a satellite screwed up. Hell, I didn't know about any of that jazz; here I was a deck ape on a merchant ship, hooked up with a computer whiz kid…it was a perfect match."

My curiosity was getting the best of me. I said, "Where did you meet her?"

Farley said, "Where else but in a bar? Where else would two respectable alcoholics meet? We met in the financial area, where all the hot shots go, I had just come out of a sailor bar across the street, and just took a wrong turn, and fell in. I stumbled into a bar stool and turned around and she said, 'You look like you could use a drink.'

"And there she was…absolutely gorgeous, dressed to kill, beautiful long black hair, fantastic smile, great figure…she was stunning, and she was drunk as a hoot owl. As she bent over to get something in her handbag, everything went flying across the deck. We both scrambled around the deck trying to pick up all the stuff from her handbag. Anyway, I fell for her right away, she was smart as a whip, and a real looker, the kind of gal that construction workers whistle at when she walks down the street, and she was a knockdown drunk. Naturally, it was too good to be true, because she was crazier than a shithouse rat. We thought we had some kind of Kismet thing going, because it turned out we shared the same birthday. February fourteenth; we thought that was real romantic, the whole Valentine thing and all, although ten years apart, can you believe it, it seemed like a relationship made in heaven.

"On our first date, we went to a really fine restaurant on the Embarcadero, we got back to my place and the first thing she says is, 'Okay, let's get down to business, where's your liquor cabinet?' It wasn't long till I found out she was in worse shape than me. Sure she lived in a beautiful loft, and had a prestigious job, and drank expensive wine, but she was driving around in a four-hundred-dollar truck that she had got in return for trading in her one-year-old BMW while she was drunk.

"The IRS was after her for the tune of eighteen thousand dollars, and she had at least one pending lawsuit against her, but I was in love. The first inkling that I might have a problem with her was when I brought her on a ship. My Polish friend George told me, 'Farley, she's just another Polish girl hooked on the potato juice. You better get rid of her ASAP, because she will make your life miserable.' He was absolutely right. I could go on, and on... She would do unbelievable things. For a small woman she could drink unbelievably large amounts of alcohol, from gallons of expensive wine to cheap rotgut whiskey. One night we went to a special martini bar, I'll guarantee you they're still talking about us. She said to me, 'Farley, you've got to try this vodka from Holland; it's fantastic, it's like water, and you can drink it all night,' and that's what we did, and we were both eighty-sixed. We weren't thrown out on our ear for not spending money; I think we dropped three hundred dollars that night. We were on a roll.

"The next day we sobered up just enough to rent a Lincoln Towncar, and drive up to Lake Tahoe. We were living large; the best restaurants, staying in big hotel suites, it was crazy. One night, while having cocktails I suggested we live together, that's how sick I was. The next day I went to a pawnshop in downtown Reno, and bought a fifty-two-hundred-dollar engagement ring, and that night I give it to her in the hotel suite. We had room service working overtime, they brought lobsters, clams on the half shell, fancy French pastry, champagne, canapés, cordials, aperitifs, anything that sounded cool...we didn't miss a thing...I mean the works. I wanted a real intimate and romantic setting, so were watched our favorite movie, *Midnight Run*, on pay TV."

I said, "Oh yeah, what a great movie—that's the one with Deniro, and all those crazy characters, but how do you see that as romantic?"

"I don't know, we just did. Will ya let me finish my story? So we're watching the movie, and I put it on pause and formally ask her to marry me, and I gave her the ring. Later on I found out she wanted to have a big wedding in Venice, and honeymoon in Paris. Stella— that was her name, by the way—wanted to be in a white horse-drawn carriage with four white horses. Now that I think about it, maybe that was an omen of the Four Horses of the Apocalypse."

I said to Farley, "God, you guys were way out there. Where the hell were you going to come up with the money?"

"I don't know; I'm sure I didn't tell her I was the captain on my ship, she wanted us to pay guests to fly to Venice. Yeah, she took me on a ride, and I never thought I would come back, but I'm here now, and I'm sober.

"We both had a complete break with reality, it was truly nuts. We finally got out of Reno with our winnings, and on the way back to the Bay area she said to me, 'Stop the car right now, I have to get in the trunk!' She got out of the car, and opened the trunk. It was ten in the morning, and I can see her in the rearview mirror, and she was taking a slug from a bottle of Jack."

"Wait a minute, how much did you say you won?

"Believe it or not, we left with twenty-two thousand dollars. So look, I see her back there, and I was thinking, *Farley, old boy, you got yourself a beauty this time.* As I surveyed the situation, it dawned on me, this is idiotic, the car was full of hash, and God knows what else, she's half in the bag, and I'm really not sure if she is doing any other drugs, and we're both still legally drunk.

"Somehow we got back to San Francisco, and she was having problems at work, big surprise, huh? Well, one day Stella decided to go home early, and she went to 'our bar' at noon, to have a few; the bartender kept pouring, and she kept drinking. When I got there, I didn't know she had been there all day, and she was completely hammered. She couldn't even stand up. It was at this point I thought there might be a problem, I knew something had to be done. We were both sliding further and further. I checked out AA, she said she really wasn't ready, breaking up was horrible, but there was no other way."

I said, "It sounds like you had to make a decision; either her or alcohol."

"It wasn't that cut and dry; there was more to it, but if I was going to get, and stay sober, you're right, and you can only do it for yourself, and no one else. As I look back, I can see that I had two breakups, one with her, and one with booze."

"When's the last time you saw her?"

"It's been years. During the week of our breakup, I was back at the scene of the crime, the bar where we met, and her new boyfriend was there, and it wasn't pretty. I was half in the bag, and I went right up to the two of them, we got in a shouting match, and I decked her new prince. He got up and hit me with wimpy right, and it wasn't long before we were rolling around the deck entertaining the financial dinner crowd. The bartender and gutsier patron, threw me out on my ass…it was a sorry sight.

"That's when I knew I was looking at my bottom, and I was tired of digging. I couldn't stop with just AA, I had to go into a program up in Calistoga and detox, and things have been a real roller coaster ride, and it's all good. They told me I had to change everything, and I did, because I knew my life depended on it. I got a sponsor, I got 'The Book' and went to meetings.

"I was nervous about going back to sea because booze is everywhere, but I ran into this sober old-timer that worked on the waterfront, and he had thirty-four years without a drink. Can you imagine, thirty four years? 'Be your own best friend' and 'Stay connected' were just two of the helpful expressions he would say. I also took his advice and subscribed to *The Grapevine*, it's a meeting in print, and provides an excellent method for staying connected. I have six copies with me if you want one?"

I said,   "Maybe, but not now—we'll talk. That was some story—what happened to your fiancée?"

"As I said, she got a boyfriend right away, and they are probably drinking themselves to death. It was hard, because I still cared for her."

"She sounds like my kind of girl, Farley."

"Oh man, you don't know, being with her was like being in an enjoyable train wreck."

"Farley, I had no idea what you had been through, but I got to hit the sack, 0400 comes early, and we're going to be underway replenishing all day tomorrow."

"Yeah, Ted, see you tomorrow, and thanks for listening."

Chapter Twenty-Nine

Murray was in orbit; he had drunk two pots of coffee in the past two hours, and he was so spun that his eyes were crossed. The little leaping gnome had just completed his wake-up calls, and was yelling and screaming all the way back to the bridge. With Murray's tasks completed he bolted up to the wheelhouse to take the wheel. However, he made the mistake of looking at our stern just before relieving me, and I could see terror in his eyes.

There were thirteen ships lined up on our stern, and I knew it freaked him out. I could always tell when Murray was freaked. Not only did his eyes bug out, but he stunk; the smell would be unbearable. It wasn't so much that he was dirty; it was the garlic. For some reason, he consumed abnormally large quantities of garlic, and I never asked why. With Murray on the wheel, I looked aft on our port side, and there it was, a CVA, the USS *Independence*. A radio talker on our bridge said, "One thousand yards, and closing." By now, we must have had fifteen people in the wheelhouse including TT.

"The bow is even with the stern, sir."

"Very well," was the captain's response. The *Andrew J. Higgins* was no small ship, but the *Independence* dwarfed us. She was even with our stern for what seemed like ten minutes, and then she started to make her approach. Murray's fifteen minutes were almost up. I looked at my watch; three minutes left. I was now standing behind Murray. I wanted to see how much wheel he was using, and to get a general feel. When I felt confident, I tapped him on the shoulder, and as he looked back at me, I took the wheel. As Murray dropped back, the *Independence* accelerated up to our port side, and I compensated by applying left rudder. I was getting in the groove. No sooner had the *Independence* made her approach on our port side than people on our bridge began to move to the starboard side.

The *Scudd County*, an LST (landing ship tank), was making her approach, and she was loaded down to her load marks with fighting equipment. Trying to get a glimpse of the approaching ship, while staying focused on my heading, I had a feeling I was being watched. Sure enough, the captain was giving me a look, and I knew that only five tenths of a degree off course, and I would see that look again. The *Scudd County* had no less than twenty marines at her port rail staring up at our wheelhouse. Normally we wouldn't see that big a showing, and just thought their unusual vigilance was due to the females on our bridge. But this time the appearance of females appeared to bring everything to a stop on the LST. We, on auxiliary ships, had females, but on combatants it was a different story, and the marines looked as if they were going to swim over and scale up to our main deck.

It wasn't long before we had ships on both sides, with cargo flowing, and the work for the day had begun. The 4x8 was now the watch behind, and Murray would head down to after steering, and I would beat feet to the fantail. I had a rescue swim bag that was filled with all kinds of cool stuff to bring to an over-the-side helo party. Murray had been acting stranger than usual, and I could tell he was up to something. He had a goofy smile on his face, and just before Murray went below he made his way toward TT, thereby taking the long way to the coffee mess.

The Navy chief didn't give Murray any quarter; she was right in his face as she said, "You stay away from me, you little pervert, or I'll have you brought up on charges before you can say cross-dress!"

Thinking to myself, *Wow, now that's what he needed to hear!* In a second his face turned beet red, and he flew below like he was shot out of a cannon. The Navy chief, without skipping a beat continued talking in her radio headphones and acted like nothing happened. I had other things on my mind; such as my swim fins, BC vest, a knife with a blade curved just right to cut the seatbelt harness of the pilot, and copilot, and I was good to go. Being at the ready, I had a chance to reflect on my decision to be a rescue swimmer.

Just to be perfectly clear, let's see; at a moment's notice, I would hurl myself off the ship's stern, and go down with the chopper, and single-handedly rescue a minimum of two guys out of a helo that was descending in water at a rate of eight feet per second, and in any kind of conditions, day or night. What the hell was I thinking? I must be out of my mind!

When Murray and I returned for the afternoon 1600x2000 watch, we still had a ship on our starboard side. We were looking at a different ship, but the sailors and marines had that same look…the thousand-yard stare. On her main deck, all eyes were trained in our direction. This time the young lads were exercising with their shirts off, and it was weird; it looked like the Village People, and they were making us uncomfortable. The only person enjoying himself, that didn't seem to think it odd, was my partner. This was getting ridiculous, and I was curious to find out what was going on. With a break from the wheel, I went outside, and looked up at the flying bridge deck, but for the life of me I couldn't figure out what all the fuss was about. I then I craned my neck upward to the signal deck and, wow! It was a blond female, with her shirt tied above her waist was exposing her midriff, while she was sending semaphore signals across to the signalman on the LST.

It was now abundantly clear what all the fuss was about…she was putting on her own USO show, and the troops were loving it. This was an asset that somehow escaped me. Naturally, it didn't take long for the word to get out to the rest of the fleet, and ships would pull alongside with awe-inspiring enthusiasm. Guys would do any number of stupid things to get her attention, and there were no limits to creativeness noticed by the *A. J. Higgins's* Sea Goddess. When I was on standby status taking a break, I would go out on the bridge wing to get some fresh air, and shoot the breeze with my new friends in the signal department. In addition to our Sea Goddess we had a new seaman signalman striker. He was kind of a funny-looking kid from the Midwest, and his direct supervisor was the Sea Goddess. I think you can see where I am going with this.

Trying to impart some of my knowledge to the signal department, I found myself on the signal bridge with the new recruit. The signal deck had a pair of "Big Eyes." These were large and very powerful binoculars. Well, one day we were steaming along, and the bow lookout had just called in a contact. The new kid said, "Yeah, sure, I see it." He was using the big eyes now.

So I said to him, "I bet you can't read the name of that ship."

He said, "Oh yeah, just watch me! I got it." He began spelling the name. "It's the N-O S-M-O-K-I… Ah shit, aw, never mind!"

That was the last time he looked for a ship's name on the forward-facing part of the house of a tanker, and next time he would have a "weather eye" when taking advice from a merchant sailor with a touch of the smart ass. He was a good kid, and we had a lot of laughs, but he got the last laugh when I continued my lookout workshop. I was behind the big eyes trying give him some pointers, and who should make their way up to the signal bridge directly in front of the big eyes, but—that's right, you guessed it—the Sea Goddess. She not only wasn't thrilled that I had my big-eye lenses focused on her physique, but she was equally disgruntled that I, a civilian, was showing her protégé the skills of his trade.

At exactly 1900 we were empty, and of all the breakaway songs we had heard, theirs was by far the weirdest, "Adios, Arvoire, Auf Weidersein," by Lawrence Welk. With a full day's work completed, thoughts turned to the mail that had been distributed; these were the days before e-mail, and snail mail was our lifeline to the world. Naturally a replenishment ship without cargo is worthless, so arrangements were being made for a fill-up.

Chapter Thirty

Diego Garcia is not on most standard world Atlases, and unless you're looking for it in the right ocean you'll never find it. Diego Garcia is above the equator in the Indian Ocean between the continents of India and Africa. This little island that America shares with England was our "last-chance gas station" before entering the Red Sea.

We were elated at the confirmation that Diego Garcia was to be our next port of call, and we wouldn't be needing to rendezvous with a tanker in the I.O., Indian Ocean. Diego Garcia has long been a strategic base for the United States and British military. I could probably handle a short visit, but for more than a month, I would go bats. ("Daygo" is Navyspeak for Diego Garcia.) It is too confusing with San Diego and is primarily forward staging area for repositioning ships that sit with tons of military gear, waiting for the world to take a dump. Some guys enjoy this kind of duty, some guys even enjoy being stationed at the South Pole, or the Mojave Desert. It's a fact of life that the far outposts of the world need to be manned, and thankfully there are people suited for these jobs.

I was on the bow the night before arrival, and the sky was spectacular. With only a quarter moon, and with no lights from civilization, the sky was unbelievable; even the faintest star would shimmer and twinkle. Feeling unusually witty, I felt compelled to tell Joe Gonzales my star joke.

"Joe, you know, it has been said that if you look up at the sky for an hour you will see no less than ten stars, and you know what that means?"

"No, what does that mean?"

"It means the sky is falling!" He didn't think it was so funny, and the next day he said he only saw eight. I told him to go home and see if he can make eight pizzas in an hour. It wasn't funny, he knew it, and I knew it, we were all beginning to snap. With one month in a

Japanese dry dock, and another aboard, and an abbreviated stay in the Philippines, as a tease, we needed time off. We were anticipating a three- to four-day port stay, but that never materialized. You had to give the military credit for making this remote piece of real estate fit for human habitation. Of course, an argument could be made that they turned a piece of paradise into a toxic dump site, reeking with chemical and biological hazards.

There was a delicate balance between being a far-off desolate island gulag that no one wanted to go to, and a beguiling island paradise. The water was paradise water...crystal clear blue, all the way down to the sandy white bottom, much like a travel brochure, or a computer screen saver. The beaches were dotted with small sailboats, surfboards, and beach huts. Unfortunately, our daydreams of flipping Frisbees through the air on a warm beach with bikini-clad female women of the opposite sex was never realized, due to an unscheduled event.

Although Diego Garcia was in the middle of the Indian Ocean, you could almost close your eyes and here the song "Bali Hi" from that classic movie *South Pacific*. Naturally there was one minor glitch to this tropical dreamland...the military. But if you could handle paradise with lots of military ritual, and hardware, you would adapt, and do very well. Throw in a few other "essentials," and who knows, you may thrive, and never want to leave.

We were all fast in Diego Garcia at 0900, and the AB day workers where making the hose connections in preparation for loading cargo. The 4x8 had the entire day to themselves. Murray said he was going to stay clear of beach activity; even though there was a rumor going around about Daygo being a fantastic place to free dive for sponges.

As fantastic as the sponge diving sounded, Murray wouldn't set foot on the beach. Murray was just beginning to see his blisters heal from his last beach foray in the Philippines. At this time I thought it prudent not to make any more shore-excursion suggestions, as Murray might get the idea that parting my hair with a fire axe was a good thing to do. Murray wasn't humiliated — that was impossible — he was just being cautious; you see, being from another planet, he was operating from a different orientation, and different set of values.

Before any of us set one foot off the gangway, the management handed down a warning. The captain had a pre arrival meeting for the officers, and the gist of the meeting was, "For God's sake, don't screw up! The whole damn battle group and all these Shipwreck Kelly's on Diego Garcia will be watching us." Our reputation was increasing with leaps and bounds and not just our professional demeanor, or military bearing, and ship-handling skills. Once ashore, most of us went our separate ways, in typical sailor fashion (by the time you hit the beach, most sailors were sick of one another, and went their separate ways). Once ashore, only by chance did crewmembers get thrown together, and the likelihood increased if there was only one bar in town.

While Mongo and I were running down the gangway, he asked for a favor, and I willingly obliged; of course a cocktail promised at the first bar we spotted helped my willingness. Mongo, somewhat embarrassed, said he had a newspaper from his hometown, Sultry Mattress Springs, Arkansas, that was concealed in a paper bag. His plan was for me to take his picture while he held the newspaper in front of himself. Apparently, the newspaper had an ongoing contest every month, and whoever sent in a picture of themselves with the paper from the farthest geographical location from Sultry Mattress Springs would win a prize. Evidently people were traveling to the far ends of the earth to evacuate this little piece of Heaven on Earth.

Diego Garcia was the perfect location for Mongo's contest, not only because it was in the middle of nowhere, but Diego Garcia had the perfect sign. It had little arrows pointing to different geographical locations; eighty-seven hundred miles to Hollywood, fifty-seven hundred miles to Baghdad, and nine thousand miles to Manhattan. In Mongo's case it would take some additional calculations to get the precise mileage from Diego Garcia to Sultry Mattress Springs, Arkansas. As we were setting up the shot, I said to Mongo, "Hold the paper up just a little more, yeah, that's perfect."

Then we heard a female voice, "Now isn't that the nicest thing you ever saw, Marge? Will you take a look at those two big burly guys taking cute little pictures of themselves with their newspaper?"

The one that must have been Marge said, "It sure is. Hey, fella, you want to borrow my hair brush?" They both were laughing hysterically, and went around a corner, leaving us feeling somewhat stupid, and somewhat less manly. Worse than the initial insult was the that neither one of us came up with a reply, and all we were left with was a long silence.

"Will you hold still, Mongo, so I can take this damn picture!"

He said, "Hey, they weren't from our ship were they?"

"No, they weren't. I got the shot, now let's get the hell out of here." I never did find out if Mongo won the prize, but I am sure he was a front-runner. I didn't imagine many people in the States had heard of Diego Garcia, let alone knew where it was or made the journey. I handed Mongo his camera as our shipmate Joe Bones yelled coming out of the enlisted club, "Guys, get over here—we have to talk!"

"Great, now what did he do?"

"I don't know, Mongo, but let's go—he looks serious."

Chapter Thirty-One

I said, "Would you say that a little slower, Joe?"

"There's a guy in the Tipsy Skipper bar and he's asking all kinds of questions!"

Mongo stepped in and said, "Look, just slow down, and start at the beginning."

Joe began again, "I was in there having a few, and I got in a conversation with this guy, and then we started playing pool. At the time, he seemed like a regular guy, but then I was feeling like he was pumping me for information as soon as I told him I was on the *Higgins*. I didn't think too much of it at first, but then when I told him we had a couple of good-looking gals aboard, his eyes lit up, and then he started asking me about Blaze."

Mongo said, "Wow, No shit!"

Then I said, "Well, what did you say?"

"Nothing really!"

"What did you tell him?"

"Nothing"

"And who is he and where did he come from?"

"Okay, wait a second, and I'll tell you—Jesus, take it easy, will you! First of all, I didn't give him one bit of information; I just let him believe that she was still on board." Mongo and I let out what must have seemed to be a sigh of relief.

"And as for him, he's on a ship right here; he's on the *Sergeant Pomroy*, one of those repositioning ships. He wasn't giving up much information, but he did say that he and Blaze were old friends and he wanted to see her."

Mongo said, "Okay, so now what do we do, guys? You know this joker is going to call the ship, and sooner or later, he's going to find out the truth."

I said, "You're right, but up until then, we can at least try to steer him clear. Joe, what did he look like?"

119

"I know what you're getting at, and he doesn't look Italian, but he looks serious."

Mongo said to me, "You know, you guys are going have to give me a little more info about Blaze. I don't know half of what you're taking about."

I told him, "First of all, not now, Mongo; and secondly, if I told you the Mob in New York was involved would you want to know the rest of the story?"

Mongo said, "Let me get back to you on that."

Joe Bones finally said, "Maybe we should go back to the Tipsy Skipper and see what we can find? Hey, what more can we do? Look, there's a Navy exchange that is well stocked with stuff that I'm sure I can't live without—let's go check it out."

And we did. We all traipsed over to the exchange, and then I heard Mongo say, "Hey, Murray, I see you over there. I thought you would be out at the beach diving for natural sponges; I heard the diving here is world class."

"You guys really think you're hilarious don't you?"

I said, "We have our moments."

Then Mongo said, "Holy Christ, there she is, over there by the chocolate Easter bunnies, at aisle C."

I said, "Mongo, don't have a heart attack, will ya? Who is it, TT?"

"No, it's the signal chick!"

"You mean our Sea Goddess."

"Yeah, and you better stay away. As we say in the merchant service, 'If it's gray stay away,' and that applies to ships, and women."

I said, "Mongo, you do what you want. I'm just going to say hello." As I walked over to the Easter display, I saw the better half of our signal department.

"Hello there. What a nice surprise to see you cats and kittens here!"

Our Sea Goddess said, "Oh, it's you again. Isn't this nice—it's kind of a Bergdorf Goodman's in a Quonset hut." Then she turned to her fellow signal person and said, "Isn't it nice to get off the ship, just to get away from all the weirdos aboard? Nice to see you again, but we really must be getting back." So much for shore excursion social niceties; this wasn't my day to expand my horizon.

Then Mongo said, "What's Bergdorf Goodman's anyway?"

"Mongo, I never been there, but I have a feeling it's where people with too much money and time like to unload their cash on overpriced crap that's called high fashion."

Having recovered from our encounter, good news awaited us at the *Higgins*; the mail had arrived. Richard the third mate looked as if he had a head start on happy hour as he made his way up the gangway. Richard was decked out in his cowboy hat, with matching chrome-tipped boots, and his custom-made leather motorcycle jacket, blazing with silver buttons and chains. Richard's exuberance wasn't equal to his ensemble; he was in a foul mood and cursing something about his wife. He had opened a second letter, and tore it to shreds, and crashed into his room, and slammed the door.

We were scheduled to depart in two days, but rumors of a possible early departure were confirmed, and we singled up lines at 2000. Iraq's Saddam Hussein had invaded Kuwait, and we were going to be the first responders. Well, what the hay, it was about time we had a little fun! Immediately our awareness level cranked up a notch. The nearest we could figure was that the battle group was to steam to the Persian Gulf, and stand by for further instructions.

In less than twenty minutes, the ABs at the manifold area disconnected three product hoses. Murray and myself were in the process of shifting the watch from the gangway to the bridge. Joe Bones and I had a chance to discuss the inquisitive sailor back at the enlisted men's club, and we agreed that it was fortuitous that we were leaving early, and hopefully he wasn't able to check if Blaze was aboard. The harbor pilot was on his way up to the bridge, Murray at the helm, I was on standby, and Joe Gonzales on the bow. We were eager to get underway even though we had no idea what lay ahead. Somewhere below at another level, the crew was thinking, *This better not screw up our revisiting the Philippines, or going to Thailand, Singapore, and Jeddah, or any other cool ports. After all, a sailor has his priorities!* Upon making a quick disconnect and sailing short on cargo, we would follow the *Independence*. The *Independence* was much faster, and the emergency situation dictated she be on station ASAP. Her screening ships had speeds far in excess of the *Higgins*, and could keep up with no problem; the rest of the auxiliary ships would do their best. A convoy will go as fast as the slowest ship; our top sea speed was in the neighborhood of twenty-one knots…still a respectable sea speed. There is something about living in a question that makes life interesting, and that's about all we had, were questions.

Were we going up to the Persian Gulf? Were we going through the Straits of Hormuz into the Persian Gulf? Or would they direct us to the Red Sea? More importantly, what about our shore time? And of course, the recurring thought was, were Thailand and the other cool places to be put in limbo? Saddam Hussein was beginning to get on our nerves. Most of us had heard Saddam Hussein's name when it had become popularized with the Iraq-Iran war of 1988-1989, along with that other peckerwood, Momar Kadafy.

Chapter Thirty-Two

We were three hours out of Diego Garcia when I saw our jilted mate, William the Third, on the main deck, and he was acting in a most peculiar way. He had a sea bag slung over his shoulder, and was dragging two bags of clothes to a handrail. I said, "What's up, mate? Going someplace?"

He said, in a barely coherent voice, "You really want to know? Well, screw her!" And he began throwing his clothes over the side, socks, shirts, pants, and even underwear. Being on the leeward side everything immediately flew into the air, and into the seas. I tried to reason with him, but William looked to be possessed, and as I looked him in the eye, I could see that Richard was beyond reasoning. William's eyes looked like two piss holes in the snow, and he must have had a world-class hangover.

I said, "Mate, what the hell are you doing? You can't just throw your clothes out there."

"Oh yeah, I can't, huh? Just watch me. That bitch! The hell with her!" He staggered back to his cabin for a second load, and looking in our wake I could see his clothes, slowly sinking beneath the waves.

"I don't need her, and I don't need that stuff, I don't need anything!" And he was gone.

I went down the galley to grab a cup of coffee, and ran into Don Morse, and we both went to find William. Don and I spotted him dragging a half-empty bag. I said, "That's not everything is it? Mate, you're gonna need some clothes to stand your watch in two hours."

Then he started balling, "Why? So I can make money, so I can give it to her, so she can give it to her boyfriend? I'm gonna get them! I'm gonna get the both of them!"

"Richard, get a grip, get a grip on yourself. You're not going to get anyone without your clothes—what the hell did you do that for? What do you have left?"

Then he said, "I have my black socks, and these shorts I have on…." Richard was clearly a mess. Don Morse and I got Richard up to his room and pieced him back together, and he somehow sallied forth to stand his watch. The next day Richard didn't recall a thing. To not remember bits and pieces of a wild night is one thing, but he said to the captain that somebody broke into his room and stole his clothes. I have heard of blackouts, but nothing like this…he remembered nothing, absolutely nothing!

Civilians with normal nine-to-five jobs barely keep up with front-page headlines, and when a major conflict arises they run for an atlas or encyclopedia to find out where things are. I can still recall going to a globe to locate Vietnam when it made the headlines, and saying to a friend of mine while still in high school, "Vietnam, where could that be? You ever hear of it?"

"Nope, I never heard of it."

I only found it when I was staring dead at it; it was like it was invisible, unless you happened to be looking at the exact spot in Southeast Asia. Up until the 1980s, sailors, and military people in general, viewed news as a luxury, because we didn't have access to the daily news (while shore-side people were reading about what happened, we became what was happening).Then we get to read about what we did months latter. Military people in forward-deployed areas away from the continental U.S. could at best get a copy of the *Stars and Stripes* newspaper. Until recent history, the *Stars and Stripes* newspaper was a serviceman's only link with back home. The greatest single addition to a sailor's way of life in the last one hundred years, apart from unions, has been the ability to send and receive email from a ship; at sea, we use every tool we can get our hands on to stay informed. Additionally, sailors are for the most part well read; because of our peculiar situation, most sailors are voracious readers. At sea, it is not uncommon to see someone with a fourth-grade education quoting from Joseph Conrad, Raymond Carver, or Thomas Jefferson, or Mel Blank.

Steaming north at a leisurely pace, we were to reach Oman in five days to refuel three ships. On arrival, we dropped the hook, and waited for further orders.

With nothing better to do than go fishing, that's what we did. The only real snag facing our shipboard fisherman was that he couldn't eat his prize. The steward department had specific instructions that they couldn't cook anything that was caught. Company policy...something to do with the military's required diet, fear of mercury poisoning, who knows—whatever it was, it dampened our anglers' enthusiasm. However, the crew's passions were revitalized in discovering that we would be going to the ancient city of Muscat, Oman.

Our port visit to Muscat had little to do with public relations, or morale building for the crew, and all to do with loading fuel at an offshore mooring station. No one aboard had been to Muscat, Oman, and going to a new and different port always creates excitement on a ship. For us at sea, anything that is more, better, or different is always preferred. Generally, we would take on fuel from a large commercial tanker, by consol (fuel consolidation). Like an UNREP, this was accomplished while underway, and we would do it one more time before going to Muscat.

Chapter Thirty-Three

It had become painfully obvious that the 4x8 could not stay out of trouble, and this time Joe Gonzales became the center of attention. After dinner, Joe had gone to the TV room, contented with a full stomach of chilidogs and piles of goop. Innocently enough, while Joe watched his movie, he fell asleep. Joe's snoring had been the launching of numerous controversies, and this time it was no different. To arrest Joe from his deep sleep and annoying snoring, more often than not, guys would yell at Joe, or throw things; small things, like popcorn, or oranges, paper cups, sometimes a shoe, or just about anything that would wake him. This time, there was a new twist; it was November 14, 1990, 1810 local time, when a crew member couldn't take it anymore. The disgruntled crewmember hurled a humongous glob of rocky road ice cream at Joe, and it struck Joe square in the face.

Getting hit in the face with ice cream doesn't sound all that bad, and striking Joe in the face wasn't all that difficult, as Joe had an ample amount of face, but a piece of the rocky part of the road got lodged in one of his nostrils, and when Joe awoke, he was ready to kill. Once large Joe got to moving, Joe packed a mighty force, and he hit the warring food-fighting cook on the nose with a copy of Norman Vincent Peale's best-selling book, *The Power of Positive Thinking*, and blood went everywhere. Three guys trying to watch the movie classic *Chitty Chitty Bang Bang* jumped in, and soon it was a full-on gymkhana.

Had we been elsewhere, the captain would have given everyone involved their walking papers, but because of the ship's location and situation, the brawlers were given a stern warning. Listening to the captain's wrath, for what I am sure seemed to be an eternity, was enough to put the kybosh on a future fracas. After a visit to our ship's hospital, Joe was scheduled to have a medical checkup, to see if he was in fact fit for duty. With Joe's being a hundred pounds overweight, poor eyesight, and the possibility he might have a real narcolepsy disorder, Joe's maritime career was in peril, and a revitalized pizza career on the beach appeared to be on the horizon.

We were a thousand yards from the tanker, stem twister, *Overseas Vermont*, and unlike our characteristic gray paint, the *Vermont* had a red hull with green decks, and actually looked good to our color-starved eyes. The *Higgins* would make her approach from the *Vermont's* stern, and advance on her starboard side. This was another first for me, but I felt comfortable. I had been chanting like a madman, and I had gotten plenty of practice steering in the last month, with what seemed like continual underway replenishing. The fully loaded *Vermont's* forward main deck was awash in boarding seas. As we closed in on her stern, at five hundred yards, it felt like our bow would touch her stern. I was steering 085, then 086, 087, my course to steer would be 087.5, and we were doing twelve knots. The required speed was twelve knots to maximize steering; anything less would require more rudder, thereby reducing the helmsman's reaction time. The crack of our line gun could be heard as we were in position, and the men on the *Vermont* raced to retrieve it.

Our people weren't accustomed to seeing a ship operated by so few people; Gonzo, one of the AB's said, "It looks like ghost ship. Where are they?"

The *Vermont* had an entire crew of twenty-four. Compared to the *Higgins's* crew of one hundred and twenty-two, it looked like a lonely ship. A ship of our size in the regular Navy would have a crew of four hundred…different missions, differing crews. The fuel transfer took ten hours; trying to project loading or discharging time is seldom accurate, due to the size and the amount of hoses, and the flow of the cargo. Seeing the *Vermont's* stern sailing over the horizon represented a long day's work, and longer days to follow. When operating with the fleet, there is much work for our class of ship; warships have unending requirements for fuel, spare parts, mail, and food stores, etc..

I had an opportunity to compare shipboard life on a tanker with that of life sailing with the fleet. After completing my assignment on the *Higgins* I was assigned to a black oil tanker, and I can recall, in my first days aboard, saying, "Is this it? Is this all there is? Where are the choppers, the forklifts, the people, and where are the rest of the ships?" Going from point A to point B, with the only break in monotony being tank cleaning, in my opinion, at best becomes dull and boring. Having an aircraft carrier on your port side, with Harrier jets taking off, while transferring fuel, and having helicopter operations on the stern, and forklifts moving cargo, and a warship approaching your starboard side at fifteen knots, lends to an excitement level that is hard to replicate.

AFARTS, the American military television station, informed us that we were in an operation called "Desert Shield," and the news got better when we discovered we were the first on the scene. However, being a first responder is one thing, but being a first responder that remains on the scene for months is a very different thing. The *Higgins* was put on a Mod Loc, Modified Location, and that meant just that. With no place to go, we would travel in circles, in squares, rectangles, and sometimes just drift and dream. The military has many word compressions (acronyms) that sound ominous and mysterious, and repetition brings familiarity. Mod Loc wasn't a fun one.

Chapter Thirty-Four

It was a bright and sunny morning, as our day began with the *Independence*, and behind her was an awe-inspiring collection of needy warships, with an insatiable appetite for fuel. The *Independence* accelerated to our port side, lines were passed, and cargo was flowing. The captain, along with the Navy communication chief, and the usual complement of people were on the port bridge wing, and about two hours into the replenishment, it happened!

The hose at rig station #6 burst, and fuel went everywhere. Rig station #6 was directly in front of the bridge, on the port side. The forward-facing windows on the bridge were covered in fuel oil, with everyone on the bridge wing getting soaked in fuel oil. The first indication that something was amiss was the captain's arms thrust into the air. The captain was heard saying, "Goddamn it, what the hell is going on down there? Who dropped the ball?" The radio person communicated to all essential personal, and an emergency shutdown commenced, and the chief mate came to the bridge to relieve the captain. Not ten minutes went by, and the captain was back on the bridge, with business as usual, and sporting a clean spiffy uniform.

The rig bosun, along with sailors, was on the main deck and the bridge busy cleaning up the mess that seemed to be everywhere. The captain was now looking down to the main deck and forward at #6 rig station, and we knew he was looking for the rig captain, who happened to be my buddy Joe Bones. It didn't take long, and as soon as the captain spotted Joe, it was an another Touchdown. The captain was yelling, and using his unusual style of body language to convey to Joe to get up to the bridge, and pronto. All eyes from neighboring ships were directed toward the *Higgins*, and it must have been a great show. If Joe Bones never considered jumping over the side, this would have been an opportune time for Joe to calculate his odds. The rig bosun and a couple of AB's got the burst cargo hose down, and were making a close inspection.

The captain and Joe Bones were face-to-face on the port bridge wing, and the old man was letting him have it. The captain's arms were up in the air, and then they were on his hips, back up in the air; he was working harder than a *Monday Night Football* referee. The captain then went for his radio, and the expression on the captain's face immediately changed. The captain then walked back over to say something, and you would have thought that Joe and the captain were old high school buddies. I knew Joe Bones was smooth, but he wasn't smooth enough to talk himself out of a situation this huge. Evidently, the hose had failed, and was not attributed to human error, meaning Joe, the human, was not responsible for the hose breaking. Although Joe and the crew were relieved at the outcome, we also knew that somebody down the line would catch it for not making proper maintenance inspections.

A rig captain has an enormous responsibility, not only for the gear, but for the many people working for him that are not even in the same department. Many of the people that make the UNREP evolution happen come from the steward department, and that is a colossal headache, with differing nationalities and languages. When the sun set, at least no one was hurt, repairs were made, and we were up and running for the next job.

In the following two weeks we did one more consol, and then we were headed for Mysirah, Oman. As one gets closer to the Persian Gulf, you get to experience the aroma of an occasional sheep ship. These ships come up from New Zealand and Australia to service the needs of the mutton lovers of the Gulf. In extreme heat, we would keep the exterior doors closed, not only aiding in comfort, but to protect the electronic gear. There are some odors that can penetrate any barrier, and one day someone said, "I don't see anything, but does anyone else smell that?"

The second mate said, "Yeah, sure do, I have him on radar at 19.3 miles out, and two points to starboard." Sheep ships can be detected long before they can be seen. When up close, the sight of them is almost worse than the smell. Four to five above decks, jammed with sheep, and that's not to mention what's below. Just the thought of working on one of these ships can bring on the horrors.

At Mysirah, helicopters would labor to transfer all types of dry cargo to us, but foremost in importance was our mail. Daily we had been doing helo operations on the stern, and it was becoming routine. I was really beginning to become fixated with these ungainly contraptions that flew through the air. The helicopter is really the strangest, most awkward thing to watch, and almost looks as if to defy nature. It is equally amazing to think it was invented by Leonardo da Vinci (1452-1519), right around the time Columbus discovered America. When you have the boring task of lookout, many strange thoughts can make their way into your head. Joe Gonzales said to me one day, "Just look at that thing! Why on earth would they name these things helicopters, especially after the airplane was in existence—why wouldn't they name it an airscrew? After all, that's what it really is."

I said, "You're right, the chopper is nothing but a screw—it winds up and it winds down, and it can't glide. Heck, choppers don't even appear to want to fly in the first place. I wouldn't want to get in one of those machines. I'd rather get on a roller coaster, or even bungee cord jumping headfirst off a bridge into a dried-up riverbed. You know Joe, just maybe I am spending too much time on the stern looking at these things." Which took me back to Nam, and I said to Joe, "In Nam we had this guy flip out one day, because he was paying too much attention to helicopters. My unit was on the beach, and day in and day out, choppers would make runs up and down the surf line. Then one day, this guy Whitey got out of his rack in the morning and thought he was a helicopter. We tried to reason with him, but he was gone. He had his hands up in the air, and was waving them around and going *whoosh, whoosh, whoosh!*"

Joe said, "Well, what happened to him?"

"He was sent back to a psych ward in Yokosuka, and last we heard he was on a bus with a shore patrol escort, and he wouldn't get off the bus, and it took a half a dozen shore patrol types to get him off the bus and back to the hospital without killing himself or anyone else. He was harmless until he did his whoosh-woosh-whoosh thing and start throwing things at people, and that really upset the locals."

Chapter Thirty-Five

The oil embargo against Iraq had left hundreds of oil tankers idle in the Persian Gulf, as well as the United Arab Emirates seaport of Fujiarh. We estimated one hundred empty oil tankers were swinging on the hook in the Fujiarh harbor. As we made our approach, low cumulus clouds were dancing on a backdrop of Sorrento blue sky. I was on bow lookout, and an odd thing was happening as we made our approach. A small cloud was moving with the ship, and stopped at the bow. The cloud was only four to five hundred feet in elevation, and when it got to the bow it opened up and dumped buckets of rain, and as quickly as the cloud arrived, it left. This would happen three times. At first, I thought my paranoia was kicking in, but when I was soaked for the third time, I just considered it a freak act of nature. I imagined my plight looked amusing from the bridge, that I was being pursued by a cloud.

Not to be distracted, while looking through my binoculars, I spotted a high-speed gunboat coming my way. I reported the boat to the bridge, and while training my binoculars on the gunboat ahead, I glanced to my right and there it was! That dopey cloud had returned, and it was more menacing than before, as it began to let go another torrent. The bridge said, "On the bow, look aft, and to port." As I turned my head, and without warning, there was a chopper, and both pilot and copilot were looking straight at me. The helicopter had positioned itself on our port bow as we steamed into the harbor, and the helo stayed level with our main deck. The chopper might have had their M-60's, and .50-cals., but I had my ass-kicking 7x50 binoculars and radio. It was a good thing they were up in that chopper, and not on my bow. I was starting to get worked up. "And if they knew what was good for them, they would back off. Who the hell did they think they were, sneaking up on me like that? They should show a little professional courtesy."

I looked at my watch, and mercifully, it was time for my relief, and Gonzales did get to the bow on time, and breathing like he had been doing wind-sprints. "Hi, Joe. I see you have your raingear; you know it's not going to rain for the next four hours!" And it didn't.

Then Joe said very seriously, "Any contacts?"

"Well, let's see, Joe… Things are kind of quiet. I see about one hundred tankers riding high, at anchor, and then there's that chopper at thousand yards to starboard, and five hundred yards on the port beam you've got that gray gunboat, but that's about it."

Joe already had a radio, so I gave him my spare battery, and he said, "Okay, I got it!"

When I got to the bridge, everyone had to tell me what a great laugh they had, watching me fend off the local clouds, plus the U.A.E. air force and navy.

Almost as quickly as the last line was made fast, the gangway hit the dock, and the crew set a track line for the Gulf Hotel. The rig bosun, a reliable asset and good judge of character, had reconnoitered the area previously, and provided reliable intelligence, that female women of the opposite sex frequented this establishment, along with a great selection of high-quality spirits. Fujiarh proved to be a port we could live with, and we were all eager to return.

The next day, an interesting thing happened. A half a dozen guys talked of having a new girlfriend, and when comparing notes, it was discovered that they were all in love with the same girl that shared the same features and social skills. Secretly, those involved were hoping it wasn't the same girl working the whole crew (these things happen). The fresh supply of mail from the States appeared endless, and as fast as we received it the mail was distributed to the rest of the fleet ASAP.

As I look back, I can appreciate more fully our safety record given the activity, and to the pilots' credit, I never saw a near miss. The superstructure of the *Higgins* had what we called a truck tunnel, thereby allowing forklift trucks to transit the stern through the house on the main deck, and forward up to the forecastle. After making a trip to Mysirah, it wasn't uncommon to see our main deck loaded with pallets of mailbags. The mail was being flown to Oman by large fixed-wing craft, and then heloed out to us for distribution to the fleet.

The *Higgins* was at the end of the mail chain, and whenever it arrived it was always a welcome sight. It wasn't unusual to see Murray at the head of a mail line, but now the third mate was showing unusual interest. The uniqueness of wearing clothes from the ship's store or donated rags by crewmembers was losing its luster, and I am sure Richard was tired of looking like a real *Higgins* poster boy.

After our initial port stay in Fujiarh, we began going into United Arab Emirates, U.A.E., on a regular basis. The main attractions were the duty-free shop and the Gulf Hotel. The Gulf Hotel was a local stop for employees of Gulf Air, wayward sailors, and flight crews on a layover. Stewardesses looking for an evening of recreation with an Arabian prince or a swarthy eligible sailor need look no further. Not to fear! The crew of the *A. J. Higgins* was not unfamiliar with the rigors of recreating.

Seldom am I shocked at people's creativity when it comes to the subject of recreation and how they spend their time. From the relatively civilized decks of the *Higgins*, across the dock, and about a half a mile away, the rocky parched dirt began increasing in elevation, ascending to the most uninhabitable landscape on the planet. My partner and I were positioned at the gangway, in the sweltering heat; when out of the depths of the engine room, a creature came forward. This inelegant-looking vision from engine room's gang dressed in lederhosen, a Tyrolean hat with a feather and a knapsack walked up to my partner and my watch partner said, "If you're a vender or yard worker, I'll have to see your I.D."

The engine room guy said, "I work here, I don't need I.D. You mean you've really never seen me before?"

"No, I have never seen you before, and I have my rules and regulations, and if you're going to give me trouble, I will have to call the mate, so wh...."

I couldn't stand it any longer, and said, "For Christ sake, Murray, you idiot, this guy is a crew member on here, and he works in the engine room, and he's leaving the ship, and not boarding."

Then the funny-looking guy said as he pointed toward a mountain range only fit for a yak, "Thanks. See over there—that's Mt. Abdul Bin Crotchety Itch Something or another," but no one was really paying attention to the wing nut except Joe Bones, who was always on the lookout for the weird.

"I'll be going up there. If any of you guys are interested you can come along. I'll be doing a geological investigation, studying igneous and sedimentary rock."

Joe Bones took one look at the guy and said, "You know, you could save a lot of time and effort and just take the rocks out of your head, and put 'em in your knapsack!" We figured this guy had already spent way too much time in the heat.

Being in the wheelhouse for most of my waking hours wasn't the best way to stay in good physical condition. And the time had come for me to begin cranking up an already weak training and conditioning schedule, and start some serious drills. In 1983, I began practicing a mysterious Korean martial form, called "Kuk Sool Won." It was all-inclusive, with lots of kicking, with an emphasis on pressure points, and joint locks, breaks, acrobatics, lots of weapons, and ritualistic bowing. I trained like a maniac in the early years, and after a couple of chipped teeth, a broken collarbone and a few other incidentals, I was awarded a black belt in 1986. I always admired the Koreans' fighting prowess, and had some firsthand experience with the R.O.K.s in Vietnam. I thought if I was ever stupid enough to get involved in martial arts, it would be a Korean style... Fighting is a way of life for Koreans, and not just a sport.

Just last year, in Pusan, Korea, I was in a taxi traveling downtown, and observed two businessmen dressed with suits and ties, and they were kicking the daylights out of one another in the middle of the afternoon, and nobody seemed to think it unusual. Altercations are a common occurrence on Texas Street in Pusan. Sailors, and Russian fishermen and local Korean/Russian bar thugs are always hashing it out, but in the downtown financial area of Pusan? Koreans, obviously, aren't one bit shy about self-expression.

I am not sure what that says for their society, but there is one thing I am certain of, and it's that these people aren't driven by political correctness. You can also bet that half their population isn't bipolar, and on ten different kinds of medication, and spending their money on self-help this and that, and paying a personal trainer to baby-sit them through life. The *Higgins* had a well-equipped gym; we had a heavy bag, a speed bag, with free weights, and accompanying machines. On days without UNREPS, and over time I would visit the gym to break a sweat.

The gym, although well equipped, was not a space of huge proportions, and I was sharing the room with a fellow shipmate, the radioman. One day, while working on my skills, I was doing a series of spin kicks, and out of nowhere the ship took a freak roll, and I went airborne. On my return to the *Higgins's* deck, I landed on the radioman, and it was as much a shock to me as it was to him. The unsuspecting radioman was quietly stretching several feet from me, and he bore the full impact of my descent. As I touched down on his ankle, he let out a war whoop that could have been heard all the way to the bridge. If his ankle wasn't broken, the swelling told a tale of further injuries, and either way, the ship's nurse wanted it x-rayed. Both the radioman and Joe Gonzales would be on the next helicopter to the *Independence*.

I was trying to cheer the radioman up, just to ease his pain, and fear of helicopters. "You and Joe Gonzales—what a couple of lucky guys!"

Radio guy said, "And just how are we so lucky?"

"Are you kidding? You both get to fly in a chopper to the *Independence*."

He said, "Yeah, I know. I have been thinking about that, and there's got to be another way to get over to that ship, other than helo. Isn't there any other way you can send me over there? Don't you have a basket that is used for transferring personnel? I am definitely not comfortable with this."

I said, "Forget that, you'll have the time of your life. I have done the personal transfer, and it's a gas. Trust me—it's a lot scarier and more dangerous. Plus, there's no way the *Independence* is going to come alongside just for a couple of crewmembers. Just enjoy the ride—you'll probably never have the thrill of going straight up in the air like a rocket for the rest of your life."

"I guess you're right... Like a rocket, huh? And what choice do I have ?"

Joe Gonzales had a different concern; Joe was concerned that he might miss lunch, and he was curious as to how many entrées the *Independence* might have, and if their quality was up to his standards.

Chapter Thirty-Six

The captain, along with the military department, wanted a full explanation for the radioman's accident, and they had some creative suggestions for my future workouts. The radioman, along with Joe Gonzales, got their chopper ride to the *Independence*, and Gonzales was to get a full medical checkout for his sleep problems, as well as an eye exam, and an official weight in. The Navy had their own way of dealing with obesity. The Navy would put their overeater on the "fat boy" program. The program would include a special diet and exercise regimen that provided an amount of time to lose the weight. And if the pounds weren't given the heave-ho by the fat boy, then the fat boy was given the heave-ho by the Navy...real simple. Now Joe, being a fat boy civilian, was subject to a different set of rules and regulations, and the fat boy program wasn't applicable. The radioman was happy because he didn't have a broken bone, and Joe was going home; he was deemed medically unfit for duty, and a relief was on the way.

However, I thought it strange, that in the face of adverse news, Joe was uncharacteristically happy. Was he happy because he got a ride on the chopper, or because got to he visit the *Indy*, or perhaps it was their food? Either way, I bet a strong case could be made that chopper rides should be given as prescribed therapy for future ailments. They both admitted that going aboard the *Independence* was awesome, and Joe gave a complete critique of the menu and meal on the *Independence*. I was jealous.

The *Higgins* was now on a milk run to Misirah, Oman, from Fujiarh. That in itself was okay, because we could at least go ashore in Fujirah. Misirah was out of the picture, because there was no there, there. Misirah was an airstrip in a desert incapable of supporting life. On arrival, we wouldn't even drop anchor, we would "heave to," or in landlubber's vernacular, "float around," and that gets very old very fast. Receiving word that Muscat, Oman, would be our next port definitely piqued the crew's enthusiasm. Muscat had a rich maritime history, steeped in ancient sea stories, such as Sinbad the Sailor, and the Seven Seas, and other mythical seafaring men.

The *Higgins* would be one of the first ships in Muscat's harbor in many a year, and it would be nice to have Muscat on our roster of port visits. Muscat provided a much-needed supply of finished products—jet fuel, aviation gas, diesel—that were being consumed in huge quantities. Even with the addition of Muscat, the months were going by slowly, and we were getting frustrated that there appeared to be no end in sight. In October, we were told we would be rotated to back to Yokusuka, Japan, it was then pushed to November, and then we were promised December. The public at home was for the most part supportive; we were getting mail from many differing people, and to be expected, there was the element of the sick and weird. We only had one rule when it came to mail: "If you open it, it's your responsibility to respond, no matter what!"

Farley and I were in the library one day, and he said to me, "Why don't you try reading some of this mail? It isn't that bad. I have only received one bad letter, and it was from a guy in Berkeley, California. Can you imagine, this guy accused everyone on the *Higgins* of being baby killers."

I said, "Ouch, that's a might bit harsh, don't you think, Farley?"

Farley reminded me, "Everyone has a right to an opinion; after all, this is America."

I said, "So do I. Do you still have that letter? Because if so, I would be happy to share my opinion with him."

Farley continued, "No, I mailed a return letter out last week, and I tried to explain my point of view, an…"

"Darn it, next time you get one of those, I want it. I'll write him a barn burner." Muscat had a single-point mooring, meaning that being pier side was out of the question, but we would have a launch service, and that was good news. At first light, AB Stan would drive us in. As we made our approach I was leisurely checking out the headlands of Muscat, with its steep cliffs surrounding the harbor, as well as the approach, that gave the appearance of middle-aged ramparts and parapets. The style of construction reminded one of medieval castles and fortresses, and the harbor was naturally fortified by its unique topography of walled rock.

The first launch was packed. Farley, Joe Bones, Stan and myself, along with the steward, were the first in the launch. The steward had said that he had begun sailing when he was sixteen, and at sixty-two, would be retiring in a year. The ever-inquisitive Farley knew this, and asked the steward if he had any sea time in the North Atlantic during World War Two. What Farley didn't know was the length and depth of the steward's adventures. Our hour-long ride into shore was made a lot quicker as the steward began telling of his recollections of World War Two.

"Like all of us, I was just a kid back then, but I grew up overnight. We were in the North Sea the first time I got torpedoed, but the Gerry's didn't sink us, so we limped back in, and made it up the Clyde River in, Scotland."

Joe bones said, "The Clyde, isn't that the river were all those famous ships at Cunard have been launched, like the *Queen Elizabeth 2*, and a slew of others?"

The steward said, "Yeah, you have been doing your homework; you're right, but keep in mind, that coincidently, there have been over a hundred wrecks on the Clyde. See this tattoo of a ship blowing up? I got it in Grenock, as soon as I got off that ship, just as a reminder of World War Two, and what it was like being a sitting duck, and just waiting to get blown out of the water."

We were riveted to the steward's every word. "The second time I got hit was when I was on the *Ferndale*. It was broad daylight, and we were smack-dab in the middle of the Atlantic when the U-boats struck. We were the last ship in a convoy, and were steaming at twelve knots. The next thing I knew, I was in the water looking up at my ship going down in a fireball. I had been doing maintenance on one of the gun mounts. When the first torpedo hit, I was thrown over the side with a large piece of the ship's handrail.

"We were hit below the waterline, and up forward, by the foremast. I can still remember these high sheets of flame, and at the very end one of the explosions, green flames shot seven hundred feet in the air, and she went down like a crowbar. Immediately, I looked for something to grab on to, and as I turned around, I couldn't believe it, but there floating right in front of me was an SS *Ferndale* life ring; the ring had been attached to the handrail that had gone over the side with me, and it sprung free."

Slim, one of the *Higgins's* deck mechanics, said, "Get the fuck out a here!"

The steward continued, "I know, it sounds unbelievable, but that's what happened. When I landed in the water, I cracked some ribs, and later found that I had broken my ankle. There was one explosion after another, bombs and ammunition were being ignited, and then the boilers blew, but the worst part by far was that, above the noise, I could hear the sound of men yelling and screaming. I was able to hold on to one guy, but he didn't make it through the first night. What I couldn't understand, was why the convoy didn't stop. I was told later that it was the beginning of a major assault with more subs and planes, and the battle was a pivotal part of the war. Two days later, I was picked up by a destroyer, and we went back to the Brooklyn Navy Yard.

"Two months later I caught another ship that convoyed back to Europe, and the whole time I was aboard I couldn't sleep. Every time I heard a strange noise I thought it was a torpedo, and I'll be a son of a bitch if we didn't get hit again, and once more I got thrown over the side."

Slim said, "Oh, get outta here, you got to be jiving!"

"I'm not kidding, but this time I wasn't as lucky, but at least lucky to make it. I got burned real bad, and I almost lost my arm when a cargo boom hit me. It was in 1943 toward the end of the war, and we were way the hell up by Greenland, Convoy SC-22. A lot of guys didn't make it; the water was brutally cold. I got snatched out of the water by a picket boat; it was just me and two other guys. The rescue ship, a minesweeper, was heading to the East Coast, and in three weeks we were back in Manhattan telling our stories. The three of us planned to stay in touch, and in two weeks after returning I got a phone call from Ed, one of the survivors, and he told me that Bert, our third survivor friend, was dead. Bert had been run over in New York City by a getaway car that was in the middle of a bank robbery."

And then Ed said, "If it weren't for Bert being hit by the car and killed, the robbers would never have been caught, go figure. In another month the war was over, and that was fine with me, 'cause they wanted to send me back on another ship—can you imagine? I was thinking, I mean, Christ, how many times do I have to go through this shipwreck thing? I mean it was getting mighty old. But

I'll tell you one thing, back in those days, I'd go into a bar back then, and I don't think I bought my own beer for about three years."

Slim, the deck mechanic, said, "Here we are! Tell you what, I'll buy you the first drink, stew!"

Once again, we were reminded to be on our best behavior. The captain seemed unusually concerned; perhaps it was because Americans hadn't visited Muscat in a long time, and all of us were "ambassadors from the United States," and we were representing mainstream America (That alone, was a scary thought).When we finally got ashore, we felt as if we were on the Discovery Channel, we literally felt as if we were walking back in time. The souks were a main attraction. They were a Mid-Eastern equivalent of a strip mall, with differing types of shopping specialties, gold, vegetables and fruits, clothing, tobacco, you name it.

As for whiskey and women? Well, those activities would be put on stand-by. The locals were shocked by our appearance. You would have thought these people hadn't seen outsiders since the days of Christ, and acted as if we were Martians, and just jumped out of a flying saucer. I can't speak for the rest of the crew, but I felt more like a dreaded tourist, armed with camera, tote bag, and Bermuda shorts, than a sailor out for a robust time of celebration.

As we made our way into town in the ninety-degree heat, we evidenced the remains of British occupation by seeing locals playing a spirited game of cricket. At this time I made a suggestion to my partner. "Murray, you know, with this scorching heat, I bet it would be great to take a swim in that beautiful water."

He said, "Get lost!"

"You know something else? These waters here in Muscat are some of the best in the world for viewing marine life, and the chances of any sharks out here are minimal, and just take a look at that beach, doesn't it just reach out to you and say jump in?"

"Drop dead!" Murray took the less adventurous route, and decided to view the marine life through binoculars while safely aboard the *Higgins*.

Chapter Thirty-Seven

The waters of Muscat had incredible marine life, and being a gangway watch provided ample time between launches and other duties to peruse the waters. On just such an occasion, I can recall a school of fifty sea rays swimming down the side of the ship. My partner said that he had seen hundreds of huge sea turtles coming to the surface; of course he also swore that he saw his first mermaid that day. We from the United States had never seen anything like it.

The strangest marine life by far was something that appeared to be a cross between a fish and a snake. The ship was in the middle of a routine weekly fire and boat drill with the lifeboat in the water, and the boat crew took the opportunity to explore. The crew came upon this odd fish/snake creature that had a long nose, and a very long, thin body with fins. The mystery creature surfaced right by the boat, and of course our boat engineer's first instinct was to beat it over the head with an oar.

Then somebody yelled, "What the hell are you doing, you idiot? Use the boat hook; it's got a better reach!" And that pretty much ruined any photo opportunity. After the sea monster came around, it decided that it had had enough, and went back down to the depths from whence it came. So much for the aspiring Jacques Cousteau and Marlin Perkins wannabes.

Undoubtedly the strangest creatures of the day were aboard our returning liberty launch. Sober, quiet sailors returning from a full day and evening on the beach at a new port of call was definitely a rare sight. A break in the fast-paced marine action occurred the day we had a close call with our cargo hose. A single-point mooring has two integral large moving parts. The first one is a very large buoy that connects to another large part, and that is the submarine hose on the ocean floor. One end of the hose goes to the oil terminal ashore, and the other end goes to an offshore ship that is connected to the humongous buoy, with a large hawser.

It sounds simple enough, and with only a few large moving parts, what could possibly go wrong? Well, for one thing, it is possible that the hawser would have too much slack, and take a turn around the buoy, and of course, that is what happened. And when all hell broke loose, the 4x8 was just happy to be off watch. We were in step with the good side of Lady Luck, and were developing a habit of being off watch when bad things happened.

Along with fixing the problem, there was interest in fixing the blame, and it appeared that the standby on 8x12 watch would have some explaining to do. Part of his job was to check the strain on the buoy attached to the hawser, and to report anything unusual. Under the category of unusual, taking a turn around the buoy was high on the list, and evidently it wasn't noted, or at least thought of as a big deal by the standby. When Burt Enfield, the standby, was questioned, he had an interesting reason for the mess, and it made complete sense to the deck gang. He said he was "Head over heels in love with one of the cadets, and couldn't think clearly, and blamed his horrible behavior on springtime in the air." Either way, it was considered a big deal by most, because the twelve-inch hose was carrying jet fuel. After the situation was corrected, and all proper people were advised of their legal rights, and chewed out royally, things went back to normal (normal for us was somewhere between FUBAR, and SNAFU).

Chapter Thirty-Eight

On a damp, wet, very rainy day, we made our departure, and we were looking forward to a return visit to Mysiarah, even if we couldn't go ashore, because we would at least receive mail. Our employer had the bad habit of promising reliefs, and not delivering. After six months at sea, most sailors were more than ready for vacation, and if you didn't have a personality disorder when signing aboard you most certainly would if you went past your relief date. This time the company delivered on its promise, and there were five happy crew members aboard, because they knew their reliefs would be waiting at Meseriah, on our return visit.

On our return trip, as expected, two AB watch standers, two maintenance men and one ordinary for Joe Gonzales were helicoptered out to the ship. They arrived on the helo deck, with all the normal fanfare that a Hollywood celebrity would expect, and were then introduced to their supervisors and work stations, and quarters respectively. This was all very normal, and procedural, except for one thing; we were now on the lookout for one of Frankie Scarpino's lads that was instructed to see that Blaze would be swimming with the fishes.

Joe Bones and I were scrutinizing the new reliefs' every move for anything that appeared to look suspicious, or mob related. Joe said, "I guess we should be looking for stuff like any showy gold jewelry, slick black hair, and pinky rings, or loud clothing, right?"

I said, "Yeah, I guess so, but that description could fit a few ex-wives and girlfriends as well."

When the first two of the reliefs hit the deck, Joe Bones looked over at me and then did a double-take at one of the new-bees. I could only interpret that second look as either a look of interest or skepticism. I found out later I was wrong; Joe's look was one of confused apprehension, along with a mild case of acid reflex. The first arrival under the discerning eye of our gangster-detecting microscope was

Fuzzy B. Culpepper, the new ordinary seaman. Fuzzy Wuzzy (his immediate nickname), was a new hire, and he was ecstatic to be aboard the *Higgins*. Fuzzy could have been mistaken for a number of things, but a mob hit man he wasn't.

We had never seen or heard anyone talk as fast as Fuzzy. Upon introduction, he would tell you his entire life story, from day one to present, if you let him. It could be said that Fuzzy was motivated; Mr. Fuzzy B. Culpepper had decided what he needed was a new occupation, because he figured his mid-life crisis was somehow connected to living in the Midwest, and he was feeling smothered.

With Fuzzy Wuzzy's gift of gab, Joe and I figured Fuzzy for a door-to-door vacuum cleaner salesman; however, Fuzzy had been a successful crop duster in the Midwest. In addition to being motivated, Fuzzy was desperate. He said, "I don't care what it takes; I'll do anything to see water, any kind of water." He said crop dusting was making him bonkers, and he was going to sea, "even if it meant being on a ship with a bunch of screwballs that didn't know if they were afoot, or on horseback." We weren't sure, but we thought we were insulted.

As more was revealed from Fuzzy's background, in no time, he would become an inspiration to us all. Out here, you get to know people rather quickly, and we thought having a pole dancer for a wife was like finding that pot of gold at the end of the rainbow. Even more incredible was that Fuzzy's father-in-law owned the strip bar that his better half worked in...well, that was over the top! Fuzzy was an overnight superstar with the deck gang, and treated accordingly, and could do no wrong.

Unfortunately, Fuzzy didn't last long. Not that the requirements were too stringent on our fine ship, it's just that the captain discovered that Fuzzy had a glass eye, and being that Fuzzy was the lookout on the 4x8, something had to go, and it was Fuzzy B. Culpepper. The scuttlebutt was that Fuzzy was very proud of his glass eye. (Evidently, he lost it in a barroom skirmish, when a bar patron hit Fuzzy in the eye with a 1960s mood ring, and he felt compelled to tell everyone.)

Fuzzy wasn't totally innocent. He said the incident happened when he was trying to introduce someone's girlfriend to the fine art of pole dancing, and the offended raging bull took it as a personal affront. Fuzzy would have done very well on the *Higgins*, but as I said, "He couldn't keep his big mouth shut," and eventually the captain got wind, and that was that. We never did figure out how Fuzzy passed the physical in the first place, and we were never really sure if the eye was glass or not. Don and I even tried the Sammy Davis Junior thing…that's when you try to see if both eyes look in the same direction when they move. I have no idea what Fuzzy is doing today, but I would bet everything I own, it isn't crop dusting acres of corn in the Midwest for chicken feed.

Shanghai Cid was another welcome piece of work to the *Higgins*. Cid was a so-called "outlaw biker." But as Cid put it, "No, it doesn't mean I rob banks and rustle cattle when I'm riding the range on my iron steed." Whatever Cid was, he was hard-core all the way. Tattoos? You bet! Cid left nothing to chance; he reckoned even if he got involved in a horrible accident and was either comatose or dead, he would not be forgotten. Shanghai Cid had the engine-casing I.D. numbers of his scooter tattooed on his arm, as insurance against having his parts mistaken for someone else's. No one was sure if that was to identify the bike's parts or his parts, but he seemed to have it figured out. Shanghai Cid made a big deal out of being in a club, and not a gang, and what the differences were…most of us didn't give a hoot.

Years later, I heard one of the leaders of the H.A.'s say, "Look, the Hell's Angels aren't a motorcycle gang, we're a motorcycle club." To me, it sounded like a semantic word game. For example, when a merchant vessel is departing or arriving, we have a gang call, and it means all hands are directed to go fore and aft; we don't have a club call. Whatever the group is called, it's simply an assemblage of like-minded people with common goals and interests. Some of these assemblages like to meet and discuss social issues and problems, and some groups like to discuss the nuances of rape, pillage and plundering. The Rotary gang, The Commonwealth gang, a motorcycle-riding social club, call yourselves whatever you want, such seriousness is silly.

Shanghai Cid was more suited for the deck than the bridge of a ship; he was built like a gorilla. Central casting couldn't have done a better job when searching for a deck-ape knuckle-dragger type that looked as if he had the capability to bench press a garbage truck. Cid was to be on the 12x4 watch, and there he would stay for the next three months. Just to look at Cid would make most people uneasy, and he said that on several occasions, he would be invited in a nice way to leave bars and restaurants, because he was scaring business away.

Although Cid was a calm and mellow kind of guy, if you were using your God-given brains, it would be wise not to annoy him, and stay clear of Cid's dangerous semi-circle.

While in Fujirah, there was a time we found ourselves with some spare time and money. Cid got an idea. "Hey, what the hell, let's go out and destroy some brain cells!" We found ourselves in a low-life bar of our choosing…you could only go so low; after all we weren't in San Pedro, California. We matched each other with shots and beers until we were both in a self-induced comatose state, and then plotted a course back to the ship. We jumped in a taxi, and halfway back, Cid got in a verbal exchange with the cabby over the fare, and Cid almost took the back door off the cab. We got out of the cab, paid the guy with the turban on his head, and walked back to the ship. As we approached the gangway, Cid reached into his pocket and pulled something shiny out, and said, "Oh shit, I forgot to give back the guy's door handle!"

Contrary to his looks, Cid usually got mellower, the more he drank. He told me his greatest fear was to get completely shit faced, and get whooped by a thirteen-year-old girl arm wrestling… Cid was definitely different.

Jimmy Bowes went to the 8x12 watch, replacing Stan. I never really got into Stan's head, but I got some of the highlights of his background, and it was not to be confused with a conventional person. Evidently Stan wanted to become a licensed officer, and his next destination would bring him back to school at a turnbuckle tech academy. Stan was, without a doubt, one of the most unusual men I met while on the *Higgins*. For starters Stan said that he had spent five years in Mexico as a midwife delivering Mexican babies. And Stan, being very Irish…well, it just struck me as being very strange. Stan had a wide array of interests; he played piano, jazz guitar, he spoke a number of languages, and was a martial arts practitioner that gave up the crack pipe and brewskis. He told me that the midwife thing, and being into herbal medicine stuff helped him stay clean and sober, as he said, "Alcohol and crack cocaine brought me to my knees."

I wish had gotten to know Stan better, and I admit I was impressed by his openness. He said, "I suffered from the consequences of my drinking for years. At one time, I lived on an island in the South Pacific in a cave with enough alcohol for a year, and you see these native tattoos here? I had them put on the old-fashioned way, and they got infected, and in a living hell and almost died." He said, "I had to keep drinking, because of the horrors of the DT's, and the terrible pain from the screwed-up job on the tattoos. I eventually checked into a hospital in Hawaii, and had the infected tattoos cared for and got a handle on the drug and booze thing."

Chapter Thirty-Nine

Jimmy Bowes was another new hire that had been inspired to go to sea during the course of his lifetime. And as he put it, "All my life, I wanted to go to sea, and this Desert Shield is going to finally let me do it. I seen it was going to help me, even though I don't know nothing about the sea except for those movies *Moby Dick*, and *20,000 Leagues Under the Sea*, with Kirk Douglas!" Then he went into a rendition of one of the movie's songs, "I've got a whale of a tale, of a tale or two. I swear by my tattoo, there was mermaid Minnie...."

Joe Bones overheard what was going on, and said, "That's great! It's always good to see someone keeping the classics alive, but let me ask you this, can you do any real authentic sea chanteys? See, we only have one guy that knows 'em all."

With that, Jimmy said, "No kidding, and who might that be?"

Joe Bones said, "That would be Murray Katz—we call him Murray the K., and he's sea-chantey-singing fool if there ever was one."

"Murray, that's an unusual name, isn't it?"

Joe said, "It is, and he is—you guys might hit it off just fine."

I said to Joe Bones, "Now what did you do that for? This guy seems like a good enough guy."   "Yeah, I know, but he was getting on my nerves, and besides, you ever get to where you just can't help from saying stuff—you know, it just kind of comes out, and you don't even know why, and a lot of times it's just a bunch of stupid bullshit?"

"No, Joe, I wouldn't know anything about that."

"Yeah, well, that's bullshit too!"

Jimmy was a likable guy, but he was a might old for any entry-level job, let alone going to sea. We could care less that he was pushing sixty, all that mattered was whether he would pull his own weight. He was the type of guy that was conscious of his age and compensated by overdoing a normal job, if you know what I mean. Here was a guy fulfilling a lifelong dream, and even if the realization didn't measure up to his rainbow chasing, all he had to do was walk down the gangway.

My first bosun, an old Swede, liked to give bosun locker speeches, and over a couple of beers in the line locker he said, "Never forget that the gangway goes in two directions, and when you feel yourself going crazy, get off before it's too late. Many sailors forget this, and just keep riding ships and lose touch with the real world, and before they know it their shore-side coping skills are gone."

That old Swede bosun was right; I have literally seen guys that didn't know how a bank account worked. No kidding! The basic things that people take for granted, like buying a piece of property, would completely confound some guys. I knew another guy on a cable ship that had been aboard two years. We were in a tavern in a little seaport in Scotland, and I heard a sailor say to a mate, "I have been on here two years and three days. Nobody has ever said anything to me about getting off; how do I get off?"

The mate said, "Are you nuts? You can get off anytime—what the hell's wrong with you?"   And the guy answered the mate with a straight face, "Mate, when I was in the Navy they told me when to get off and on ships, and I didn't have to do much thinking about it."

The mate said, "Well, see me in my office tomorrow and we'll get the paperwork going if you're still interested in getting off."

"Off where?"

The mate said, "Never mind, just show up!"

Compared to other countries, the United States needs to do more for its own merchant marine service; a national crisis is the only time people show any interest, and then it's a last-minute scrambling for ships and qualified sailors. Sailor unions are under constant attack by big business. Most disturbing is in a time of so-called environmental concerns people look past the obvious flaws in environmental policies regarding shipping.

The Untied States has millions of tons of cargo brought to our ports by foreign governments, with foreign ships, foreign crews, and foreign registry, and if you think they care about our environment, or waterways, or the handling of hazardous and toxic materials, you've been reading fiction, and need to start reading some nonfiction. It's "Big business as usual!" Big business will not be happy until they have replaced every U.S. flagship with foreign crews, and the average American has no idea what is going on. Any sailor today will tell you living conditions and wages are under constant attack. If ships coming into our ports are to have responsible people that have a vested interest in our country, the crews should be paid a fair wage consistent with conditions in the United States, and not Bangladesh.

Chapter Forty

None of us recognized the two guys that came aboard in Misirah, and that in itself that wasn't strange; it was more of an attitude than anything else...a look, a swagger, a gaze, or maybe the strut...only time would tell. Of the two, one would be a mess man in the galley, and the other would go to the deck department as an AB. Later we would find out who the cold-blooded killer was.

Right away, I could see Joe Bones sizing them up. The ship's bosun showed them their rooms and gave them a brief tour of the ship. Later on, Joe and I caught up with the ship's bosun, and asked him a few pointed questions, and what he thought of the new crew members, and he said three words, "They're bad news!"

Joe said, "What do you mean, Boats? What do we have on our hands with these guys?"

"Well, for one thing, neither one of them knows shit from shinola, and for another thing, they don't look like they want to learn. I could be wrong, but if I were you guys I'd watch my back."

I said, "Boats, come on now, how can you tell so much when you were with these guys only a few minutes? And just 'cause they don't know much about the business it doesn't make 'em all bad."

"Look, I have dealt with damn near every kind of personality, and I have seen them all, the good, the bad, and everything in between. I'm not sure about the new mess man, but I'll give you both some advice, don't turn your back on the one called Tony."

"Bosun, you got a few minutes to spare? Joe and I have got something we have to tell you, and it is probably more important than anything else on this ship right now."

"Yeah, sure, like what—what is it?"

Joe and I detailed the entire mess to the bosun, and then we had to talk him out of going to Touchdown Barney. The news would have put the old man over the edge, and what's more, we really didn't have any proof, so we were forced to deal with these characters in our own way. The bosun's reaction was not what we expected; he completely caught us off guard.

"Wow, right here on the *Higgins*! It sounds just like Hollywood!"

Joe said, "Boats, get a grip—will you come back to earth? When these Italian meatballs come flying at you with guns and knives you're going to think different."

"I know, I know, I was just having a little fun. Hell, I'm glad the sonofabitch is here—by the time me and the gang get done with that greaseball, he'll wish he never set foot on the *Jolly Higgins*. Argh!" Boats went on, "But guys, help me out with this, maybe I'm missing something! I don't understand—if the guys coming aboard and the guy in Diego Garcia are Mob connected wouldn't they have a criminal record a mile long? You know as well as I do that you have to go through a major background check to get out here."

"Yeah, I know, Boats, it seems unbelievable, but they have unbelievable connections, and who knows, maybe the guy in Diego Garcia was already in place on a ship, and Scarpino's people just made a phone call, and the two guys that just came aboard are legitimate new hires with no priors. I know it sounds far-fetched and coincidental...I'm just doing some brainstorming."

"Yeah, Joe, well let's just see what we have with these two, but I'm warning you now, they're hard core!"

Chapter Forty-One

As we approached the coast of United Arab Emirates, we were making eighteen knots. At precisely 1910, on the 4x8 watch, on a clear evening two loud explosions sounded over our heads. This reads like a deck log because that's what it is. On the bridge it sounded like we were taking fire from a .50-cal. Heavy-barrel machine gun, or a 20-millimeter cannon. However, the second mate had another point of view, speculating that "Maybe something falling from space had broken the sound barrier." With all the space junk up there we thought it sounded plausible, and it sounded better than explosive rounds coming our way, but no one really fell for the mate's explanation.

Murray had a unique interpretation, and ran up to the bridge and proclaimed that the blast was a "heat explosion!"

The second mate and I, in unison said, "Heat explosion, what the hell is that?"

Murray went into some screwball explanation. "When it gets hot and dry enough, the surrounding air bursts into spontaneous explosive gas."

We had no idea what he was talking about, but regardless of the source, it was clear that our new hire, Billy the ordinary seaman, wasn't feeling especially comfortable on the bow. This was Billy's first bow lookout, and it was one that he would be talking about for days to come. Billy was many things, but he wasn't shy, and he wasn't afraid of letting us know of his displeasure, and although the second mate tried, he wasn't reassuring Billy. The second mate said, "Oh yeah, we heard it too. It's just one of those low-flying heat explosions in the earth's atmosphere."

Billy on the bow, answered back, "Well, when's the next one?"

The mate said, "Can't tell from here, but just mind your lookout—we have things covered—and just let us know if you hear or see anything strange."

The bow lookout came back, in a jittery voice, not caring about respect for rank and privilege, and said, "You've got things covered my ass—we're taking fire from somewhere, and wasn't that explosion strange enough?"

It was kind of funny. The chief mate and captain had just arrived on the bridge to catch the last bit of conversation with the lookout, and they were equally stymied, and it was a sure bet they didn't want the lookout to abandon his post. What did the trick was when the chief mate heard all the commotion, and said, "If you leave the bow you're fired, and you will be on the next plane to the States."

Just arriving on the bridge, our other new man, Shanghai Cid, looked at me and said, "Low-flying heat explosions in the earth's atmosphere? What are you people talking about?"

I said, "I have no idea, but it's getting pretty good up here, and I think it just might keep Fuzzy Wuzzy the crop duster on the bow."

We never did find out what the explosions were; we just chalked it up to "things that go bump in the night."

Every morning the AB maintenance/day men assembled on the fantail and were informed of the day's events, along with work assignments from the bosun. As watch standers, we weren't involved, but this was to be our new hire Tony's début, and the deck force would get its first look at a "real live mobster," and they were excited. Rumors were flying; Tony was tried and convicted even before he set foot on the fantail that day. The rumors ran the gamut; there was even a rumor that Tony was actually from the Capone family, and was Al Capone's second cousin removed. The steward said Tony has John Gotti's hairstyle.

Tony carried himself with a confident air that broadcast loud and clear "Mess with me, and I will tear your head off."

With no hesitation, the bosun said, "In the back! New guy! Get that cigarette out of your mouth! There's no smoking out here, what the hell is wrong with you?" And then the bosun laid out the day's work, and said to Tony, "I want to speak with you after muster." The sailors disbursed, and Tony and the bosun went into the bosun locker and shut the door. Ten minutes later, Tony came out by himself. Tony didn't say a word. Without a word said, or any ceremony, Tony and two sailors went to the paint locker to get set up. Joe Bones and Don

Morse had spent the morning with Tony, and gave me the heads up at lunch.

Evidently, Don and Tony were painting the side of a bulkhead, and Tony started asking questions.

"How many chicks do you have on board? Where are they? And what do they look like?" Then Tony said, "I don't know about you guys, but I prefer dark-haired women. Anybody seen any on board? What's the mater? None of you guys wants to give up any info—you scared I might horn in on some of your private stock?"

Don started talking about Blaze, and had gone into detail, and then Don said, "You sure ask a lot of questions," and Don told him, "We just had one nut-up on us a little while ago in the galley." And Don explained everything, how she went into a fit and started flopping around the deck like a fish, and they had to medicate her, and get her off in the Philippines.

They said that Tony flipped out, and said, "What do you mean? I can't believe it. She couldn't have been here that long. I was hoping to see her. She was a real looker, right?"

Don overdid it, and for my money he passed too much information to our mob coworker. Then Don said, "You bet, she sure looked out of place out here. I mean she was showgirl material, you know, the classy kind you see at Atlantic City, or Las Vegas."

Tony said, "That sure sounds like Asia; she is a serious babe. Tell me one thing, Donny boy, when and where is our next port?"

"First of all, it's Don, and I ain't nobody's boy, and it's Fujariah, in three days. Now let's get this bulkhead painted by coffee, or the bosun will have our ass."

"Yeah, yeah, knock yourself out, Donny, I got things to do, sucker!"

When the bosun got wind of what had happened, he got the chief mate and they went right to Tony's room, but no Tony. They were too late. Tony didn't know, and even if he did, he wouldn't have given a damn about the chain of command, or any other kind of protocol... He went straight to the captain's stateroom.

Once at the captain's door he began knocking and yelling, "I want off this ship, and I want off now. I know you're in there—open up."

It didn't take more than thirty seconds for the announcement over the 1MC (the ship's public address system): "Now hear this! Will the ship and rig boatswain lay to the captains' stateroom immediately."

Chapter Forty-Two

With the increased military threat, tensions were building, and everyone was beginning to stress, and what was needed was a good old-fashioned beer bust on a pier, any pier, anywhere. Fujiarh in November was ninety degrees, just perfect for filling a couple of shit cans full of beer, and ice, and that's what we did.

Unfortunately for my partner and I that had to work, we would watch the festivities atop the gangway on the main deck, as every beer was drained with gusto. Once the party began we could see in the background a few of the locals working the terrain with picks, shovels, and wheelbarrows on landscape that looked as rugged as the face of the moon. Murray and I had no idea what they were doing; to us, they were simply busting big rocks into little rocks in the sweltering heat, and they appeared to be having the time of their lives.

Our crew, being somewhat more casual, and not two hundred yards away, was consuming ice-cold beer with delight. The liquid gold was being rationed like a war supply, not for supply purposes, but for the more obvious reasons. The sailor's lament of always being pissed off and tired was given fuel, but their pursuit of a good time wasn't dampened, because of prior knowledge of another source of alcohol. The duty-free shop on the pier in addition to a selection of watches, and electronic gear, and foreign candy was also stocked with a vast assortment of high-quality spirits. Unfortunately, this prior knowledge wasn't a secret, and the gangway watch was given instructions to search luggage for booze when people were returning to the ship.

The days of rationed and approved alcohol on US Navy ships went out with flogging years ago, and if you're a sailor that enjoys the pleasures of drink, you will have to be resourceful. Making sure you have an ample supply for your next voyage is critical, and can lead to some higher mathematical calculations to determine the right amount. Speed, consumption rate, time, distance, and a vast amount of other statistics when factored in will come up with the correct amount of alcohol for any voyage. Watch standers didn't have an axe to grind in either direction, but having to police our own crew was not a pleasant assignment. Enforcement of the new search-and-seizure regulation was a joke, but we had to make a show. Later on that evening, we had our hands full just making sure no one got killed or maimed when returning, let alone trying to search bags for jugs.

In the wee hours of the morning, two of our shipmates, after a long day of sightseeing and debauchery, got themselves in a predicament. In returning to the ship, they had traveled as far as the container crane adjacent to our ship, and then sat down on a piece of the crane's structure near the wheels to take a respite from their reverie. Then they passed out underneath the inactive crane, while the crane operator was unaware of his inert passengers. The crane was ready to go to work, and did what crane operators do...he started the crane. My partner and I heard the crane start, and then we heard the motion alarm, and Murray yelled, "It's moving!" And sure enough, the crane was moving, and it was headed our way with the two knot-heads passed out on it. We both ran down the gangway, knowing full well that getting the operator's attention would be fruitless, so we ran to the crane, and one at a time pulled our crewmen off the crane. Reasoning with them was out of the question, and as we attempted to revive them, one of them took a swing, and the next thing we knew all four of us were at it.

As if things weren't bad enough, an official-looking car with flashing lights was speeding toward us. My partner and I were now shoving these two ungrateful idiots up the gangway onto the ship, as we spotted the local gendarme coming our way. I was thinking, *Is it possible for this situation to get any worse?* You betcha! We explained to the police that if we got the two dumbbells to their rooms all would be okay, and it looked like they were buying it.

Then something odd happened; in the middle of our explanation it became apparent that the police were visiting the *Higgins* for another reason. In the course of the evening there was a bit of a scuffle at the Gulf Hotel, and one of our colleagues was involved. It was hard to make out the details, but we heard the word "stewardess" twice, and the word "sailor" once, and that was enough information.

It wasn't so long ago that a sailor would be ready for a full-on nuclear exchange if it meant defending a stewardess's honor. To be fashionable, airlines have gone to great lengths to transform the stewardess's title and job description. Flight attendant is more socially and politically correct these days, because airlines of course, want to include everyone as a candidate to be employed in the friendly skies.

There are flights that have all-male crews, as well as flight attendants reaching the upper end of old age, and some people would view these new developments in the skies as a positive breakthrough for everyone, with at least one exception...sailors, and or any straight man that has the gift of vision.

I do get sidetracked. Back to the *Higgins*. Murray noticed something moving in the police car, and said, "Jesus Christ, it looks like there's a bear in the back of the police car!"

And I said, "You're right, and it looks angry!"

And Murray said, "Where did it come from?"

And I said, "I don't know, let's find out!"

And then the large figure in the back appeared to be getting off the floor of the car. Then Murray said, "That's the new guy!"

I said, "It sure is."

The figure was none other than our newly acquired AB, Shanghai Cid. And by the looks of things the local police were not one bit entertained or happy with Big Cid. As the story went, Shanghai Cid the biker had gotten fairly well oiled up, and by all accounts, removed his clothes, and went a-callin' on one of the stewardesses. This is just the sort of activity frowned upon in these Arab countries, but our motorcycle friend apparently hadn't gotten the word, and was not familiar with local mores and customs. In all fairness to Cid, we heard that the stewardess got Cid excited when the talk turned to tattoos, and the gal said she wanted to see Cid's bunny rabbit tattoo on his stomach. Once Cid got going he lost control, and felt obliged to show her and everyone in the bar his extensive ink work. We wanted to be around when Cid had to explain his Kabukiesque strip show to the captain.

There seems to be no limit to a woman's guile in making grown men do stupid things. As an ardent fan of all womankind, I still have to remember what an acquaintance of mine told me after a horrible divorce, that "All women are bimbos, except your mom, and mine." Perhaps a little harsh, but it keeps things in perspective for me. Just recently I read that, according to Greek mythology, Pandora was the first woman. The gods who were angry with Prometheus for making a man out of mud and then stealing fire from them made her. Making a woman was their REVENGE. They gave Pandora the box. Prometheus begged her not to open it. She opened it. Every evil to which human flesh is heir came out of it. It's a depressing story, but I didn't make it up, the Greeks did, and oh yes, the last thing to come out of the box was hope. It's easy to dismiss this story, saying that ancient Greeks were just a bunch of fruits that ran around in white sheets with too much time on their hands, but as Joe Bones said, "I'll give it some thought the next I'm getting a table dance."

Farley appeared to be the only sober person on the ship, and after giving him a rundown of the evening's events, we agreed that watch standers were grossly underpaid, and babysitting shouldn't be in the scope of our work.

When the watch shifted from the bridge to the gangway, we worked out our own work schedule. Murray and I were at the close of our watch at 0800, and once again, the unexpected happened.

Chapter Forty-Three

I have always considered it fascinating that in the worst of situations the most committed of enemies can learn to work together. Throughout our watch we were actually working together to solve shared problems, and thereby creating an outward similitude of a bond. This same bond might be compared to the warring nations of earth coming together to solve the problem of being invaded by deadly space aliens. We were both working as though there was no underlying problem, and that felt alien. Murray commented, "This watch has been one mess after another, and finally it's almost over."

And before he could finish the sentence, I said, "Don't be so sure—look what's coming down the pier!"

At 0730, a military vehicle was heading down the pier toward us. The vehicle stopped at the gangway, and two uniformed police and two undercover men got out and came forward.

Murray and I were at the head of the gangway when Murray got a call from the captain. "Murray, be on the lookout for an official-looking vehicle."

Murray said,   "Well, it's almost here, sir, with four guys, and it's pulling up to the gangway right now."

The two men in front wore marine uniforms, and the two in the rear had on dark civilian suits. As they approached us at the top of the gangway one of the suits did all the talking and asked only to see the master of the ship, and to be taken to him immediately! I called up the captain on the ship's phone and the captain said, "Have them come aboard, and escort them to my stateroom!"

"Yes, sir!"

I remained at the gangway, and Murray dutifully marched up to the captain's stateroom, and within fifteen minutes, I saw Murray leading the crowd coming down to the main deck. There were the four military-police types; the bosun, the chief mate, and Tony their new friend, and he wasn't looking especially comfortable in his new wrist jewelry. As the group passed the gangway, Tony lifted his head long enough to look straight at Murray, and under his breath we heard, "I won't forget you!"

Murray jumped back, and said, "What! What does he mean?" And then Murray looked across at me, as I gave him a big *Higgins* smile, and that was the last we saw of Tony!

I was making the final entries in the gangway log to close out our watch, and I said to Murray, "Well, we earned our money on this shift."

Murray said, "Did you see what just happened?"

"What do you mean? I thought it went rather well, all things considered."

"All things considered? It's not funny, why are you smiling? How does he know me? And what was the deal with the mess man—what the hell did he do, kill someone? And do you know that those two guys were federal marshals! Blah, blah, blah!"

To avoid a huge explanation, I let it rest. I simply said, "I don't know, but the rumor is that Tony is connected with the Mob."

"The Mob? What mob? What are you talking about? Hey, come back here...!"

The party and soap opera were over, and it was time to do what we did best; get back to the fleet and underway replenish.

Not long after our departure, we began a series of underway replenishments that would take us into the evenings. We were several hundred miles from Iran, the *Independence* was on our port side, and an LST to starboard. The visibility was fantastic. Twenty miles is as about as good as it gets. The sun was slipping under the horizon, and we were all waiting to see the "Green Flash," a natural phenomenon that occurs at sunset when conditions are right. From the flying bridge above, we heard, "Two points to starboard, small craft going starboard to port."

I had just rotated to the wheel, and it is hard to describe the scene, but I will. Picture three warships steaming together, on a sea of glass, at twilight with multicolored chemical lights attached to various lines and rigging, and a horizon clear enough to see almost past the curvature of the earth. All the while these splendors of nature and man were unfolding, something else was unfolding. A lone boat, a small, slow-moving boat that didn't appear to be altering his course or speed. All of us were on a collision course. To expand on the scene, two warships and an auxiliary ship transferring highly flammable fuel were bearing down on a small craft with a closing CPA. The scenario was a captain's worst nightmare, and it didn't take long for people to spring into action. The mate on watch attempted radio communication via channels sixteen and thirteen, and even the signalman used flashing light to no avail... the small boat did not respond.

Three ships of the United States Navy bearing down on a twelve-foot boat would have alarmed most boaters, but not this guy. He was now dead ahead, with a range of two miles, and then he stopped. Touchdown! Our captain went nuts! "Who the hell does this guy think he is?"

Things were getting serious, and it had become very quiet on the bridge. The captain had two walkie-talkie radios going, and was communicating with the ships on either side. Then the order came. "Come right one degree, to 298." The next command was 299, and to everyone's amazement, the small boat appeared to be steering right for us! At this time, the boat was five hundred yards away, and it wasn't going to clear. Murray was behind me ready to relieve, and the captain said, "Mind your helm at 299, and stay your relief." The little boat was actually going between the *Independence* and us, and down our port side. Obviously, I couldn't see, but I was imagining what was happening with a one-hundred-foot clearance between the ships traveling at twelve knots. The captain was heard saying, "What kind of wacko is this guy?"

By this time everyone except for myself was on the port bridge wing looking down at the boat. The captain told Murray to relieve me, and being the inquisitive type, I wished I could have seen the action. When I got off the wheel I talked with the signalman striker, because he had a clear view of the action, and he said, "The crazy guy made it all the way to the stern after spinning around four or five times. Luckily there wasn't anyone behind us." He also said, "Of all the times to not have a camera, this is the kind of thing that no one would believe." And he was right.

The captain stepped inside saying, "Well, that's it, I can now say I have seen everything."

The signalman also said, "There were gunners mates positioned with weapons at the ready." In the not-so-distant future, this would have never happened. The boat would have been considered a hostile threat, and a warning shot would have been dispatched to the yachtsman's head. As I walked into the crew's lounge I could hear the sea stories booming over the TV. The topics were the usual, preceding this kind of event; who had been in the worst collision, who had survived a sinking, and groundings and varying types of fires...you name it. Then I ran into the ship's bosun, and we both agreed that we had never seen anything like it before. Then the talk turned to Tony, and the bosun said he regretted not having the proper chance to show Tony around a little more; perhaps Tony might have enjoyed a tour of the bosun locker with a few of us.

We agreed that it was fortuitous that we weren't back in the States, because the press not only wouldn't rest until this story was on the front page, but there would be a pilot to launch a twenty-episode miniseries. Blaze was going to have a tough enough time trying to stay one step ahead of Frank Scarpino, and she didn't need press problems. I was lamenting the fact that I never even got to first base with her, but then again I didn't have a death wish. Plus, how was I to know what her crystal ball would predict? She was a dangerous lady.

In the crew's lounge, the conversation was stuck at shipwrecks. Shanghai Cid and I were talking for a while, and I asked him, "Cid, you've been around for a while, you ever go down in a ship?" "Go down in a ship—let me think, have I ever gone down in a ship? No, but I've got a great collision story for you."

One of the ordinaries said, "Wow, I'd like to hear that!"

"Okay then... Well, I was on another fleet oil can, the *Nebraska*, and we were in the North Atlantic, with naturally rough seas. She was an old converted oiler with two houses, forward, and aft, and we were doing an underway replenishment, with a destroyer on our starboard side. We had been pumping bunkers to her for about a hour, and everything was running smooth. I was on rig station one, and I looked over my right shoulder, and I saw the bow of the destroyer fall back, and the next thing I saw were the hoses flapping in the breeze, and cargo was flying everywhere. Her bow kept going to her port, and she slammed into our starboard quarter, and with all the sparks flying I was surprised there was no fire.

"If the cargo had been jet or aviation gas and not bunker C we would have gone up like rocket. Anyway, that bow of hers just started slicing through our after house like it was butter, and I jumped off the rig, and went back to see if I could help. Luckily the crew was on deck, because the collision took out almost all the berthing spaces, and until we could get to a port, the unlicensed crew had to sleep up in the forecastle just like the old days. Later on, after the huge mess was cleaned up, we found out from the captain that the destroyer had lost power, and couldn't regain it. It still blows my mind when I think about it, because I saw the whole thing. And because I did, and had the best view, I had to go before a JAG review board... it was a big deal."

"Then what?"

"Well, we made our way to Southampton, got paid off, and that was fine with me, because I had already been on that rust bucket for six months."

Chapter Forty-Four

"Did I ever tell you about the time I was up in Alaska purse seine fishing, and I got dumped in the water?"

"No, I think I would have remembered that one. But go ahead, I wanna hear this."

"Even though it wasn't a ship, and only a small boat it's still a sinking."

"Ted, will you just tell the story."

"Okay, here goes. Well, it was the summer of 1972, during a college break, and I ran into a couple of Seattle gals visiting Sausalito, California, and we met in one of those trendy wood and fern bars."

"Can you skip the *Dating Game* stuff, and get to the action?"

"Yeah, but just listen, it's part of the story—and try to have some patience! See, I found out they were driving back to Seattle in two days, and when I asked them if I could help them with the drive, they agreed to take me along. When we arrived in Seattle, I immediately went to the fisherman's terminal, and spread the word that I was an outstanding commercial fisherman and that I was looking for work. I got a job on a boat called the *Prowler*, and a week later we were headed up through the Inside Passage up to Petersburg, and Ketchikan in Southeastern Alaska.

"To be honest, I really had no idea what commercial purse seining was, but I had seven days to figure it out. You didn't need to be an astrophysicist to figure it out, but as I was trying to acquire knowledge, I didn't want it to appear that it was my maiden voyage. The time came when the captain said, 'Okay, it's time to go fishing.'

"I guess I bluffed them pretty good, because I fit in without any problems. The only essential requirement was an ability to party, and I had a black belt in partying. The stern is where all the gear was stacked; you had the lead line, the corks, and the webbing. The jobs of cooking, being on deck, and driving the seine skiff were rotated.

"The seine skiff looked like a big aluminum bathtub with a powerful Ford Lehman engine, and I loved it. I would get that engine revved up until I thought it would fly apart, it was great. The only drawback was when the engine cover got so hot that you couldn't keep from getting burnt. After about the second month, it was my turn to drive the skiff, and as time went on, we just weren't catching any fish. Out of desperation the captain hired a local fish guide, and all of us resented the little wise ass, but we figured if he could help us catch fish, well, what the hell. At that point, even though I went fishing to make my fortune, and it looked like a bust, I was having a ball.

"The Skipper, being a family guy with debts and responsibility, was going nuts! On this one occasion, the fish guide (a kid of about nineteen years old) wanted to drive the skiff. I was on the bow and the kid was on the wheel, then the little shit started hot-rodding as we were pulling the net off the stern of the fish boat. The kid had the engine at full throttle, the tow line got fowled, and the skiff's stern was dragged under. And with the blink of an eye, we're both in the drink. To make matters worse, there was two-foot chop on the water, with the added excitement of jellyfish.

"Decked out in my full commercial fishing ensemble, I had my rubber hip boots on, a heavy leather jacket, a sweater, and tons of gear. My boots were filling up with water, and I was going down. The kid was swimming around with no problem, because he wasn't loaded down with gear. By this time I noticed the big jellyfish in the water, and I noticed something more important, an empty jerry can! A World War Two jerry can that was in the skiff and luckily the top was on tight. I grabbed it, and it had just enough buoyancy to keep me afloat, and my head out of the water. Coming up fast was another boat to our rescue, and the two of us couldn't get on their main deck fast enough. I can still remember being on deck, peeling my clothes off, trying to get the stinging jellyfish. The only thing comparable to that day was a motorcycle accident that happened in later years. It all happens so fast that before I knew it I was either in the drink, or on the pavement.

"So, that's my sinking story, Cid. What do you think?"

"I got to tell you, it's different, but what happened to the guide?"

"His career with us was over, and I never saw him again."

"What did you do next?"

"Well, as for the boat, fortunately there was a line attached with a float to help in retrieving the skiff, evidently it wasn't the first time a skiff had gone down. We hauled the skiff out, dried her off, went fishing, and finished the season. The skiff was on loan from the cannery, and they took charge of the salvage mess."

I asked Cid about the outcome of his collision, he said that "Neither ship was in danger of sinking, but it looked like world war three. Since we were two hundred miles from England both ships limped back to a dry dock in the U.K. The whole thing was all pretty embarrassing, and luckily no one was killed, just some minor injuries."

"Cid, let me tell you about the time we did a round haul in a shallow slough, and we got the net hung up on some rocks, as the tide was coming in. We tried to pull it free with the power block, and the strain pulled our port rail under, and we started taking on water."

"Look, I've got to eat and get to the bridge. We'll talk sea stories later."

"Sure, fine. They're still probably talking about that fish boat that came down between us and the *Independence*."

"Did you go back for another season of commercial fishing ?"

"Heck no, but I thought about Alaska for a long time; I was in love with the place. I almost went back to try my hand at setting chokers in a logging operation up in southeastern, but I found myself selling electrical appliances door to door in California."

Cid said, "Electrical appliances? What are you talking about?"

"You know, vacuum cleaners?"

I went back to my room to unwind, and practice with my Bokkun, and I could hear the Thermo Kings screaming. Thermo Kings were refrigeration container boxes that had to maintain a set temperature and would start to howl when temperatures would rise, and preset alarm settings would kick in automatically, and set the motors off day or night. Four feet from my window, in front of my room, facing forward on the main deck, was a row of reefer boxes, and they were loud.

My first thought was, *Okay, I'll just face in another direction;* then when that didn't work, maybe I could turn the bed around—no way! Naturally the bed was welded to the deck. Maybe what I really needed was better sound insulation, or maybe having the referrer boxes moved. None of the above worked, and that's when I discovered the world of silence, through earplugs. Earplugs are great for shipboard noise, but they are ineffective against vibration. On a ship, vibration is something you just have to live with; I have been on ships where the vibration was so bad, that you could feel the fillings in your teeth come apart.

Chapter Forty-Five

The chief mate, glancing at the deck, said, "You guys on the 4x8, if you're interested in some overtime, you can strip and wax the bridge deck. Murray, I know you're a wiz with sanitation."

It sounded simple enough, and we both replied, "You bet, we'll take it!"

We set out to do a routine job that quickly became our nemesis, and in a nanosecond, our wax job became the talk of the ship. It was a complete nightmare! What would normally take two people two days, took us a week. For starters, Murray insisted we use his special wax stripper that Mom had sent from home, and subsequently had to replace ten linoleum tiles, due to the industrial-strength, high-grade wax stripper. The stripper not only removed the wax from the deck, but it discolored the linoleum, and would have to be replaced. When I told him we shouldn't be using cleaning supplies from his mother, that the US Navy and Murray's mom may not be on the same page, he took it personally, and I thought he was going to have a nervous breakdown on the bridge.

Murray started hyperventilating, and the second mate had to get the ship's medic, and Murray was given a mild sedative. The chief mate and I got Murray up to his room, and then the chief mate went ballistic, because in the mate's own words, "There was so much crap in Murray's room that we could barely get to him."

The next day, Murray was fine, but the chief mate was out of sorts, and he was on the warpath, and wanted to do an inventory of Murray's room. The real crazy part was when the chief mate discovered that all the stuff in Murray's room was indeed Murray's! Evidently, his mother had been sending him cleaning gear for over a year. At this point, we weren't sure who was crazier, Murray or his mother!

Once we got the new linoleum down, Murray was insistent we use a polish that his mom had sent. Murray was giving a sales pitch on the merits of his mom's wax: "Spanish Carnauba is used by all top-flight hotels across Europe and the finest apartment buildings in the United States." I had heard of Carnauba wax, and it has always been touted as great stuff, but Carnauba floor wax was to be used on wood decks and we had linoleum. He had gear no one else had ever seen, and with Murray's hardware store/cleaning locker, the chief mate appeared to be in over his head. We were fairly certain the mate hadn't seen this behavior before, and doubted his academy had addressed Murray's condition at length... We imagined the mate would have to go to the captain for advice on this one.

In spite of ourselves, we finally completed the job, and it amounted to $750.50 in overtime, and the chief mate said, "How can you expect me to pay you for a botched job?" And they weren't going to pay. To add insult to injury, we were being accused of destroying government property, and threatened with disciplinary action for our incompetence. After the smoke cleared we each received $135 for busting our butts for a week...a meager sum for our efforts.

I tried to sell the cost overrun angle to the chief mate, but he wasn't buying. I even tried appealing to the chief mates sense of humor; he wasn't buying that either, no dice! The chief mate said he should never have had us on the job in the first place, and we could forget any future extra work. I thought it was funny. Hell, if that was his idea of disciplinary action, heck, I didn't care if I ever worked again after suffering through the last overtime campaign with Murray.

By now, Murray was using so much garlic, that the chief steward told him he had to sit at the end of the mess deck area when eating, because he was grossing out the crew with the stink, and they couldn't eat. The list of stupid weird things goes on and on. All I wanted to do was put some distance between myself and Murray. My buddy Don Morse was complaining about a toothache for a week, and finally the corpsman onboard said the tooth should be looked at.

Don was scheduled to take a helo ride to the *Independence* aircraft carrier and get his mouth fixed. The helo was hovering over our flight deck at 0700 to pick up Don. Shanghai Cid had last standby, and he said, "If Don was nervous he didn't let on."

I was on the stern when he arrived after his dental work, and he looked like a different guy; you could tell he was jazzed. Don said, "I felt like a V.I.P. Everywhere I went I had a marine guard, I felt like the Goddamn secretary of defense.

"While I was waiting for the dentist, the guard and I walked to the galley area to get a cup of coffee, and on the way we passed this oval room with all these guys in uniform smoking big cigars, and it looked like Dr. Strangelove, or Dr. No. You know what I'm talking about—this was some high-powered action."

"Wow, you lucky bum. Sounds cool. What else happened?"

"Well, I didn't go in and introduce myself, and tell them I was an AB over on the *Higgins*, and just wanted to make sure things were running smooth; besides, I had G.I. Joe on my ass, so we went back to the dentist, he yanked my tooth out, and we marched back to the helo, flew back, and that was the whole shebang."

I said,   "I can't believe it—you got to do all that just for some lousy tooth? Man, I have to come up with a plan to get a chopper ride, and get over there on that bird farm."

"Hey, let me tell you something, the grass is greener on the other side. Our guys want to go to the *Independence*, and the *Independence* guys want to come here to introduce themselves to our Sea Goddess. I'm just glad I got back without having another look at my breakfast, what a ride! Straight up! It was awesome!"

"What do you expect? It's an airscrew, not an airplane, Don."

"Where'd you get that from anyway?"

"I don't know, I think I read it somewhere."

Shanghai Cid wanted to know all about the helicopter ride, and what it was like being on the *Independence*, and if they had hard liquor for sale in the ship's store. And said, "What were you saying about our very own Sea Goddess? Did you say that all those guys are trying to get to my girl?"

We both piped up, "Your girl?"

"Well, yeah, sort of. I asked her if she wanted to see a movie with me, and she said she was flattered, perhaps another time or place, but no thanks. Could it be that maybe I am not as attractive as I think I am?"

"Cid, anything is possible, maybe you should tone that biker edge, just a touch."

"No way! That's all I got going with her. You know she asked me to take off my shirt, 'cause I told her I had some special tattoos."

"Not again. Didn't you learn your lesson in Fujiarh?" Don said. "Cid, how do you think that's going to look? A forty-eight-year-old man parading around with his shirt off just because you got some tattoos that a nineteen-year-old gal in the US Navy ain't seen? Just get a mental picture of it before you make an ass of yourself."

"Yeah, maybe you're right, but check out this bunny rabbit!" As Cid lifted his T-shirt.

Chapter Forty-Six

The months were going by, it was now November, and we were now in the advent of the holidays. For some, our isolation, and being cut of from the mainstream of life drove us into the mailroom as never before. I had been corresponding with a half a dozen people that had interest in our ship and its mission. The questions were wide and varied, and letter writing was an education, for certain, there was no shortage of opinions from people back home. From our point of view, we thought the questions and comments were entertaining, because most people haven't got a clue about life at sea.

An older woman wrote, "What do you do at night when you are at sea, do you stop your ship and turn the lights out, or do you leave a light on?"

A couple from Iowa asked, "Do you see whales every day? And does it rain when you're at sea?"

One of my favorites was from a guy in Oregon, "How many miles of anchor chain do you need to have on a ship? Do you need thirteen miles or more in case you're at the Mariana's Trench, that I read about in a magazine?"

We had two guys aboard that probably had absolutely nothing to do, and they sponsored an adopt-a-ship program with schools. It shows you that some people would do anything to keep from getting bored out of their skulls.

Collisions at sea are tragic, a near miss although not tragic, is equally nerve-wracking, and one morning we had a near miss with another ship that had the captain running to the bridge in his jockey shorts. During operations Desert Shield and Desert Storm we were assisting the Navy with security during the blockade. Typically, we would contact a suspicious ship and ask questions; what was your last port, what's your next port, the kind of cargo, that sort of thing. Brother Don Morse, not thrilled with our new job, told me, "It's not our job, it's a military function," and he had a whole explanation and justification.

I thought Joe Bones' answer was simple enough: "What's the difference? It all pays the same, and in case you haven't noticed this ship is gray, and we are part of the Navy's mission."

On the fourteenth of November the lookout reported a contact on our port quarter, and it was closing in on our port bow. The second mate was doing the standard Q-and-A routine, and he wasn't satisfied with the response, and began using flashing the light. Using the light was a common practice when hailing, just a simple Alpha, Alpha—still nothing! We were now on a collision course, and radio contact was finally established on channel sixteen. Second mate, on the radio, requested the ship to come to his port. There was still no change in course or speed. The second got back on the radio, and in an aggravated voice said, "Would you alter your course to port?" Still, no deal. Then to everyone's amazement, the other ship altered his course, but it was to starboard, thereby putting themselves on an intended collision course with us. There was no doubt they would have T-boned us on our port side.

At the helm, I was awaiting a rudder command, and the second mate froze, I said, "Mate!" I heard nothing.

Then seeing the extremis position, the second began yelling into the radio, "No! Come to port, not starboard."

I looked at the mate once more, and said to myself, *Somebody's got to do something*, and just as I was about to come right, the mate gave the command, "Hard right!" At full sea speed, it didn't take long for our ship to respond, and as the ship heeled over I eased the rudder to right 15. We continued swinging to starboard and made round turn, and not a minute went by and the captain shot up to the bridge in his jockey shorts. The captain was as cool as could be, and we just watched the ship pass our stern, and in so doing providing a look at her stern, and it was the *Polo Swan*. The captain immediately called his superior, and let them deal with the matter. The second mate and myself aged about ten years on that one, and I am sure we will be telling that story for some time. For a man of thirty-two having a premature bald spot on top of his head is not that unusual, but his premature balding was attributed to his own doing. He would literally stand in front of the radar and pull his hair out, one strand at a time.

We continued doing our Q and A that was designed to let commercial shipping know that we were paying attention. Later in the war a full-on board and search with more teeth would be used by qualified naval warriors. Desert Shield had become more real to us when we discovered that the *Independence* had lost an aircraft and the pilot had not been found. What made this particular incident eerie was that the crew had witnessed the fatal routine touch-and-go flight operations that the pilot had crashed and burned. Most of us were civilians, and had been on station for four months, and would not be going home for the holidays.

Our time with the *Independence* battle group was over, and we were to take on another mission. In mid-December we rendezvoused with an eight-ship amphibious assault group to perform varying exercises. The *Higgins* found herself joining forces with what was shaping up to be a convoy, and we were doing special maneuvers and underway replenishments with as many as twenty-five ships at a time and it was exhausting, and dangerous. One ship executing the wrong command can put an entire fleet in harm's way, and jeopardize an entire mission, and we witnessed just such an incident while executing a battle turn. We had a full day of drills with our newly assembled group, and we would do leapfrogs, racetracks, and the first drill to be performed was to be a battle turn.

A battle turn is an effective strategic maneuvering tactic that when executed properly commences with a column of ships following one another on matching course and speeds. When the command "Execute" is given, the column will come to a predetermined course at exactly the same time. A ninety-degree turn to starboard was the objective on the command execute. However, it seemed one ship in our group already had a "Wrong-way Corrigan" reputation; its name is not important now, but then, one need only mention it, and visions of F-Troop, or the Keystone Cops came to mind. On execute, all eighteen ships put their rudder over to starboard, and came to a new course of 096; however, there was one exception, and it was passing 348 as she was turning to port, and it appeared the ship turning in the wrong wasn't going to try to correct her swing. They would continue, and go a full 270 degrees until they steadied up on 096.

On our bridge, I can still hear the our captain: "I can't believe it, they're coming to port."

There are few things that are more embarrassing for a captain or helmsman or for that mater anyone on the ship. And when something like this happens you don't even want to know anyone on the ship. Hell, you don't even want to be in the same time zone! Even with a helm safety directly behind the helmsman, it took two people to make that mistake. Once a ship starts her turn, with a rudder hard over it takes plenty of time to recover and steady up. Being on their bridge would have been better than Showtime or HBO; the captain's conversation might have had this tone: "Goddamn it, you idiots, keep her coming to port, and steady up on 096."

Chapter Forty-Seven

After making a trip to Muscat, and loading jet fuel and diesel, we were bound for the fleet. Our watch was coming to a close with ten minutes to go, a fresh pot of coffee was made, and Murray was polishing the inside of an ashtray. Then I heard a voice; it was Murray, and he was mumbling, "No one cares, no one gives a damn. If I don't do it, no one will. There's spots here, and spots there, and damn it, look at that will yah! There's water drops in the ashtray!"

And then it hit me like a bolt! The perfect plan. A couple of water droplets, a little push, and, "See yah, in the Sierras, Murray!" When relieving one another, we would pass down information, such as course, RPMs, and or anything else we should know. The next day, on our morning 4x8, I let Murray know the coffee was made and everything was prepared for the next watch. However, I added a little something extra, and said, "And by the way, Murray, this time the ashtrays are clean and dry." What makes this information significant is in knowing that the chief mate had jumped Murray for some dirty ashtrays about a week prior. Now all I had to do was keep my mouth shut and get ready for the fireworks. Everyone was in their regular positions: I was at the helm; next to me, the helm safety; the second mate on the radar, and the captain on the port wing, with the military contingent.

Not more than thirty seconds went by, and in a loud voice, "There's water droplets in the captain's ashtray!" Bingo! Murray was yelling, "There's water drops in the captain's ashtray!" Then Murray stomped up to the steering console, where the helm safety and I were, as he continued bellowing with ashtray in hand. I couldn't believe it. Even for Murray, this was crazy. He was now holding the ashtray at arm's length from me as he was yelling.

I said in my most obsequious voice, "Would you please let me do my job. I am having trouble concentrating. We can talk about whatever is disturbing you later."

I heard the chief mate say, "What in the hell is going on over there?" And Murray, like a rabid dog, was still screaming about the water droplets.

The chief mate in an aggravated voice to my right, yelled, "Murray!"

Meanwhile the entire bridge was looking in our direction to see how this daytime drama played out. I looked back at the compass, and I was one degree off course...oh shit! And looking outside, I saw the captain's hands reach for the sky, and he screeched through the bridge door, "Mind your helm! Don't make me come in there!"

The next scream out of the chief mate was, "Murray, get off this bridge, and lay below right now!"

At the end of the day, it's just you and your marbles, and as far as I am concerned, the one with the most marbles wins. At times it requires doing some unpleasant things to keep your own marbles, and it can be viewed as a chess game for mental survival. Shanghai Cid was to be my new watch partner, and Murray was shunted to the 8x12 watch by popular opinion, because Murray was considered unsuitable for the 4x8, due to his sanitation mania, and laundry list of other peculiar quirks. In the event of a collision at sea involving three naval ships, if upon investigation it were uncovered that the catalyst for the collision was related to an overzealous sailor performing sanitation duties on the bridge... that was something the captain did not want to explain in a court of law. JAG lawyers are notorious at being sticklers for detail, and relentless in their quest for the truth.

The shipboard squabbling was behind us, and in the coming days we would have something to really whine about, and it would make water droplets in an ashtray more laughable than it already was.

An amphibious assault group was our next assignment, and with it providing a new level of exhilaration, and tension. The general feeling was that something big was about to happen, and if we were lucky, it would include us. We have had that feeling before, when we first arrived on station in late August, but somehow this was beginning to take on a new element. We were getting a look at war equipment that appeared to be more serious; tanks, armored personnel carriers, more ammunition ships, landing ships, and helicopter ships with marines loaded to battalion strength.

Thanksgiving had come and gone, and Christmas wasn't far away. The Indian Ocean doesn't lend itself to anything that can be construed as festive in the Western sense. Holidays at sea are always difficult for people with families, but for the lone albatross sailor, it's a Godsend. For him it means more overtime, and fewer reminders of a family way of life that never worked, and not having to cope with the constant reminders of past holidays.

One day, Joe Bones told a couple of us that one of the guys was in a jam, and we were going to take up a collection. Joe said, "Ralph R. Snapp just got word that his new bride of eight months was in the hoosegow in someplace called West Monroe somewhere in Oregon, I think—anyway, the point is he needs three thousand dollars to get her out, and that's not the worst of it."

Joe went on to say it seemed that she had been writing Ralph for a couple of months, telling him how great the convenience store was doing in their new enterprise, when in fact, she had a small time methamphetamine business going with her folks. To add insult to injury, Ralph was now a wanted man, and there was a warrant out for his arrest as an accessory to the alleged crimes she committed. Ralph was to depart the *Higgins* on the next helicopter on a personal leave, and he was handling that part just fine; what seemed to have him keyed up was that his new bride and family represented themselves as real "Christian folks," and now Ralph was having doubts.

Ralph said, "I had been searching for different ways of meeting single women, and met her at a religious serpent-handling celebration, and it was love at first sight, and never once thought she was capable of running and operating an interstate pep pill operation." Unanimously, it had been decided we would chip in what we could afford, and send Ralph off with some monetary help, as it was painfully obvious he would need all he could get.

Chapter Forty-Eight

The Persian Gulf and surrounding deserts have strong seasonal winds that contain very fine sand that can wreak havoc on man, machine, and beast. These winds are called Shamals, and they can be seen for miles forming huge clouds of sand. The *Higgins* hadn't seen rain in months, and it wasn't long before the entire ship was covered in fine sand. Modern warships have exterior sprinkler systems for combating bacterial and chemical agents, and now sand was added to the list of irritants.

In the Iraq/Iran war of 1988, I was stationed in Bahrain on patrol boats, and had firsthand experience with the harsh climate of the region. Sandstorms blasting the paint off our equipment were not uncommon, and we managed to keep the equipment in top condition. There was the time we had just finished putting fresh green paint on our boats, and someone looked up and said, "Hey, what in the hell is that coming this way?"

Someone else said, "It looks like locusts, and they're headed right for us!"

"No way, it looks like flies." In fact it was a giant Shamal zeroing in on our freshly painted boats...no big deal, we now had Mother Nature's non-skid, not United States Navy regulation, but we could live with it.

At six knots, the *Higgins* was steaming down the coast of Oman, and comfortably positioned in the middle of an amphibious group. We were all proceeding on a slow bell, at five knots, with just enough headway for steering. Along with us was the ammunition ship *Versuvious*, a mile ahead off our port bow. Shanghai Cid, my new partner, was driving, Jimmy on the bow, and I had the last standby. There was nothing unusual about the morning. I had gone through the routine of calling the next watch, and made coffee. When Cid was relieved on the wheel we went below together, and Cid started in on his favorite subject…two-wheelers. I was telling Cid, "I've only had two motorcycles, and managed to wreck them both."

Cid said, "Yeah, well, let me give you a rundown on some of my more colorful and memorable bike accidents."

He had told me of a particular misfortune that put him twenty feet into a pet shop, and in so doing broke his right leg, and lacerated his right arm to shreds. Cid didn't have a gift for telling a funny story, but later when I thought about it, I couldn't stop laughing. He said, "I was in so much pain I couldn't stand it, and the shopkeeper was yelling and screaming at me in Chinese. Hell, it's not like I aimed for the most exotic fish tanks in the store, it just happened. And there were these stinky, smelly fish, and kelp, and gravel everywhere, plus there was this dog cage that got all busted up."

Shanghai Cid continued, "The dogs were barking, and licking me, while the Chinese guy was yelling, and I could barely move." Cid said he was on the floor for half an hour before the paramedics came and rescued him from the mess. When I asked him if the dogs were okay, he said, "Heck, they were fine. They were having a good old time. They were just thankful for some excitement." Cid also added, "I smelled like fish and dog shit for a week."

We were all beginning to become frustrated, because we knew something big was about to happen, but no one was talking. Trying to get information by normal methods was not working, and the reality was that no one really knew what our next move would be.

The following morning was more of the same. The 8x12 assumed the watch, Jimmy would be on the wheel, and Murray on the bow, and Ralph would be on standby. With no underway replenishments scheduled, the after steering watch and rescue swimmers were not required, so the morning was free. I had stopped by the galley, and decided against breakfast, and headed back to my room for a rest.

I was in my rack, with earplugs set, and was just drifting of to sleep when I felt something very odd. After being at sea for months, you get familiar with the ship's noise and vibration, and the slightest change is immediately noticeable. At first, there was a slowing, and a kind of dragging/pulling, and then a complete stop. My eyes went wide open. I pulled out my earplugs, and waited a second or two, and then looked at my watch; it was 0810. My first thought was, *Thank*

God I was off watch! Something was very wrong! I didn't know what, but I had to find out.

Immediately, I jumped out of bed, I put on my clothes, and proceeded to the main deck. Whatever was happening was not on a schedule that I was aware of, and not twenty minutes had passed since I was on the bridge. When I arrived at the main deck, I was alone, and it was very quite, not a sound. I walked ten feet forward of the house, and to the port side, and finally I saw one of the rig captains.

Until I saw the rig captain, my thoughts were, *Did I miss something? Maybe I didn't get the word, and we are in the middle of a drill.* I asked the rig captain, "Did you feel that?"

"You're damn right I felt it; it almost knocked me off the shitter. Let's see what's going on! This isn't normal whatever it is."

Neither one of us had a clue. I went over to the port rail and looking over the side. I could see a red substance beginning to surface. "Hey, you got to see this, look over here!"

Then the rig captain said, "You're not going to believe this, check this out!"

Just as he mouthed the words, these huge air bubbles started surfacing, and we both looked at each other as if to say, "Well, we've done it this time!" At first, we thought the red substance in the water was our bottom paint, but with closer inspection, we knew all too well that it was red algae coming from a reef. Things were beginning to accelerate.

The rig captain, Ralph, shouted, "Look over there, that's oil!" And it was, but not black oil; we were a product carrier, not crude. Nevertheless, it would have been a gross understatement to say we had problems, because huge amounts of product were now bubbling along the port side of the ship. Ralph said, "Do you think this is going to screw up our stay in Thailand?"

I said, "Thailand? From the looks of things, I think this will screw up our stay anywhere, except a dry dock."

Curious people were beginning to make their way down to the main deck. Shanghai Cid came ambling over and said, "Hey, what the hell is going on? We're dead in the water!"

I said, "Yeah, you got that right, bubba. Take a look over the side—what do you suppose that stuff is?"

Cid said in his nonchalant manner, "What's the matter, you never seen oil before? It's a leak. We sprung a leak, big deal. I'm going in to finish my movie. By the way, do you think they're still serving chow?"

"Hell, I don't know. You might have a minute or two, go check it out, and while you're halfway through your grits and eggs, we'll be slowly going to the bottom."

Cid said, "Don't be so dramatic! What do you want me to do? If you guys want to wring your hands and worry about it, that's your business. See yah—just let me know when we go to the lifeboats."

Timing is everything, and we on the 4x8 had much to be grateful for; in our case, twenty minutes made all the difference in our world. It was now 0832, and just being off the bridge was a relief, but for the men on watch, whether they were found at fault or not made little difference. Going hard aground is serious business, and guilt by association is, for want of a better word, bottomless.

Chapter Forty-Nine

The uh-oh squad was on their way! And within a half hour, an inflatable Z boat with six divers approached our port side, and they were looking very businesslike. Fortunately I was off watch, thereby providing me an opportunity to rubberneck. The captain and chief mate were talking with the divers that had come from the ammunition ship *Kaboom* to survey our situation that was deteriorating rapidly. We weren't alone in this mess; the *Kaboom* had also struck a different reef/pinnacle, and managed to shave off a foot of her screw (propeller); however, she was not in jeopardy of sinking.

The *Higgins*, on the other hand, was in a much more perilous situation. With her bottom torn out, she had come to rest atop a pinnacle three quarters way aft, just forward of the house, and directly under my room ten decks below, at the keel. The dive team's leader immediately had his men in the water with wetsuits, tanks, and multiple underwater cameras. The divers began at our bow and worked their way aft, doing a complete sweep of the *Higgins's* hull, taking pictures and checking for structural damage.

The shallow-draft amphibious ships ahead of us could navigate in shallower waters, and because a pinnacle by its very nature doesn't indicate depth gradually, the change in depth was never noted. We were in charted waters that weren't normally used by the military and merchant shipping, making it impossible to forecast what lay ahead. The *Kaboom*, grinding its way through the pinnacle, never had time to warn the *Higgins*. What saved the *Higgins* from a horrific wreck was our slow speed; had we been traveling at normal sea speed of eighteen knots plus, and not six knots, there would have been little doubt of our fate, and we would have joined the bottom feeders straight away.

As the day wore on, we were the center of attention, and for all the wrong reasons. I recall Farley saying to a couple of us after about two hours into the grounding, "I can see the home-made T-shirts already, with us teetering on a big old pinnacle, rocking back and forth." And Farley was right, even before we arrived in a dry dock for repairs, there were no less than four designs for T-shirts by entrepreneurial crew members. The circus was in town, and it was us. Fortunately, we were on the other side of the world, and away from media attention.

Joe Bones and I had time to discuss the recent events, and Joe put it correctly, when he said, "Can you believe it? This shipwreck/grounding, Blaze/Mafia thing? Heck, the *Higgins* should have its own press corp." Indeed, the press would have taken the ball and run with it all the way back to the States.

The impact to the environment was minimal, no one was killed or injured, and what cargo did go into the water dissipated, unlike a thick heavy black crude oil. Looking back from this direction, given the situation, we were all rather lucky.

As an addition to the bizarre atmosphere, we noticed these warrior fellers on our main deck, that appeared from nowhere wearing black ninja outfits…most unusual! These guys had on safety helmets, with Kevlar body armor and weapons slung over their shoulders. Shanghai Cid, just coming up from the galley, said, "Who are these people? What do you think, are these guys our reliefs, or what?"

Farley Cranpool was a special-operation nut, he had read all the black-operation books, and subscribed to *Solider of Fortune* magazine, and he had all the jargon down. Farley was getting a kick out hobnobbing with the SEALs,

"Wow! Check these guys out, will yah!" And Farley went on about insertions, and extractions, and fast rope techniques, and that the SEALs did a simple insertion on the *Higgins* via fast rope from a chopper. Farley told us about a three-day *SOF* convention he went to in Las Vegas, where he got to shoot a .50-caliber machine gun. He said they took over a casino and on the second day some of the guys got too worked up after the hand-to-hand combat training, and the police got involved. On the third day there were seminars on blasting agents and explosives, but the turnout was low because twenty-five percent of them were in the Las Vegas poky.

Cid said, "Now that sounds cool," and asked, "But did they have any tanks?"

Farley said that they were supposed to, but the tank had been hijacked in San Diego by a guy that was drunk and he drove it up on a highway center divide, and it screwed up the whole event. Naturally the guys fast roping from the chopper weren't our reliefs—it's just not done that way, and they seemed a bit too eager. We had learned Farley was correct, and that it was a SEAL team on the *Kaboom* that decided what better time to play war games, and use the *Higgins* as the opposition force in a terrorist drill. Part of the drill was to board our stern from a helicopter, and all of this to be done in a stealthy fashion. We didn't know what the SEALs expected of us, but the *Higgins* crew was too busy to play games; our only strategy was to extricate ourselves from the mess we had gotten ourselves into.

Being rendered high and dry is not the most comfortable feeling. We literally could not go forward, and could not go astern. By early afternoon, the divers were able to examine the photos with the experts to make critical decisions. We were amazed at the swiftness of their findings. The *Higgins* had been severely damaged. The pinnacle had not only torn through our steel plate, but longitudinal support members of the ship had been severely damaged.

One need not be a naval architect, or an expert in salvage to see that the integrity of the ship was in question, and we all were wondering what really was keeping us afloat. The big question was, "What next?" Should we try to set the ship free from the reef with the next high water? Or should we sit and wait for tugs to assist? Or should we remain stationary, with the knowledge that movement from the seas would enlarge the already widening hole in her bottom? These were hard choices, and decisions had to be made quickly. A decision was made, and that evening we were going to give it a shot, and make an attempt at backing the *Higgins* off the pinnacle. There was one small problem; we had one hundred thousand barrels of cargo aboard, plus tanks containing dirty ballast, and a hole in our bottom.

The 8x12 was on watch when things came to a grinding all stop. Our new hire Jimmy, from the streets of Oakland, was at the wheel and was heard to have said, "I guess that's it for my career; that will be my last time at the wheel."

Of course, Jimmy had nothing to do with the grounding, and neither did the bow lookout who thought, *I should have seen it coming.* He said, "I was going to run for the brake," and the man on standby was completely out of the loop, because he was making his rounds.

The first attempt to set the *Higgins* free from the pinnacle was on the 4x8, and the bridge was standing room only.

With the sun just slipping below the horizon, and daylight diminishing, the entire scene was beginning to resemble a Hollywood production. A high tide at 1806 dictated the optimal time to depart, and as time was nearing, the level of tension was in the eyes of those in charge. I was at the helm, and standing in front of me was an officer in the Navy. Time permitted, and I took notice of a few interesting things about this officer. It wasn't difficult to see that this officer stood out from the rest. He was wearing a Navy SEAL insignia, and if that wasn't enough, he wore the Congressional Medal of Honor, and a Sea Bee patch. Unlike the officers that arrived from the Navy's JAG team, he was wearing fatigues, and no other ribbons or medals were displayed, but we were sure he had more than the national defense ribbon at home. We had no idea what role this officer played in our predicament, but it was good to see he was on our side. Our captain didn't appear to have slept in the last twenty-four hours, and we could tell he was anxious to get things moving. I imagine fewer things can be more disconcerting than to be in command of a vessel that is aground for the entire world to witness. The order was given, "Dead slow astern!" Within a few seconds, we on the bridge we could feel the rumbling below, and after a minute, we were looking for any sign of movement, then the captain increased the engine to slow astern. As the vibration increased, so did our expectations, but still nothing. The *Higgins* hadn't moved an inch. I was then ordered to exercise the wheel hard to port, and then hard to starboard. Nothing! We didn't budge! Differing maneuvers were being employed; next we went to all stop, and then captain then gave the command "Slow ahead" with rudder amidships; still nothing. Once more, after trying astern, the ship continued to vibrate, and then it was decided to wait until the next day to make another attempt.

I said to Cid, "Whoever up here is calling the shots must know a lot more than we do. What do they think is going to keep us afloat?"

He said, "Don't forget, you don't run the train, you just ring the bell."

Shanghai Cid had an expression for every occasion; he is one of those people who can come up with an expression, and you'll be left scratching your head saying, "Where in the hell did he get that from?"

THEODORE CARL SODERBERG

Like most ships, we were of single-hull construction, with the engine spaces being double bottom. An argument could have been made that if we had double-hull construction from stem to stern, this mess would not have occurred, but in the real world of military budgeting and prioritization, we never had the chance to find out.

In the morning, Cid and I discovered that a nearby tanker would come alongside to take our cargo. Until then, the ship's crew was doing its best to maintain stability and protect the environment. We stood a normal watch on the bridge, and as my partner and I were heading below we could see a large tanker approaching our port side, under the watchful eye of an escort tug. My partner was a bundle of nerves, and he went below babbling about "What will happen if we can't control our list, and how does the captain know we won't sink...?"

Chapter Fifty

It was a gray gloomy morning, as we watched the tanker *Vermont* ease to within one hundred feet of our port side. She had her port anchor at the water's edge, and ready to let her go. After a pause of five minutes, with a roar of the anchor chain the anchor crashed into the water, and sent a geyser of water into the air. We could only see the *Vermont's* bow that had been engulfed in a cloud of rust and dried mud, with chunks of debris flying everywhere.

To keep the *Vermont's* stern from swinging, the tug had passed a line up to the *Vermont's* stern, and the deckhands made it fast. Once the *Vermont* was in position, a floating hose was paid out that would connect both ship manifolds, and then pumping would commence. Discharging our cargo would take a good portion of the day, and the sailors would make sure the tank tops and manhole covers were airtight. We were visited by several small boats and helicopters throughout the day, and there were some very serious faces coming aboard. The word on deck was that there were two bigwigs from the Navy's legal department.

I was telling Shanghai Cid, "These are the guys that get paid to take scalps legally."

And that prompted another Shanghai Cidism. "All I have to say is, 'Heavy hangs the head who wears the crown.'"

I said , "Ah yes, the burden of command."

And Cid said, "Don't forget, it's a short walk from the penthouse to the shit house."

"Enough already. I can't take it anymore—see ya later."

We would sit and wait for the evening's high tide. The deck department had worked feverishly and our preparation was complete. Some additional facts were beginning to surface; like the fact that we were nine miles from shore, and nowhere on the charts was any notation of pinnacles or reefs, or any other navigational hazards. In addition, I can recall that the fathometer didn't look right.

The night before, at the helm while we were trying to back her off, I was looking at a fathometer that was reading sixty-seven fathoms, more than enough water for any ship.

I didn't mention anything at the time; it's just not something you start talking about as it was apparent careers were on the line, and nobody was ready to listen to some wise-ass AB say, "Hey, look up there on the fathometer—it says sixty-seven fathoms. Maybe were really not stuck up here on this pinnacle like a bunch of dorks, and it's just someone playing a practical joke." We were indeed teetering on pinnacle, and there were some very grim faces on the bridge. As more was revealed, keeping quiet was the right choice. The fathometer mystery was solved; apparently the transponder for the fathometer was located forward and there indeed was sixty-seven fathoms of water at the bow. The tide was to be its highest at 1804, and that coincided with the discharge of our cargo, and we would not miss the opportunity.

With time drawing near, the bridge was becoming crowded. I would have the helm, five military personnel, two mates, my partner Cid, the captain, and God knows who else. And in the corner next to the coffee mess was one more tourist, my ex-partner Murray. The clock was now approaching 1810, and still nothing from the engine room, and at 1815, the captain spoke to the chief engineer, and in two minutes we could feel the familiar rumbling, and hear an engine room coming to life. The rumbling intensified, and then was accompanied by more vibration, and then there appeared to be some movement, then ever so slowly, the *Higgins* was actually moving astern. Someone yelled out, "We're moving! We're moving!" Simultaneously, people began to cheer on the bridge.

Then the captain shouted, "Quite please!" He knew exactly how perilous the situation was. At this point, my rudder was mid ship, and I was awaiting my next rudder command. As the *Higgins* slowly moved astern, all of us on the bridge were witnessing our bow moving to port. The movement that began slowly, was now increasing, and we were swinging hard to port. My rudder was hard right, and I repeated the rudder angle, and was told to shift my rudder to hard left. I wouldn't even pretend to figure out what the captain had in mind, because there were too many variables in the mix, tides, currents, etcetera, plus the *Higgins* had twin screws with variable pitch, and bow thrusters. The initial elation had within seconds turned into panic, as we were about to witness a collision with the *Vermont*. The red tanker that so obligingly took our cargo and was working to assist now became another threat, and it was now fifty yards away, and closing fast.

The captain was issuing orders to the engine room, and the chief mate was on the radio talking to the tanker, "Do you see what's going on? Here we come, get the hell out of the way!" The chief mate was now on a different radio talking with the tugboat telling him to get the slack out of his line, and start taking a strain. My partner and I were watching scene by scene as the drama unfolded before us.

Then Navy chief shouted, "There's a guy over there running up to the bow!"

And sure enough, an AB on the *Vermont* began running forward on the *Vermont's* main deck; he flew up a ladder to the bow and headed right for the wildcat. We could hear the AB as he was banging on the starboard pall, the pin was stuck and he couldn't free the pall, and we could hear people yelling at the AB, "Get a bigger hammer!" He was wielding a nine-pound sledge, and as a blow landed, the pin shot out, and the pall went up, and he started releasing the break. There wasn't enough time to heave the anchor free of the bottom; it would have taken minutes, and we needed that tanker clear in seconds. Slacking the anchor chain and paying it out was the only solution, and that's just what the AB did. There was the possibility that the *Vermont* might run out of anchor chain, and pull out the pin in the chain locker, but that would have been a small calculated loss, given what was at stake. With the clock ticking, it appeared as if the *Vermont* AB would have just enough time to release the brake, and have two shots of chain to spare. Simultaneously, in a coordinated effort, on the *Vermont's* stern, we could see huge billowing clouds of black smoke, and hear the roar of the tug's engine. The towboat was a powerful oceangoing sea tug that was up to the job.

The *Higgins* continued coming to port, but her rate of turn was slowing, and was beginning to correct. As the anchor chain slacked, the *Vermont* finally began to ease astern, and missing our bow by twenty feet, as we were still swinging at a fair rate of speed. We now had two things to cheer about; first, we were dislodged from the pinnacle, and second, we didn't have a collision at sea with another ship. This was shaping up to be quite a day.

On the bridge, there was a cautious cheer, as some of us were wearing life vests (some of the crew were still convinced the ship was going to roll over and sink!). Once we started moving, it wasn't long before we were clear of the pinnacle, and began slowly drifting astern. As the *Higgins* was settling, it was difficult to ignore our fifteen-degree list, which we were thankful did not increase. Shanghai Cid relieved me on the wheel, the captain and the chief mate proceeded ahead on a slow bell, the tugboat was directly on our stern, and would serve as our escort.

Shanghai Cid said to me, "See, that wasn't so hard. I don't know what all the fuss was about. Now that I have the wheel, why don't you go make coffee for the oncoming 8x12. Do you remember how Murray likes his coffee?"

To Cid I replied, "I'll take care of the call-outs and coffee, but just in case you haven't noticed, there's a fifteen-degree list in your coffee cup, Cid!"

Chapter Fifty-One

We were steaming on a northerly track as our list varied fifteen degrees in either direction. For the first ten minutes to the next twenty-four hours the shifting list was rather disconcerting, but the crew was working on the problem, to pursue the best method for stabilizing the ship. Some of these methods included different types of transfer of water, with dirty ballast, and air pressure, plus the additional burden of tank cleaning. Plans were made to obtain another tanker to discharge our dirty ballast. The elimination of all cargo had to be done ASAP, as we were leaving a rather unsightly sheen of petroleum in our wake.

Grateful to be underway, and free of the pinnacle, we would remain in hand steering, because of the ever-changing dynamics of the ship's stability. Shipmates from below would cycle up to the bridge to see how things were going, and see what our next move would be. Don Morse dropped by one evening, and we got into a conversation about religion, which was usually not a good idea. Politics was another bad idea for what would begin as a light conversation that at anytime could erupt into a heated and sometimes downright violent debate.

I had twenty minutes to kill, and Don being a homespun kind of guy, opened the topic.

"So what do you think of religion, what do you believe in?"

I knew this was trouble, so I tried not to get in too deep. I said, "Don, you know this is a hell of a time and place to bring up religion, and why now?"

He said, "How come every time I ask you a question, you answer me with a question?"

I said, "Why not?"

"I don't know. Look, are you going to listen or not?"

"Sure, go ahead."

"I was just thinking about today's organized religions, you know, what they have been battling about, and fighting, like which one has the right answer? Well, I think I have some of it figured out."

"Well, you've gotten this far, I'm dying to know." I wasn't about to stop him.

"Here goes… See, each religion thinks they have the inside scoop on Christ. You know, the Catholics think Christ came and went, and he's coming back. The Jews think he came, but it was the wrong guy, and the right guy is on his way. The Adventists think he never came and he is coming. The Hindus, and Moslems just think he was a nice guy doing good deeds, and most of the rest of the world is confused. What do you think?"

"Don, I got to tell you, after hearing that, I guess I am with the rest of the world."

"Yeah, I guess I am too. I thought I had it figured out, but I'm just as confused as I ever was."

"Say, listen, by the way do you have any idea where were going?"

"Well, let's see, it being daytime and the sun is over there, and the compass is over here, and that little arrow is pointed that way. I would say we're going north."

"God, you can be irritating!"

"Seriously, all I have heard so far is that we are to rendezvous with a tanker tomorrow morning, and offload whatever we have left, and after that it's anybody's guess. After that, I would bet that we would be steaming to the nearest dry dock, ASAP, before anything else goes wrong, and we go the bottom."

The third mate came up to me and said, "Here's a letter for you; it's from Brazil!"

I said, "From Brazil? I don't know anyone in Brazil" And then it hit me. "Wait a second, I think I do—let me have that letter!"

Chapter Fifty-Two

The letter was indeed from Brazil, and it was from Blaze, the newest resident of Rio de Janeiro. I couldn't believe it! I thought I had seen and heard the last of her in the Philippines. Immediately, I opened her letter. Blaze went into detail how she had been taken to the Navy hospital in the Philippines, and had undergone many and varying tests and examinations and the doctors weren't able to find anything physically wrong with her. The physicians were looking at the possibility of an epileptic fit, or an alcohol-induced seizure, or the more obvious, that she was indeed okay, and faking.

Blaze said she was getting concerned that perhaps the doctors would discover that she falsified her seizure, and she was scared to death that she might be sent back aboard. Blaze's fear-based decision motivated her to give another performance, and according to Blaze, "You would have been proud of me, my last attack was brilliant."

Evidently, so much so, that it was her grand finale, before being sent back to the states, via Clark Air Force Base, on to Hawaii, and then Oakland. She knew that once on the West Coast, in Oakland, California, it wouldn't be long before she was processed out of the company and back on the street, to face Frankie Scarpino and his goons. She said that when she arrived in Hawaii, she had enough time to contact a friend for help. This was a smart move on her part, because arrangements for new identification and documentation and a ticket to Brazil would thereby eliminate any delay in Oakland. Blaze also had a new perky name; Whitney Dallas. She added, and I'm not sure what she meant by it, that, "The sky's the limit!" Whitney Dallas also said this would give her enough time to have Frank's money routed to South America. With that little piece of information, she made me think that this lady must either have a death wish, or be incredibly stupid, or some combination. Blaze/Asia/Whitney also wanted me to know that she was eternally grateful, and if I ever got to Rio de Janeiro to look her up. I was beginning to think I had grossly underestimated this gal; she was working every possible angle to the max.

That evening, I composed a letter for the next outgoing mail (early retirement in South America with an Italian beauty was beginning to sound like a good idea). The thrust of my letter was that I wanted Blaze/Asia/Whitney to know that Tony the Gombah/Sailor was on her trail, and she'd be wise to move quickly, and cover her tracks.

Steaming north, the 12x4 spotted our tanker at 0315, and we made radio contact with the Greek tanker *Isabel*. The *Isabel* was apprised of our situation, and she was told to stand by until 0630 for further instructions. Our captain had been on the bridge for two hours, and was getting anxious, so he took command from the second mate. The plan was basic seamanship. Have the tanker come alongside, and make ourselves fast, and then use Yokohama bumpers for protection. There was nothing complicated about the evolution, and discharging our dirty ballast would be our final step before going to a dry dock inside the Persian Gulf. While the *Isabel* was made fast, both ships would steam at a civilized speed of eight knots. The *Higgins* was dead in the water when the *Isabel* came alongside, and we had two Yokohama bumpers rigged on our starboard side. She made her approach ever so slowly, and we had a healthy list of ten degrees to port. I went down below with my partner to assist with the tie-up. We doubled up all lines fore and aft, and the Yokohama bumpers fit perfectly. The captain of the *Isabel* was micromanaging his people and shouting directions instructing his people, and the connection was to be made with an eight-inch hose. Joe and Don and the ship's bosun went over to the *Isabel* to lend a hand. The *Isabel*, a ship of Greek registry, looked as if it had seen battle during the Peloponnesian wars. Today she was sporting the cheery colors of fire engine red, and Christmas tree green, and appeared to be out of a Looney Tunes storyboard. Everything about the *Isabel* was cartoonish… Joe and Don came back to the *Higgins* and gave us a full description. Joe said, "You won't believe it over there, it's like watching a Saturday morning kid show. That crazy captain looks, acts, and talks like Yosemite Sam. He's a little short guy with a handlebar mustache, and he's wearing a cowboy hat with shorts, and boots…I tell you, it's the craziest thing I have ever seen!"

I said, "Are they Greek?"

"I have absolutely no idea. They could be from anywhere, probably someplace in the Soviet block, who knows, and what's the difference?"

Don added, "I thought any minute their captain was going to say, 'Great green horny toads, this is the rootenest tootenest ship in the whole dad burn Indian Ocean!'

"The *Isabel* had a forward and an after house, and the ship was run by the captain's family that spent its time on the bridge with the family dog. The dog was thought of as part of the crew, because she was the lookout. If there was traffic to starboard, the dog would bark once; if the pooch spotted traffic to port, she would bark twice. It's safe to say this wasn't a strong union ship. As for the bridge, it had all the latest navigational innovations of the 1930s. The ship's wheel looked like a Hollywood prop; it was a monstrous wooden thing with spokes. The ship's radio was one directional; you could send, but you couldn't receive. The captain said, 'People with radios talk too much, and radios were just a distraction from operating the ship,' and that radar was something you might see on a thirty-five-foot pleasure craft, and not a thirty-five-thousand-deadweight-ton tanker."

Don said, "We thought they were about to serve a meal on the bridge. Pots and pans were everywhere; there was even a hot plate and toaster next to the radar. The bridge had become a multi-purpose room, and it made sense when you are trying to run a ship with just your family, and a few pets."

Joe said, "Back in the States the Coast Guard would have loved to come aboard that tub. We never got to the engine room; we just assumed there were more relatives down there, with a similar living situation."

Discharging our tainted ballast had begun, and both ships would begin to increase speed to eight knots. It would take an entire day for the transfer, and all the watches would get a turn at the wheel. To communicate course and speed changes, it was necessary to use walkie-talkies, and two of our finest were elected to go back to the *Isabel*. Shanghai Cid and a new twenty-three-year-old third mate went back with walkie-talkie radios and spare batteries.

When they arrived at the *Isabel's* bridge, it was empty. An empty bridge is definitely not a normal occurrence for a ship at sea under power, so they began to investigate. Their investigation led them up one deck, to the flying bridge, that had become a modified sun deck.

When the screaming stopped, the *Isabel's* captain, out of nowhere, shot up the ladder to the flying bridge. At the flying bridge, as rigid as stone, were Shanghai Cid and our youthful third mate, and before them lounging on the deck, the two loves of the captain's life. The captain's wife and buxom daughter were enjoying the afternoon sun European style, sans clothing, and were now huddled in a corner draped in towels…an embarrassing moment for all concerned. The captain blurted in broken English, "Jumping Jiminy! Vat are yous tink yous are doing up here?" Cid swore that he thought he saw steam coming out of the captain's ears.

The third mate piped up, "Ahhhh, sir, ahhhh…we're here to give you these radios, and breasts… ahhh, dahhh…I mean, ahhh…batteries and the radio is preset to channel five, and here are two extra batteries. We really must be on our way. We will give you a radio check when we get back."

The captain replied, "Very well, will give check of radio, now get outski, and offski ship!"

The third mate and Cid came back aboard with big stupid grins, and went directly to the cargo control room. With necessary radio checks done, we increased speed with a course of 045, while our dirty ballast was being transferred.

Don was the first to ask, "So tell me, Cid, what was all the commotion over there? What on earth did you guys do?"

Cid said, "We were doing our job. We went to the bridge, and it was empty. I mean no one; zip, nada, zilch, no one at all, not one person there, zero…."

"Okay, we got the picture, there was no one there."

Cid continued, "I don't know what kind of ship they're running over there, but I have never seen anything like it. We went looking 'round for any signs of life, and trying to find their captain, and you won't believe what happened. Me and the greenhorn third mate stumbled in on his daughter and old lady in the buff sunbathing. Shit, I thought I was going to have a heart attack. Christ, I haven't seen that much skin all in one place in a long time." And we all had a good laugh.

Don said, "You think maybe we can get a peek?"

"Are you out of your mind? That crazy old captain's probably standing guard over them with a sawed-off shotgun."

With *Higgins's* personnel back aboard, both ships increased engine RPMs to make eight knots through the water. After steaming with the *Isabel* for three hours our ten-degree port list diminished to three degrees, and we would have to adjust the lines. In another three hours, the mooring lines would be adjusted once more, to accommodate the differing ship heights. Joining us on our starboard quarter was the *Scwalfinder*, a sister ship, and our escort tug. We were nearing the Persian Gulf, in Indian country, and their support was appreciated, in case we had to circle the wagons. The coast of Iran was approaching fast, and it was determined that a course change would be made, because we still had remaining fuel to pump to the *Isabel*.

Changing direction with two ships married together would have to be done one degree at a time, and done slowly. This would be one of my more memorable times at the wheel. We did a complete one-hundred-and-eighty-degree course change, with the *Isabel* alongside. And get this! Due to the *Isabel's* manpower constraints, their captain was at the helm, while his wife was communicating course changes to him as both ships continued on a one-hundred-and-eighty-degree turn.

As our cargo tanks were emptied, they were cleaned with hot water under pressure. This was hot and dirty work for the deck gang, but necessary to make the ship gas free before any hot work could be done in a shipyard. We had the list controlled at twelve degrees to port, and the thermometer was climbing rapidly as we approached the Gulf. With a hot breeze blowing at eight knots relative we approached the Persian Gulf optimistically making our way north. On our stern we could see sunspots on the setting sun as she slipped beneath the horizon.

Chapter Fifty-Three

We new knew Shanghai Cid and the third mate were anxious to our recover our communication gear on the *Isabel*, even if it meant having to deal with Captain Yosemite Sam. Borscht, the family dog/lookout/gangway watch, had excellent instincts, and would watch your every move. Even if you only looked as if you were coming aboard the *Isabel*, the animal would charge like a bull. This time, Captain Yosemite Sam was going to be ready for Shanghai Cid and the third mate. He wasn't about to have them wandering around his ship running into any more of his family members caught in compromising situations.

As Shanghai Cid stealthily hurdled the Yokohama bumpers to get aboard, Borscht barked like a machine gun while making a run at the brigands. It didn't take long for the captain to get to the main deck with radios and batteries to stop the detail in their tracks. The third mate grabbed the communications gear, and the two of them wasted no time getting back aboard the *Higgins*. Once our men were safely back aboard after evading the jaws of Borscht, the cargo hoses were disconnected and we began to let go all lines.

When both ships were clear, we waved goodbye to the *Isabel's* captain and family, and we continued our journey northward to the Persian Gulf. With cargo discharged, and the dirty ballast gone, we had done all the damage control we could, but we still had an eight-degree list. The plan was to get to a dry dock as best we could, before a full-scale war broke out. The closest shipyard would be in Dubai, inside the Persian Gulf.

Occasionally Shanghai Cid and I would get in a discussion that never went anywhere, but it helped to pass the time. This time, it would be my favorite subject, cars. Within the subject of cars we settled on "what was the best car we had owned?"

Cid began, "It's going to take me a second or two—let me think. Okay, how about you? What do you consider the best car you have ever owned?"

I said, "For a car nut, that's a big question. For me, that would have been my 1955 Chevy. I had a part-time job in high school, and I saved three hundred dollars to buy a 1955 Chevy two-door that ran. I had two other cars never did run, a 1953 Oldsmobile, and a 1953 Chevy convertible. Cid, this car was a mover, and a looker, the engine was a 283, bored out to 301, it had a three-quarter race cam, and a four-barrel carburetor. It also had a three-speed six-cylinder transmission, with low gears in the rear end."

"Where did you buy it?" Cid asked.

"That's another cool part of the story. See, I had this friend John, and we spent a lot of time hot-rodding around in his car, and I was dying to get something like his Chevy. One hot August night, we were in Danbury at a carhop drive-in place, it was straight out of the movie *American Graffiti*... Cool cars were everywhere! My partner John had a two-tone, blue/white 1956 convertible, and I wanted to get something similar. As we pulled into the carhop place right away I saw this 1955 Chevy two-door painted primer, and it was love at first sight! Man, it looked cool, and it had a sign on it that said, 'For sale, three hundred dollars.' I said to the guy behind the wheel that had a mouthful of cheeseburger, 'How about a ride? I'm looking to buy a car exactly like this!'

"He said, 'Sure, if you're interested in buying,' and I said, 'You bet I am. I have been working all year to get something just like this.' So we pilled into the car, and went for a spin down a back road. After about a mile he came to a stop, he revved the engine, popped the clutch, and pulled the front wheels off the ground, and burned rubber forever. Man, that was all I needed to see. John and I both freaked out. John looked at me, and said, 'You got to buy this beast!' Over the roar of the engine, and the tires, I yelled at John, 'You're darn right I do!'

"I said to the driver, 'I want this car! Here's the deal, I'll give you twenty-five dollars now, and I will meet you here tomorrow night with the rest.' I was nuts. All I knew was that the car went like hell, and it was the coolest car I had ever seen. The entire car could have been put together with duck tape and paper clips, and I wouldn't have known or cared. Like I said, it was love at first sight. I still remember bringing it home, and my mom said, 'What on earth is that?'

"I said, 'What do you think? It's a car!'

"Then she said, 'I know, I can see that, but where's the rest of it? Where's the front bumper? And where's the paint?' Mom was always funny.

"I said, 'You have to get with it, that's the style, that's what's going on today, Mom.'

"And she said something like, 'Look, it's 1964, and I am as progressive as the next person, but that's just plain stupid!' She couldn't complain too much, because it was my money that bought it. Living back East, all the cars had rust, and most cars needed bodywork, and my newly acquired purchase was no different. But I was unaware of the rust holes on the inside of the trunk. On the second day I had the car I was out trying to impress the locals with my out-of-town hot rod. Check this out…one night I wheeled into the town shopping center, and spotted some of my friends; this was their first look at my new ride, and I wanted to leave a good impression. I revved the engine and popped the clutch, I must have burned rubber for two hundred feet. After all the screeching and noise and smoke cleared, I was forced to pull over."

"Why? What happened?"

"The tire smoke in the driver compartment was so thick I couldn't see or breathe. I didn't dare go back, because I could barely see in front of me, plus it would have been way too embarrassing, if you know what I mean."

Don said, "Yeah, I think I do, but why didn't you smell the smoke earlier when you test drove it?"

"That was my first thought. All I could figure was that the guy that sold me the car must have put rags or something over the rust holes in the trunk. The next day I patched up the holes, and put big wide-ass racing slicks on the rear, and that did the trick. I was pulling the front wheels of the ground in first and second gear, and after a drag race, I didn't have to open the doors to clear the air in the driver's compartment."

Cid asked, "Did you race for money?"

"No, I never went for that, I just wanted to street race for fun. After a couple of months I painted it 1963 Chrysler metallic red."

"You do it yourself?"

"Yeah, it was no sweat. I painted it in my garage. I prepped it, masked it, and sprayed it five coats, and it came out great. But when I painted it I never thought to get an exhaust blower, so the inside of the garage had five coats of 1963 Chrysler metallic red. The folks didn't care for that too much. I finally had the car just the way I wanted, but it was getting expensive. I had blown a clutch, chewed up the brakes, replaced a throw-out bearing, and universals, you name it! Then one day I was cruising along, minding my own business, and I saw this guy in my rearview mirror on a motorcycle. I recognized him as a local guy, George Saco...a real bike nut.

"Newtown was a small town back then, and word got around fast. George motioned that he wanted to race, and as we came to an intersection ahead, we squared off. The traffic light changed, and we came screaming off the line. I slammed it into second gear, and at six thousand RPMs the engine let go, and it locked up tight, and shit went flying every which way!"

"Hi, Joe. Sit down, listen to Fireball Roberts here."

Cid said, "And then what?"

"I'm not exactly sure, but a big chunk flew through my right front fender as the engine froze up solid."

Joe said, "Wow, what were you racing against?"

"I was racing a motorcycle!"

Joe said, "A motorcycle? What kind of dumbbell races a car against a motorcycle?"

"This kind of dumbbell. Will you let him finish?"

"Well actually, that's the end of the story, all I could do then was call up the garage where I worked, and have the car towed home. With my buddy's help, we hooked a chain fall around a tree limb, and yanked the engine out. This was a first for the both of us, and as the engine reached the level of the fender the limb snapped, and my beautiful 301 fell back into the engine compartment."

Joe said, "Get out a here! You snapped the tree limb?"

"It sounds like you were having a long day. Then what did you do?"

"No shit. Well, the two of us pushed the car over to another tree and finished the job, and set the engine down to get a good look at the damage. I got so disgusted and pissed off, that I figured what the hell... since everything was in parts, I would sell everything for parts, and that's what I did. But you know, even with that bad luck, I considered myself luckier than George. George Saco's luck ran out when he had his last bike ride the following week, when he slammed into a huge maple tree at an estimated eighty miles an hour on Brushy Hill Road."

Chapter Fifty-Four

"Okay, I got one for you, but you know I'm not really a car guy... you know, my thing is motorcycles, but I got a dumb-shit-of-the-year-award story, with a truck."

"Heck, that' sounds better. Shoot!"

"It was about 1968. My folks owned a bakery, and they were doing good, and one year they went out and bought a brand-new panel truck, right off the showroom floor, and man, was it cool. You should have scene this truck. I couldn't wait to get my hands on it. It was a Chevy, with four-wheel drive, with a big V8 engine, stick shift, painted bright orange, and it had a big-ass snowplow on the front."

"Wow, that does sound cool!"

"My running partner was Archie Proudfoot, and out of the blue one day he said to me, 'How about we race, and I'll spot you five car lengths.' I said, 'Bring it on, man.'"

"Wait a minute, you were going to race this guy with a snowplow on the front?"

"Yeah, sure, why not—it had a V8?"

"A V8 is one thing, but for Christ sake, a snowplow on the front?"

"Well, I told you it was a dumb-shit story, so will you listen? That next Friday night, we got lined up at The Dinglebrook Bridge. The bridge was where everyone drag raced, and our race was the main event, and we put fifty dollars on it."

Then I said, "Well, are you going to tell me what kind of car he was racing, or what?"

"Oh yeah, this is another good part—It was a Hillman Minx!"

"What in the hell is that?"

"It was this little shit-box foreign-looking thing, with a four-cylinder engine, and a four-speed transmission on the column."

"Let me get this right, you were going to drag race a Hillman Minx with a four-cylinder engine, a four-speed on the column, against a four-wheel-drive panel truck with a snowplow on the front, and you were going to do this on a bridge?"

"That's right, and did I mention, it was nighttime, and for fifty dollars hard cash?"

I said, "Let me guess, you had chains on too?"

"No, wise guy."

"Man, and I thought I did some stupid stuff, but this is in a whole different league of stupid. What in the hell were you guys thinking?"

"Alright, alright, I know. Look, this happened in like 1965 or so, give me a break."

"Come on now, we got to know what happened," says Joe.

I said, "Will you let him tell the story."

"Okay, Sherrie, the starter, brought the flag down, and I popped the clutch. The truck leaped forward, and I couldn't see Keith in his Minx, and I thought, 'Oh man, I got myself a quick fifty dollars.' As I hit second gear, the front end jerked up, and the plow made a weird noise, and then I heard a clang under the truck, and the motor started to race out of control. I had to shut it down 'cause I thought it would blow."

"Then what happened!"

"Well, the first thing that went was the front universal, the damn thing just blew off, and then the drive shaft twisted up like a pretzel. I figured it was a factory defect, and the cheap parts couldn't handle the extra torque and weight. Hell, I don't know, I guess it was too much. Also I was trying to go from four-wheel drive to two-wheel when I hit second gear, and later someone told me that it isn't a good idea to do that."

"And then what?"

"Well, what do you think? Keith in his foreign shit box went flying by, and I lost the race, and the fifty bucks, and ever since then, it has been motorcycles."

"Yeah, that's a good idea, stick with something that's safe, that you can count on that you won't get into trouble."

Joe asked, "What I want to know is how you explained that to your mom and dad?"

Cid said, "Simple. I told them the truck was stolen and wrecked. I made it sound like the truck was ripped off in a shopping center by some kids that went joy riding and left it in a cornfield. The whole thing worked out perfect; my parents bought it, the cops bought it, and the insurance people bought it... pretty cool, huh?"

Then I said, "A cornfield?"

"Yeah, that was the tricky part. A friend who worked in a service station had a wrecker, and he helped me get it out there at night."

Then Joe Bones, of all people, said, "Cid, how do you sleep at night?"

"Just like everyone else, with one eye open."

Cid said, "Sure, Joe, you mean when you were a kid you never did anything stupid with a vehicle? Come on, give me a break."

"Well, now that I think of it I do remember this one time I was out screwing around with my partner Sandy in an old piece of junk that I just bought, so I guess I could say there was this one time, but it really wasn't that big a deal. In high school I bought my first car with seventy-five dollars. It was a 1955 Plymouth Savoy four-clyinder flathead engine with automatic push-button on the dashboard."

Cid said, "Real high tech, huh?"

"Yeah, for its day it was... My buddy Sandy and I were out bombing around in the thing after I had it about a month. One day we skipped afternoon classes, and got a bottle of this stuff called Tango... it was a mix of orange juice and vodka. Oh yeah, and one more thing before I go any further—I should let you know that Sandy's father was our driver's education instructor; for some reason I always felt like I was corrupting the guy.

Cid said, "Yeah, for some reason? A real big mystery, right?"

"We hit the back roads that were less traveled and more fun. There's something about bombing around an old dirt back road that's a gas. The radio was blaring, and we didn't have a care or a brain in our heads, and then bam! The right front tire blew, and I wrestled the old junker over to the soft shoulder to a stop. It was fall and leaves were everywhere, and we got out to change the tire. Sandy was jacking the car up with one of those old piece-of-junk jacks that was missing the base part, and I was getting the spare out of the trunk.

"Sandy, as he was trying to get the car jacked up, bends down to see why the car isn't going up and the jack is going down into the dirt and he yells out, 'Holy shit, there's a fire under the car!' We both freaked out, and were yelling 'do something, do something!' So I looked underneath, and sure enough the emergency brake part under the car was in flame. I guess I left the brake on, and it got hot and caught fire. I said to Sandy, 'Give me your jacket and I'll try to fan the fire out.' That didn't work, and all I did was ruin the poor guy's jacket, and the fire started to spread. I said, 'Shit. See if there's a screwdriver somewhere.' Sandy luckily found one in the trunk, so I took the license plates off the car, and said, 'Let's get the hell out of here!' And we did."

"Christ, you just left it there? Then what did you do?"

"We got out of there as fast as we could. I thought the whole thing was going to blow. We kept looking back, and about a mile down the dirt road we stopped for a few minutes to look, but we didn't see smoke or anything, so we just kept going till we got to town."

"Then what?"

"What did we do? That's easy—we got another bottle of Tango and went over to Sandy's house and got his car."

"But what about your car, and what about the license plates, and the registration? You're not going to tell me they never tracked you down, that the cops couldn't figure out whose car it was... they're not that dumb."

"Oh, yes, they are; they never came after me. You know though, now that you mention it, a couple of days after it happened I heard about a forest fire on the outskirts of town, and thought there might be a connection. And I think the reason no one ever came knocking on my door was because I never took transfer of the title when I bought the car, and three months later I was in Vietnam."

Cid said, "That might explain a few things."

Chapter Fifty-Five

President Bush had given Saddam Hussein an ultimatum, and time was running out. That's about all the crew of the *Higgins* knew as we approached the Straits of Hormuz. We were still on schedule to enter a dry dock in Dubai in United Arab Emirates. Shanghai Cid said to Joe as the three of us were looking over the side at the coast of Iran, "Joe, what do you want to talk about now?"

"Cid, I don't know. How's about chicks? You remember your first chick and what she was like?" Joe said, "Oh, man, I'll never forget her. Here name was Karen, and...."

"Excuse me, guys, but doesn't it bother anybody here that we are now entering the Straits of Hormuz, and we are painted gray like all the other Navy warships, and we have only shotguns, and billy clubs for protection, and that President Bush has given Saddam Hussein an ultimatum and full-on war is eminent?"

"Ahh relax, Ted. What's the worst that could happen? You think we might get torpedoed and sink? We already have a hole in the bottom."

"Well, Cid, that's what I am talking about. It wouldn't take much to...you see that jet coming over this way? That's one of those new stealths."

Cid said, "Yeah, I see it. There are guys, and they're all over the place, if anyone's gonna sweat the load, it should be me, I got plans."

Mongo and I both said, "Like what?"

"First thing I'm gonna do is take my scooter for a ride, and then go for the old lady, and if she's not home, I'm going for the dog... just kidding, guys. I'm gonna have a chunk of change when I get off this lash-up, and for once, I'm gonna do something with my money that makes sense. I been hanging out with this old heifer for a while now, and I think were gonna get spliced, and maybe buy a chicken shack up by Elko, Nevada."

211

Mongo said, "Terrific. It sounds like true love. Are you going to have little Shanghai Cids?"

Cid interjected, "Ah, come on, I'm trying to be serious. You know I'm too old for that nonsense; beside, having a couple of parents that are gas pipes ain't the best way to go for a brand-new kid, plus I can't deal with a house full of crumb snatchers. I found me an old lady that will put up with me, and this sailing game, so what the hell?"

Chapter Fifty-Six

Shanghai Cid was feeling especially good in the morning as we finally entered the Straits of Hormuz.

"So we have an eight-degree list, so we are painted gray like other warships that have big guns and missiles. A little risk is good for the soul, and builds character, and really, what's the worst that could happen? I mean after all, we're not far away from the protective umbrella of the battle group."

Joe said, "You know, I keep hearing, what could go wrong with this, and what could go wrong with that, and things keep going wrong. Speaking of which, we are now in the Persian Gulf."

Cid said, "Hey, partner, we got to get going. We better get to early chow. I got first wheel."

Mongo said, "I'll tag along."

"So, Mongo, what are you going to do when you get paid off?"

"I'll tell you what I'm going to do, I'm going to take my money and get back to the Philippines as soon as I can, and buy myself a fish boat, and try to make a go of it. I want to stay closer to home and be with my family. I plan on selling my store; I think I already have a buyer."

I said to Mongo, "I thought you liked the store, and you were doing well?"

"The store's a pain in the ass. You might not know it, but I run a jitney when I'm not shipping, and I want to get few more."

"How about you, Ted, what you got up your sleeve?"

"Me, I'm not sure yet, but whatever it is, it'll be great. I don't know about you guys, but half the time I make these great plans, and get all excited, and then a month or two go by and I get bored with the plans. Then I will start on a new set of plans for vacation, so when I actually hit the beach after a long trip like this I almost have no idea of what I am going to do. Does that sound familiar, or what? You know, a guy told me this while I was in a diner, and it made a lot of sense then and still does."

"Can we do this while we're in the chow line? What are you having? Check it out, T-bone steaks."

Mongo said, "Ted, what were you going to say about the guy in the diner?"

"He said, 'If you ever wanted to know what you wanted in life, look at what you got.'"

"Not bad. I kind of like that, that's pretty heavy," said Cid.

"I don't get it."

"What do you mean you don't get it, Mongo? How can you not get it? It's about taking responsibility for your life, you dumbbell."

"I'll have the fried chicken, and can you give me one of those ears of corn, and dump some gravy on those taters."

"Will you keep moving down there?"

"Oh, responsibility…yeah, okay, sure, like I'm running my show right or wrong, and I am at cause, and not effect in my life."

"You got it, Mongo. Bon appétite!"

Once pier side we tied her up for the last time in Dubai, with what would be a lengthy shipyard stay. Part of the crew would be paid off and put on vacation, while others would be reassigned to different ships. The crew was beginning to line up outside the purser's office for that final payoff and discharge. We all had plans as to which route we would lobby for, and how long we would stay at differing locations, and who our traveling companions would be. There were some of us that had not only spent hours daydreaming about what country to visit on the way home, but a couple of guys had even gone as far as buying language tapes and books of their country of interest. Only to find out that getting airline tickets at the last minute to some of these exotic places were so expensive that alternate choices had to be made.

The following day we were transported to our new digs, a major luxury hotel in downtown Dubai, and here we would stay until we had a flight out. As the doorman opened the huge gold and chrome doors of our new temporary home I can recall Shanghai Cid saying, "Now this is why I go to sea. Just check this lobby out, will you?"

"Look at that gold leaf over there, and that art stuff on those bulkheads, and will ya take a look at these marble decks."

When the first fifteen of us arrived, we went about the business of checking in at the front desk. At the outset, it was abundantly clear that we would fit in perfectly, and we scanned the lobby for a place to unwind. We found it and we took over. In the middle of the main lobby a group of us were seated in big overstuffed chairs and couches. Adding to an already soothing atmosphere was Mozart being performed on a grand piano...clearly an experience we weren't used to. Several waiters approached us, and asked, "Would any of you gentleman care for a cocktail?"

Bill, one of the deck mechanics, said, "Hey, you slobs, we must be the gentlemen; I think that waiter is talking to us! Do we want a drink?"

Cid said, "Does the Pope poop in the woods? Is a bear Catholic?"

Mongo said, "Do pigs fly, do ducks fly backwards?"

Farley then said to Cid, as he was reading the local newspaper, "Cid, will you guys tone it down a touch, were not on the Hotel *Higgins*; we're in an A-rab country, and who knows, they might cut your tongue out for swearing?"

Cid said, as he addressed our waiter, "Yeah okay, excuse me, your rag headship, but we will have four cool ones over here."

Then Farley said, "Christ, let me handle this. Please bring a round of draft beers, and I will have an ice tea stirred with a twist of lemon." And than Farley said something interesting as we started to feel a little more comfortable.

"Do you knot-heads have any idea what today's date is?"

And we answered up with a resounding, noooo. "Well check it out, it is January 19."

And Mongo goes, "Okay, soooo are you going to tell us, or what? And what's it got to do with us?"

"Well, for one thing, it says here in this *Gulf Gazette*, that President Bush gave an ultimatum to Mr. So dam Insane."

Mongo says again, "Soooo."

Farley leaned forward in his chair and said, "Well, sports fans, that ultimatum day is today!"

I said to Farley, "You've got to be kidding! What do you think'll happen, Farley?"

"I don't know. I don't think anyone knows; it just depends on how determined Bush and Hussein are, but the main thing to realize is that we are right in the middle of it."

Shanghai Cid said, "Waiter! Yo, yo! Over here, we're going to need more of everything over here, and maybe something stronger. It's catch-up time, keep 'em coming!"

The hotel lobby and the surrounding area was spectacular, especially when compared to shipboard accommodations, and especially after consuming copious amounts of alcohol. I didn't need a bellman to help me with my sea bag, and found my way to the right floor and room. My security card opened a door to pure luxury, and as I opened the door, I stopped to look at what would be mine for the next thirty-six hours.

But before I turned on the large-screen TV and got too comfortable, I contemplated how enjoyable it would be to shower with the piece of mind in knowing that I wouldn't be interfering with a deranged neighbor. As I toweled off, I threw open the curtains to the vast desert before me, and took a selection from the mini-bar. I then put my feet up with remote in hand, clicked the TV to Stateside news, and within minutes was asleep.

The next sound I heard was Don Morse was knocking on my door.

"What in the hell is all that banging, and who's at my door? And this doesn't look like my room!" I jumped out of my monster bed, looked at my watch.

"For Christ sake, it's 0530 in the morning!"

I opened the door, and standing in front of me in his skivvies was Don Morse, and he said, "We're screwed, the Americans just started bombing up north, and we'll never get out of here!"

I said, "We are the Americans," and he said, "Yeah, I know that, but we're not the Americans in jets shooting down those Scuds with Patriot missiles and bombing the bejesus out of the place. Go ahead, turn on your TV."

I said, "Wait a minute, calm down. How do you know for sure?"

Don said, "I've been watching this for the last ten minutes and this is it, that's how I am sure. Hell, they're going to shut down the airport! It's all over the TV, turn on CNN!" As I was turning on the TV, he said, "You feel that?"

I said, "I sure did, and I know exactly what that is—those are bombs, and not artillery. This thing is going down now."

"That's what I'm trying to tell you." The both of us were now watching night bombing runs, and Scud and Patriot missiles hurtling through the skies, with different targets blowing up.

I said to Don, "I'm calling the front desk to find out if they know anything."

As soon as I said it, Farley came in and said, "Guys, I don't want to rain on your parade, or cause any trouble, but the airport has been shut down, and we're not going anywhere!"

Don said, "That's just great. I told you! Can you believe the timing... Is this too much or what?"

Chapter Fifty-Seven

We didn't have much choice when we were told to stay close to the hotel until we departed. Staying close presented no problem, probably because we knew there was enough booze in the hotel to keep us drunk for up to a week, but after that we'd be forced to storm the gates. After another full day of pool antics and general reverie, the airport opened, and we were cleared to go. We repacked our valuable keepsakes, and said our goodbyes to the cordial staff that was saddened by our departure. Those of us that were able left in the first cab and were whisked off to the Dubai airport to put the *Higgins* in the background, and looking forward to new adventures in the foreground.

Farley, Don, and myself entered the duty-free shop at the airport with two hours to kill, and we made an important discovery; inexpensive beer and liquor for sale. Farley, with more sobering thoughts, said to the guys, "Now will you look over there... When's the last time you've seen a new Rolls Royce Silver Spur and 850I BMW for sale in a duty-free shop?"

Along with the rest of the crew, Don, Shanghai Cid, Farley, and myself had purchased assorted souvenirs that we couldn't live another day without, and were anxiously awaiting our flight to Bangkok. The time came, and we boarded the plane with extremely tight security, with the double-edged sword of inconvenience and reassurance. Aboard, and winging our way in a westerly direction, there wasn't much that could dampen our spirits; even the news that our stay in Bangkok would be only one hour only mildly dampened the mood.

One hour in Bangkok is not what we had in mind, and our next party opportunity location would be the Philippines, and this would more than fulfill our expectations. Manila was smelly, crowded, and polluted, and the airport was a nightmare, and the temperature and humidity were well into the nineties. We weren't prepared for the intense security, German shepherd guard dogs, automatic weapons… these people were serious.

Mercifully, Manila wasn't our final destination, and we made it back to the Olongopo area in a vehicle for hire to the Barrio Beretta on the beach, and even more specifically the Half Moon Hotel. The Half Moon Hotel has been a second home to wayward sailors since the dawn of civilization—well, almost.

Let the games begin! Hot, sweaty, and thirsty, we checked in at the lobby of the Half Moon Hotel. Cid said, "I want the best bungalow you have, and I don't care if it costs as much as ten dollars a night!" The desk clerk was very accommodating attractive wisp of a thing, and she gave us a highlight of the hotel's amenities. She even took the time to point out that the hotel even had an Alcoholic's Anonymous meeting list available, for anyone that thought they had a problem with alcohol, and of course we all looked in Farley's direction.

Cid addressing our group, "I don't know about you guys, but the only problem I have is that I can't find enough booze!" When the little wisp of a thing got to the part about church services, and noticing our eyes roll, she ended her homily by explaining that there was complimentary coffee in the lobby twenty-four hours a day. And Mr. Cranepool, here you are," handing Farley his key. "And at six tonight there will be a meeting over there in the cabana, and I would like to introduce you to Miss Suzy; she will show you to your room."

Farley, with a wide satisfied grin, followed Miss Suzy to his new lodgings. We had told the front desk lady that we would be in town a week, even though we had to clear it with the company. At this point, even if it meant coughing up extra cash, we would turn a layover into a play-over mini-vacation. Before worrying about crossing the T's and dotting the I's, we would finish exercising our recreational rights, and then deal with the paperwork. But just to cover our butts, Don did make a call to the home office, and we were cool. We each had a small bungalow next to the pool, and an empty beer bottle throw to the beach. Our first night out, we hired a jitney driver to get us in town, and act as a guide to the native cultural activities that would enrich our stay.

Part of our decompression regimen consisted of lounging by the pool, eating giant Malaysian shrimp and lumpia, plus copious amounts of ice-cold San Miguel beer, while contemplating the vast complexities of life, and lengthy discussions of the finer attributes of the other sex. On day two we were joined by five more crewmembers from the *Higgins* that had an extra day and a half in Bangkok. We were surprised to see them at all; there were some among them that would never have left Thailand.

Once again fooled by looks, I overheard a conversation. I saw Cid reading a book, and I head Don Morse say, "What is that you're reading, Cid?"

"It's *Fountainhead*, by Ayn Rand, why?"

"You're reading *Fountainhead*? That's heady stuff."

"That's right. Because I'm a heady guy. It's no big deal—you would think I was translating middle ages Latin to modern Italian or something. Have you read it, Don?"

"Years ago. What's the name of the other good one?"

"It's *Atlas Shrugged*."

"Yeah, that's it. Even though I haven't quite finished this, I think *Atlas Shrugged* was better, although this *Fountainhead* has some great characters, like sexy Monique Francone, and you know, I never thought being an architect would be such a cool job, but if I wasn't sailing I could see myself designing buildings...."

Don said, "I hate to break this up, guys, but anyone recognize that voice? You hear it? There it goes again, that unmistakable high-pitched whiney voice. There, hear it! I'd know that voice anywhere. Not here—why does he have to come here, damn it. It's Murray Katz!"

Shanghai Cid said, "It sure is, and he is at the coffee mess trying to explain to that little gal the Murray Katz method of coffee presentation."

I walked over to Cid and Don, and Joe Bones. "Is that who I think it is?"

Cid said, "It is, in person, and the two of you will be sharing the head in number two bungalow."

I said, "Very funny, Cid. Cid, do you ever think that maybe there is a higher, more powerful force that is continually putting things in front of you as a test?"

"No doubt about it, your test is in the lobby right now getting a coffee with cream, and five lumps of sugar. And your test is to let it be, and accept Murray into your space, and be at one with the universe, understanding that he is here to make you a stronger person is the point, and to give way to your emotions and dismember him and throw him into the fire is to surrender in defeat...it is your choice, little grasshopper."

"Most eloquently put, master. Tell me, old wise one, did you spend your entire childhood watching *Kung Fu?*"

"Not hardly. Very little TV—they don't call me Shanghai Cid for nothing. I thought you knew that I was born and raised in China?"

"No, I had no idea. You're putting me on aren't you? For all I know you came from Sheboygan; you sure don't look Chinese."

"I'm obviously not Chinese. Mom was Austrian and Dad was a roast beefer in the Royal Marines, in the U.K. I remained in China until I was twenty years old, and then started sailing foreign flag on coastal tramp steamers. Mom and Dad were always traveling, so my folks arraigned for my upbringing to be done by my surrogate dad, who was a Shaolin monk, and his name was Ying Xue-Lin."

"Wow, I wasn't ready to hear your whole life story, but keep going, it sounds interesting."

"Sure... Well, I wasn't exposed to Western extravagance, and only rarely did I get to see an episode of *Gunsmoke*, or *Rawhide*, and I have a vague recollection of the *Kung Fu* show."

Don said, "It looks like Murray is not coming over here. I think he knows better, but I am sure we haven't seen the last of him."

I said to Cid, "Tell me more of what it was like growing up with a Shaolin monk as a role model. When I was a kid the kung fu thing was cool, and we all thought having Cain as an instructor would be the greatest."

Shanghai Cid began again, "At the time, it didn't seem like a big deal, because I didn't have a reference point to compare my experience. However, looking back, I have a tremendous gratitude for what my parents provided, and when I became an adult, I was ready. I wasn't coddled and cajoled, and pampered; I was told what was right, and what is wrong, and was given standards to live by... I learned a tremendous amount from Ying Xue-Lin. The physical training was only a small piece of the picture. My training helped with the answers to life, everyday questions of survival, and living a life that is worthwhile, and being equal and ready for any task, and being able to stay up for two or three days at a time for something that's worthwhile. I also feel as though I am part of nature, and not an observer, and not being at the effect of every wind that blows my way."

Cid said calmly, "Are you catching any of what I am saying?"

Don said, "You bet. Are you ready for another beer?"

"Cid, you never talked like that before—where did all that come from?

I interjected, "Yes, you sound like a different person."

Cid continued, "It is strange, but I go around like a semi-conscious person most of the time, and then someone will say or do something, and then go into a different mode of operation. I want to say it's spiritual, but the power and the feeling I get transcends spirituality; it's as if I am on automatic pilot, and although Ying Xue-Lin has passed on, I can still hear his instructive words."

I said to Cid, "What you have is what the rest us are looking for. I don't know what you have tapped into, but I am of the understanding that a master was one that found out, and sounds like you have found out."

"What about fighting skills, do you keep them up? I mean, since I have known you, I haven't seen you in a beef, and I haven't seen you run, and we have been in some scary places."

Shanghai Cid turned his neck real slow, and said, "You just asked and answered your own question; maybe you have found out. Ted, you want to share some of your background in the arts?"

"Sure… First off, Cid, I became a steady practitioner of the arts later on in life, but I didn't let age stop me; I was fortunate to have a grand master in his fifties. If nothing else, the one valuable lesson I learned from him was to 'always go to the source.' He was unbelievable! As an example, sometimes I would just watch him. I had the impression that he had found out all he could from people, and moved to animals. He would watch tapes of animals for hours—tigers, bears, lions, snakes—you name it, he was utterly fascinated with the animal kingdom. He would watch a lion ready to move in on its prey, he would notice the lion's facial movement, he would notice the direction of the tail, a movement of the ear, he would be completely absorbed in every detail of the animal. You know, I never really thought about it, until I found myself going to the zoo all the time with my young daughter, I am not sure who benefited more from our visits to the zoo, my daughter, or myself."

Cid said, "You both benefited equally."

Chapter Fifty-Eight

It was a civilized afternoon, good food, ladies, beers, warm sun beating down, and a crystal-clear pool. Then out of nowhere Cid said, "Did you hear that?"

In chorus, "Nooo!"

Then Cid said, "There it goes again!" Then we heard a woman squeal, and then two people charged out of one of the bungalows.

Don said, "Hey, guys, that's Farley isn't it?"

I said, "It sure is, and who's the gal in her birthday suit?"

Shanghai Cid said, "Hey, you know who that is? It's the girl from the front desk, Miss Suzy!"

And Don said, "That Farley doesn't waste anytime does he?"

Miss Suzy on a dead run dove into the pool, with Farley right behind her, somewhat less gracefully. As Miss Suzy exited the pool, she let out a yelp and started running around the bar area, and Farley was a mess. Farley looked as if he had been dragged across the English Channel.

Shanghai Cid said, as he was looking at Farley, who appeared as if he might be going under, "Didn't Farley stop drinking?"

"I thought so, Cid, but he sure looks like he's had a snoot full, and this is only day two; he's got five more action-packed days ahead."

Twice Farley fell off the ladder back into the pool, and we all had our eyes fixed on Farley as he made a third attempt.

Cid said, "Yo, Mr. Rescue Swimmer, you better keep an eye on him, I don't think he can get out of the pool; this might be your first time getting wet as a rescue swimmer."

I said, "Farley is no downed helicopter pilot, anyway here he comes. Hey, what's that in his hand?"

Someone said, "It's a bikini top!"

Farley finally made it out of the pool, and spun around several times trying to figure out where he was, and then lurched forward in the direction of the bar. Then Cid said, "Woops!" We then witnessed

Farley going over backwards into the nearby shrubbery, swearing a blue streak, and then all went quiet.

Miss Suzy was peeking around the corner of the bar, speed talking in Tagalong, and pointing at Farley piled up in the bushes. Joe Bones said, "Well, guys, I think she wants her top back. At least she is laughing!"

And Cid said, "Now I think I know why he gave up the hooch. Maybe I ain't no Romeo, but I know that ain't no way to romance a lady." And then Cid walked over to the shrubs and mercifully threw a towel down to Farley, and we packed him off to his room before the local gendarme got involved and ruined everyone's day.

The following day a group of us took a van ride out to a place called Weehawken Beach. Without getting into the legal ins and outs, suffice it to say that a retired bosun had put together a mini resort, and we were going to support his entrepreneurial spirit.

Shanghai Cid said, "So, Mongo said this place is hot stuff, then where is he?"

Don said, "What, you forgot already? He's with his clan in Olonopo, but he said he might try to join us later."

Joe Bones said, "I see our ride at the driveway, let's get a move on. Uh-oh, it looks like Murray Katz is coming this way." Joe continued, "Murray, come on over here, old buddy. Come on along—we're going to need someone to help with the gear."

"You guys are on your own, I'm staying right here. Yeah, I know your game—if I don't do it who's going to do it—well, not this time. Besides, I got things to do. I got so much dirt in my room it's going to take me a week to clean it all. You guys seen Farley? Maybe I can get Farley to help."

"Yeah, Murray, I know what you mean. I hate to disappoint you, but brother Farley might not be as passionate about scrubbing floors and walls today!"

Murray and Farley never did make the ride to Weehawken Beach, and it was for the best. The four of us, and Don's new girlfriend and driver/guide boarded the van, and with what began as a paved road, ended in dirt. A one-way dirt road with an ample ditch for passing vehicles was our high-speed highway to fun. We passed scooters, water-buffalo-driven carts, and ox carts, mopeds, Carabaos, tractors, and just about every possible public conveyance imaginable, and even an automobile.

The lush green jungle, with banana trees, mangos, papayas, and rice paddies ended abruptly, and our dirt road was transformed into white sugary sand. Even before seeing the mountainous waves, we could hear their crashing against the rocks, and feel the light ocean spray.

Weehawken Beach opened before us, with a spectacular ocean view that stretched for miles in either direction, and an even more attractive open-air bar with all the tropical accoutrements. Fifty feet in front of the bar lay the beach, and another fifty feet in the water was a gorgeous out-cropping of rocks that formed a miniature tropical island with a half dozen palm trees. Our guide and driver introduced us to the owner and operator, and his name was Bugsy. Bugsy was a grizzled guy of sixty-something, with a big wide grin, and a mischievous look... it was obvious he had been a sailor.

Bugsy told us he had been a "China Coaster" for some thirty-five years; he knew all the ports from Tsing Tao to Port Klang like the back of his ham-size hand. He said, "Two years ago I said to myself, 'there's no time like the present,' and I decided to stop sailing, and drop anchor on this little oasis in the middle of nowhere."

Bugsy said, "It took me a year to build the bar, and get the beach set up just right. The place had tremendous views, regardless of where you looked. The bar was on the beach, and it was wide open, and if you were seated facing the ocean, it appeared to be the best view, but not so! Only when you sat with your back to the ocean did you notice the huge volcano protruding through the jungle canopy... it was a remarkable sight."

Joe Bones, looking at the volcanic mountain, asked Bugsy, "Doesn't it give you the heebie-jeebies having that at your back door?"

And Bugsy said, "No, but once in a while, I'll look up there and see a puff of smoke, but if she blows her stack, it will give me more beach property. Up until then, I'll just sit here, and look at the beach and the pretty girls, and enjoy myself."

Cid said, "Bugsy, you are the consummate optimist."

Don and his new girlfriend were going for a swim, and were asking Bugsy about water depths and other details.

I said to Don, "Aren't you going to introduce us to your new friend?"

"I would, but her English is limited."

"How limited? And were did you meet her, Don?"

"What is this, twenty questions?"

He said, "I met her the old-fashioned way, in a massage parlor. You see those hands? She has the most powerful hands I have ever seen. When I got my first massage I thought she was going to drill me through the massage board."

By now, Don had center stage, and we were hooked on his every word, and Shanghai Cid said, "Can she speak any English at all?"

And Don said, "English? Sure she can, she can say, 'Oh yeah,'" and with that his girlfriend with this great big smile said, "Oh yeah!"

Shanghai Cid said, "You mean, 'oh yeah,' and that's it?"

"How the hell are you going to get along, if all she can say is oh yeah?"

Don said, "You think I'm stupid? I got it figured out. I got this little dictionary right here that translates English to Tagalong, and now all I got to do is get a dictionary that translates Tagalong to English. Besides, what the hell— you don't think we're going to be discussing quantum physics, or thermodynamics, do yah?"

Shanghai Cid said, "Well yeah, I guess not. Good thinking."

And then Don's girl that had mastered the two most important words in the English language said, "Oh yeah" and we all cracked up.

We made it back to base camp, the hotel, and somehow managed to do it again in downtown Olonopo. We also caught up with Mongo and his brood, but we had to move on, because we were on a mission. Partying was to never be taken lightly, but more than anything else, just to be off the ship, and free to do as we wished, was the biggest luxury.

With the days turning into a week, it was time to leave, and we said our goodbyes to new friends, and shuttle-bused it to Clark AFB, and flew to Manila. Don Morse would be heading back to the States, with myself, Joe Bones, and Farley Cranepool. On our flight to Manila, it was agreed that we all had been on some unusual planes in our years, but our plane from Clark was literally backwards. Farley said, "I don't know about you guys, but I'm not crazy about anything named after a storm. What did that guy back there call this thing, a Hurricane or a Thunderclap?"

Don said, "I don't know, I thought he said Typhoon. Whatever it is I don't like it one bit."

The contraption was half the size of a C-130, it had two props, and it was entered via a ramp in the rear. Strangest of all was that there were no windows. And for some reason the passenger seats faced aft and not forward. We surmised the plane was used for livestock, and not equipped for humans.

Notwithstanding the fact that we weren't feeling especially human after our last evening in Olonopo, we dutifully boarded the beast. Another oddity that was making us uncomfortable was the steam rising from the floor; it could have been dry ice, but none among us had the ambition to query this mystery as our heads were still pounding from last night's exuberance.

Manila was no Garden of Eden either, and all we wanted to do was get that "Bowl of corn flakes, the duffel bag-drag, and get on that silver bird back to the world" and move on to our next destination, Honolulu, Hawaii. As mentioned before, security in Manila was extremely tight, and it was then and there that we all learned a valuable lesson; never carry a sea bag again to an airport...not for any reason, period! Security demanded that they search everything, and there is only one way to search a sea bag, and that is to dump its entire contents on the deck. Farley Cranepool was the only one not feeling like dog poop. Why? Because his one-day dance with the devil had scared him sober, and he was back on the path of the righteous and temperate.

The rest of the troop was so hungover that our hair hurt, it was a sweltering ninety-eight degrees, and a humid mother swinger, and crawling around on our hands and knees stuffing our priceless dirty laundry back into our sea bags would leave an indelible mark on our memories.

With a scheduled layover in Hawaii, it was pure joy to be winging our way to Honolulu. With only an eight-hour layover, myself, Shanghai Cid, and Don Morse went to Hotel street, where no one in their right mind goes unless they are hopelessly hungover, or drunk out of their skulls... We were somewhere in between.

Farley Cranepool led the way, trying to get recruits to go to a local AA meeting called the Twelve Coconuts, and a bit of surfing, but Farley trudged it alone. Joe Bones went to the local municipal hospital in town to take care of a social disease he mysteriously contracted. Shanghai Cid and I only had enough time for a beer at the infamous Huba Huba and Union bar on Hotel street.

Cid was chomping at the bit to add a tattoo to his already extensive collection, but he wasn't up to paying the entire price, and that would have meant missing our plane back to the world. After our high-speed cab ride, we boarded our plane, and Joe Bones said, "Thank god for modern medicine, otherwise half the crew would be blind by now. The doc gave me a shot on each butt cheek, then gave me a script for these pills and that was it!"

Just before our wheels set down at SFO, Farley mused over his coffee, "One night of 'joie de vivre,' and look what I get. I need a meeting in the worst way."

Cid said, "Why? What's the problem, didn't you just go to one?"

"Yeah, but I still feel on edge. The meeting called the twelve coconuts only had eleven, and I had to sit on the ground. Then I rented a ten-foot yellow surfboard and spent three hours trying to get up and I never did. To make maters worse, when I was going back in to call it a day I was up by the sand with my surfboard and I heard this kid yell 'Look out!' Before I could see what happened it was too late, and the end of my board hit this Asian guy in the head, and I almost knocked him out, and then a half a dozen people started yelling at me, and it almost caused a riot."

Cid said, "I didn't know you were a surfer, Farley."

"I'm not!"

We arrived in San Francisco at 11:00 in the morning, and said adios to one another. We knew we wouldn't see one another until the next time we were randomly thrown together on another ship. Shanghai Cid said he was going to rent a car and drive home, marry that gal, and buy that chicken shack. He then said to me, "What's in it for you, Ted? What's your next move?

"Cid, I will be getting my girl out of storage, dusting her off, and driving down to Las Vegas. I have a cute little card-dealing ex-wife down there that just can't wait to see me and my payoff check. Then it's off to Rio de Janeiro, Brazil, to look up a certain electronic technician friend of mine, and I might even look for some ancient Inca ceramics, and if I like what I see, who knows, I might even drop anchor for a while. But for now, I am looking for an airport shuttle. It's a great place to meet knew and exciting people; you never know who you might be sitting next to!"

The End